CHRISTOPHER BUSH
THE CASE OF THE RUNNING MAN

CHRISTOPHER BUSH was born Charlie Christmas Bush in Norfolk in 1885. His father was a farm labourer and his mother a milliner. In the early years of his childhood he lived with his aunt and uncle in London before returning to Norfolk aged seven, later winning a scholarship to Thetford Grammar School.

As an adult, Bush worked as a schoolmaster for 27 years, pausing only to fight in World War One, until retiring aged 46 in 1931 to be a full-time novelist. His first novel featuring the eccentric Ludovic Travers was published in 1926, and was followed by 62 additional Travers mysteries. These are all to be republished by Dean Street Press.

Christopher Bush fought again in World War Two, and was elected a member of the prestigious Detection Club.

He died in 1973.

CHRISTOPHER BUSH

THE CASE OF THE RUNNING MAN

With an introduction
by Curtis Evans

DEAN STREET PRESS

Published by Dean Street Press 2022

Copyright © 1958 Christopher Bush

Introduction copyright © 2022 Curtis Evans

All Rights Reserved

The right of Christopher Bush to be identified as the Author of the Work has been asserted by his estate in accordance with the Copyright, Designs and Patents Act 1988.

First published in 1958 by MacDonald & Co.

Cover by DSP

ISBN 978 1 915014 60 3

www.deanstreetpress.co.uk

INTRODUCTION

Rosalind. If it be true that good wine needs no bush [i.e., advertising], 'tis true that a good play needs no epilogue. Yet to good wine, they do use good bushes, and good plays prove the better by the help of good epilogues.

–SHAKESPEARE, Epilogue, As You Like It

THE decade of the 1960s saw the sun finally begin to set on that storied generation which between the First and Second World Wars gave us detective fiction's Golden Age. Taking account of both deaths and retirements, by the late Sixties only a bare half-dozen pre-World War Two members of the Detection Club were still plying their deliciously deceptive craft: Agatha Christie, Anthony Gilbert (Lucy Beatrice Malleson), Gladys Mitchell, John Dickson Carr, Nicholas Blake and Christopher Bush, the subject of this introduction. Bush himself would pass away, at the age of eighty-seven, in 1973, having published, at the age of eighty-two, his sixty-third Ludovic Travers detective novel, *The Case of the Prodigal Daughter*, in the United Kingdom in the spring of 1968.

In the United States Bush's final detective novel did not appear until late November 1969, about four months after the horrific Manson murders in the tarnished Golden State of California. Implicating the triple terrors of sex, drugs and rock and roll (not to mention almost inconceivably bestial violence), the Manson slayings could not have strayed farther from the whimsically escapist "death as a game" aesthetic of Golden Age of detective fiction. Increasingly in the decade capable of producing psychedelic psychopaths like Charles Manson and his "family," the few remaining survivors of the Golden Age of detective fiction increasingly deemed themselves men and women far out of time. In his detective fiction John Dickson Carr, an incurable romantic, prudently beat a retreat from the present into the pleasanter pages of the past, setting his tales in bygone historical eras where he felt vastly more at home. With varying success Agatha Christie made a brave effort to stay abreast of the times (*Third Girl*, *Endless Night*), but ultimately her strivings to understand what was going on around her collapsed into the utter incoherence of *Passenger to Frankfurt* and *Postern of Fate*, by general consensus the worst mystery novels that Dame Agatha ever put down on paper.

In his detective fiction Christopher Bush, who was not quite two years older than Christie, managed rather better than the Queen of Crime to keep up with all the unsettling goings-on around him, while never forswearing the Golden Age article of faith that the primary purpose of a crime writer is pleasingly to puzzle his/her readers. And, in contrast with Christie and Carr, Bush knew when it was time to lay down his pen (or turn off his dictation machine, as the case may be), thereby allowing him to make his exit from the stage on a comparatively high note. Indeed, Christopher Bush's concluding baker's dozen of detective novels, which he published between 1957 and 1968 (and which have now been reprinted, after more than a half-century, by Dean Street Press), makes a generally fine epilogue, or coda, to the author's impressive corpus of crime fiction, which first began to see the light of day way back in the jubilant Jazz Age. These are, readers will find, "good bushes" (to punningly borrow from Shakespeare), providing them with ample intelligent detective entertainment as Bush's longtime series sleuth Ludovic Travers, in the luminous twilight of his career, makes his final forays into ingenious criminal investigation.

*

In the last thirteen Ludovic Travers mystery novels, Travers' *entrée* to his cases continues to come through his ownership of the Broad Street Detective Agency. Besides Travers we also regularly encounter his elegant wife, Bernice (although sometimes his independent-minded spouse is away on excursions of her own), his proverbially loyal secretary, Bertha Munney, his top Broad Street op, Hallows (another one named French, presumably inspired by Bush's late Detection Club colleague Freeman Wills

Crofts, pops up occasionally), John Hill of the United Assurance Agency, who brings Travers many of his cases, and Scotland Yard's Inspector Jewle and Sergeant Matthews, who after the first of these final novels, *The Case of the Treble Twist* (in the U.S. *Triple Twist*), are promoted, respectively, to Superintendent and Inspector. (The Yard's ex-Superintendent George Wharton, now firmly retired from any form of investigative work whatsoever, is mentioned just once by Ludo, when, in *The Case of the Dead Man Gone*, he passingly imparts that he and Wharton recently had lunch together.)

For all practical purposes Travers, who during the Golden Age was a classic gentleman amateur snooper like Philo Vance and Lord Peter Wimsey, now functions fully as a professional private eye—although one, to be sure, who is rather posher than the rest. While some reviewers referred to Travers as England's Philip Marlowe, in fact he little resembles the general run of love and leave 'em/hate and beat 'em brand of brutish American P.I.'s, favoring a nice cup of coffee (a post-war change from tea), a good pipe and the occasional spot of sherry to the frequent snatches of liquor and cigarettes favored by most of his American brethren and remaining faithful to his spouse despite encountering a succession of sexy women, not all of them, shall we say, virtuously inclined.

This was a formula which throughout the period maintained a devoted audience on both sides of the Atlantic consisting, one surmises, of readers (including crime writers Anthony Berkeley, Nicholas Blake and the late Alan Hunter, creator of Inspector George Gently) who preferred their detectives something less than hard-boiled. Travers himself sneers at the hugely popular (and psychotically violent) postwar American private eye Mike Hammer, commenting of an American couple in *The Case of the Treble Twist*: "She was a woman of considerable culture; his ran about as far as Mickey Spillane" [a withering reference to Mike Hammer's creator]. Yet despite his manifest disdain for Mike Hammer, an ugly American if ever there were one, Christopher

Bush and his wife Florence in the spring of 1957 had traveled to New York aboard the RMS *Queen Elizabeth*, and references by him to both the United States and Canada became more frequent in the books which followed this trip.

Certainly *The Case of the Treble Twist* (1957) features tough customers and an exceptionally cruel murder, yet it is also one of Bush's most ingeniously contrived cases from the Fifties, full of charm, treacherous deception and, yes, plenty of twists, including one that is a real sockaroo (to borrow, as Bush occasionally did, from American idiom). Similarly clever is *The Case of the Running Man* (1958), which draws, as several earlier Bush books had, on the author's profound love and knowledge of antiques. By this time Bush and his wife, their coffers having burgeoned from the proceeds of his successful mysteries, resided in the quaint medieval market town of Lavenham, Suffolk at the Great House, a splendidly decorated fourteenth-century structure with an elegant Georgian-era façade which he and Florence purchased in 1953 and resided in until their deaths. The dashing author, whom in 1967 *Chicago Tribune* mystery reviewer Alice Crombie swooningly dubbed "one of the handsomest mystery writers on either side of the Channel or Atlantic," also drove a Jaguar, beloved by James Bond films of late, well into his eighties.

The Case of the Running Man includes that Golden Age detective fiction staple, a family tree, but more originally the novel features as a major character a black American man, Sam, the devoted chauffeur of the wealthy murder victim. Sam, who reminds Ludovic Travers of Rochester, "Jack Benny's factotum of television and radio," is an interesting and sincerely treated individual, although as Anthony Boucher amusingly pronounced at the time in the *New York Times Book Review*, he speaks "a dialect never heard by mortal ear"—an odd compounding of "American Negro" and London cockney.

The Case of the Careless Thief (1959) takes Ludo to Sandbeach, "the Blackpool of the South Coast," as the American jacket blurb puts it, with "a dozen hotels, a race track, a dog track, a music hall and two enormous dance halls." Anthony Boucher deemed this hard-hitting, tricky tale, which draws to strong effect on contemporary events in England, "one of Ludovic Travers' best cases." Likewise hard-hitting are *The Case of the Sapphire Brooch* (1960) and *The Case of the Extra Grave* (1961), complex tales of murderous mésalliances with memorably grim conclusions. The plot of *The Case of the Dead Man Gone* (1961) topically involves refugee relief groups, while *The Case of the Heavenly Twin* (1963) opens with a case of a creative criminal couple forging American Express Travelers Checks, concerning which Americans of a certain age will recall actor Karl Malden sternly enjoining, in a long-running television advertising campaign: "Don't leave home without them." In contrast with many of his crime writing contemporaries (judging from the tone of their work), Bush actually learned to watch and enjoy television, although in *The Case of The Three-Ring Puzzle*, a tale of violently escalating intrigue, Travers dryly references Scottish philosopher Thomas Carlyle's famous observation that England's population consisted of "mostly fools" when he comments: "I guess he wasn't too far out at that. But rather remarkable an estimate perhaps, considering that in his day there were no television commercials."

Of Bush's final five Ludovic Travers detective novels, published between 1964 and 1968, when the Western World, in the eyes of many, was going from whimsically mod to utterly mad, the best are, in my estimation, the cases of *The Jumbo Sandwich* (1965), *The Good Employer* (1966) and *The Prodigal Daughter* (1968). In *Sandwich* a crisp case of a defrauded (and jilted) gentry lady friend of Ludo's metamorphoses into a smorgasbord of, as the American book jacket puts it, "blackmail, black magic, a black sheep, and murder." It all culminates in a confrontation on a lonely Riviera beach in France, setting of some of Ludovic Travers' earliest cases, between Ludo and a desperate killer, in which Bernice plays an unexpectedly active part. Ludo again travels to France in the highly classic *Employer*, which draws most engagingly on the sleuth's (and the author's) dabbling in the world of art and is dedicated to his distinguished Lavenham artist friends, the couple Reginald and Rosalie Brill, who resided next door to Bush and his wife at the fourteenth-century Little Hall, then an art student hostel for which the Brills served as guardians. In *The Guardian* Francis Iles (aka Golden Age crime writer Anthony Berkeley) pronounced that *Employer* represented Bush "at his most ingenious."

Finally, in *Daughter* Travers finds himself tasked with recovering the absconded teenage offspring of domineering Dora Marport, sober-sided head of the organization Home and Family, which is righteously devoted to "the fostering, so to speak, of family life as the stoutest bulwark against the encroachment of ever-more numerous hostile forces: sex and violence in literature, films and on television; pornography generally, and the erosion of responsibility and the capability for sacrifice by the welfare state." Can Travers, a Great War veteran who made his debut in detective fiction in 1926, bridge the generation gap in late-Sixties London? Ludo may prefer Bach to the Beatles, but in this, the last of his recorded cases, he proves more "with it" than one might have expected. All in all, *Daughter* makes a rewarding finish to one of the longest-running and most noteworthy sleuth series in British detective fiction.

Curtis Evans

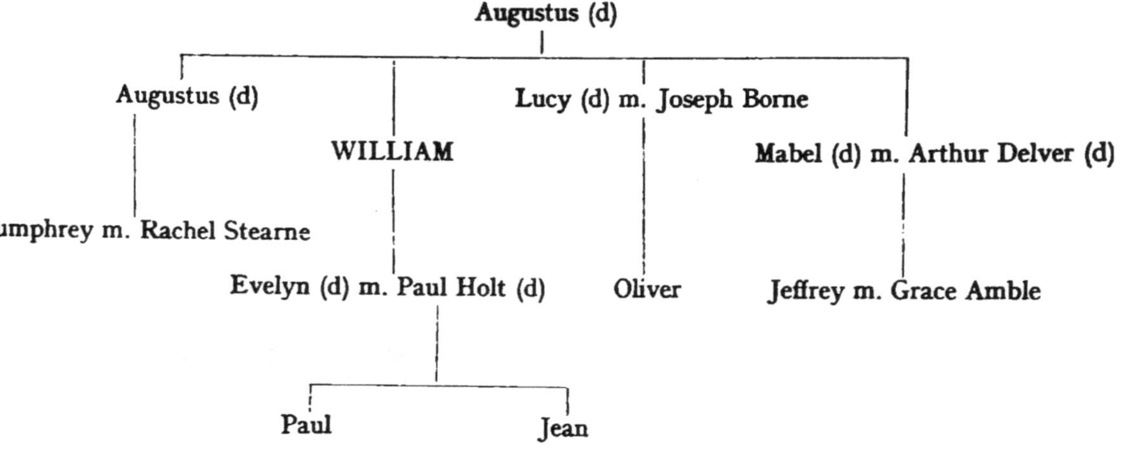

THE WEDDALLS
Augustus (d)
Augustus (d)
Lucy (d) m. Joseph Borne
WILLIAM
Mabel (d) m. Arthur Delver (d)
Humphrey m. Rachel Stearne
Evelyn (d) m. Paul Holt (d)
Oliver
Jeffrey m. Grace Amble
Paul
Jean

1. William Weddall

I OFTEN wonder why it is that so many people who have a liking for and some knowledge of what is known as antiques should regard Christie's as something remote and even somehow sacrosanct: as removed, in fact, from them and their small interests as was the Holy of Holies from the humblest Israelite. Sometimes they don't believe me when I try to convince them to the contrary.

If neither your dress nor your manners are glaringly *outré*, you simply go through the main door, pass the enquiry desk unchallenged and proceed up the wide stairway, and the auction rooms are there in front of you. For a few pence you buy a catalogue of the day's sale and then you either inspect the items or, if it is a forthcoming sale that interests you, walk round the rooms in which the objects for those future sales are on display. At no cost whatever, you can view fine porcelain, pictures, furniture, silver, textiles, jewellery and bric-a-brac, and maybe a host of other rare and valuable things which it is harder to classify.

If you are interested in the day's sale, either with the hope of buying something within your means or merely to see how such a sale is conducted, you just take a seat. Sales begin at eleven o'clock precisely, and that means exactly what it says. At a second or two before the hour the auctioneer mounts the rostrum and as the clock strikes the first lot is announced.

All sorts of people are in that room: dealers from maybe all over the world, collectors and the merely interested. I'm nearly always one of the last-named, though I'm a collector in a very humble way. It was only this spring, after two years of non-bidding, that I did buy something, and that cost me forty guineas, and I bought it only because it was a gift for my wife on the twenty-first anniversary of our wedding. In case you are curious, it was an eighteenth-century inlaid work-box.

Why do I go to Christie's whenever I have a few hours to spare? When I come to think it over I can find all sorts of answers. I love beautiful things and Christie's gives me the chance to see them, and even handle some of them, at the closest of quarters. I've both a passionate interest in my fellow humans and an incredible curiosity, so I like to watch faces and reactions. I also like to keep abreast of the times as regards the shift of prices, and it's very salutary to mark one's catalogue beforehand and note how far wrong, or luckily right, your judgment was. There's one other reason. As one who's been a modest collector all his life, besides inheriting a few valuable things, I like to be gratified by the fact that those possessions have increased enormously in value since the time they were acquired. You know, perhaps, the verses that once appeared in *Punch*. I often quote an extract and probably incorrectly:

> *If I owned a first edition*
> *I would sell without a blush.*
> *If I chanced to find a Titian,*
> *Off to Christie's I would rush.*

That's the view of the Philistine. People like me merely feel an inward warmth at the shrewdness of our earlier judgment, fortuitous though it may have been, and the knowledge that the Commissioners of Inland Revenue can do nothing about it if we do decide to sell. Which we can never do.

But even dropping in at Christie's for an hour or two has become for me a much rarer indulgence these last few years. The Broad Street Detective Agency takes more and more of my time, even if it's only keeping warm the seat of Norris, my manager, when he has to be away. And I doubt if Bernice, my wife, would allow any additions to our collection. I had the good fortune to inherit a small block of high-class flats, now run by a company of which I am a sort of sleeping director, and we contrived years ago to acquire the best flat for ourselves. It has five rooms, besides small kitchen and bath, but even so it's fairly chock-a-block. Some years back I bought a super eighteenth-century wing grandfather chair which was definitely a bargain. I paid for it, managed to get it into my car, and brought it triumphantly home. Bernice merely took a look at it. "Oh, no!" she said despairingly. "Not another chair!"

And what, you may ask, is the point of all this? Is it some subtle form of publicity? Did someone murder the famous member of the firm who happened that day to be auctioneer? Did I acquire some object which happened to have attached to it some queer mystery which nobody had suspected but my astute self? Not a bit of it. All I've been doing is preparing the ground for a meeting. You ought to know why I was where I was and why William Weddall was there, too, and how we happened to meet. But for that very chance meeting there would have been no story. And this is how it happened.

It was the late autumn of last year and I noticed in my paper that on the Friday there was a fairly important sale of pictures at Christie's. There were, for example, two Krieghoffs, that Canadian whose pictures had lately been making quite sensational prices, and I'd never seen a Krieghoff. There were, in addition to other pictures not often in the market, two Utrillos and a Monet, and I happen to own both a Utrillo and a Monet. They were among my lucky purchases when I was in Paris as quite a young man, and they were bought, by modern standards, fantastically cheaply. But don't get me wrong—I'm no genius. I've bought pictures in my time that were dear at the little I gave for them and which were later sold at a loss. I now possess only seven oils but each is excellent of its kind.

On the Thursday I slipped into Christie's, during a sale of furniture, and had a good look at the pictures and I made up my mind to be present the next day. I was lucky enough to be able to get the morning off, and, as I wanted to get another look at the Utrillos, I timed myself to be there soon after half-past ten, which meant that I might also, if I wished, secure a good seat. It was just after the half-hour on the Friday morning when I turned into St. James's and made for King Street. All the off-side of the square is used as a car park and ahead of me a not too old Rolls was backing into an empty space with the attendant giving a clear road.

As I neared, I had a good view of the man whose arm was held by a liveried, coloured chauffeur. He was short—about five feet eight—and thin, and he looked in, at least, the late sixties. He had a short grey beard that came roughly to a point, and I remember how it suddenly struck me that he was very like Joseph Conrad in the photographs one sees of him just before he died. Except that Conrad didn't wear dark glasses.

The chauffeur was also short, but sturdy. He was clean-shaven and his hair was a badger grey. His hand was just holding his master's arm as he mounted the kerb.

"Thank you, Sam. Be standing by at half-past twelve."

"Yes-*sir*. Half-past twelve, sir."

The fact that William Weddall, as I was soon to know him, resembled a famous man had been merely one of those things. But the voice of that coloured chauffeur was something different. It was exactly that of Rochester, Jack Benny's factotum of television and radio. It gave me quite a start. But there was nothing officious or obsequious about it. It was the voice of a man accustomed to speak his mind and it contrived also to have a definite respect.

Weddall moved on towards King Street and I shortened my stride. He was wearing a black homburg, a heavy dark overcoat and I could just see the faint white stripe in his dark trousers: well-fitting clothes, and expensive. He walked slowly and almost carefully, like a man whose eyes are no longer what they were. And then, just short of the right turn into King Street, something happened.

A woman leading a dog—a corgi—came round the corner. The dog swung away to the full extent of its leash, and had I not been almost at his elbow, Weddall would have tripped over it. I grasped his arm and I had to hold pretty tightly or he would still have fallen. The dog went between the pair of us and the woman was all apologies as she manoeuvred it out and shortened the leash.

"Thank you, sir," Weddall said as I released his arm. "Very quick action on your part and I'm grateful."

There was the faintest trace of an American accent, or was it Canadian? My mind, agile as ever—far too agile—was running ahead. Maybe he was going to Christie's to bid for the Krieghoffs.

"Lucky I happened to be so near," I said as we turned into King Street. "You going far this way?"

"Only to Christie's."

"So am I," I said. "You hoping to buy anything?"

"No," he said. "I usually get any buying done for me. As a matter of fact, my niece and my two grandchildren were coming to town so I thought I'd come too and drop in at Christie's to pass the time. You a dealer? Or a collector?"

"A collector in a very modest way. But, like yourself, just a spectator this morning. And I'm rather interested in one or two of the pictures."

"Thank you," he said as I stepped back to usher him through the door. I drew alongside as we went up the stairs and I noticed that he moved erectly but carefully. Through the dark glasses I couldn't see his eyes but I imagined them to be pale blue or grey.

There was a slight congestion at the head of the stairs and he thanked me again as I drew back once more to let him go through.

"Perhaps I shall be seeing you again," he said. "I shall be staying for some time."

I watched him buy a catalogue from the attendant and then I bought one too and went in search of the pictures. I ought to have known better. Most of them had already been removed to the ante-room behind the rostrum ready for the sale, so I strolled round the other rooms. I saw Weddall at various times. Some really magnificent silver was on display in a smaller room but that didn't seem to interest him. His tastes seemed to be more for porcelain and furniture, and I noted that he had a large collector's glass which he took now and again from his breast pocket as he stooped to examine something at close quarters. In another room pictures for a forthcoming sale seemed to interest him, too, and

I noticed that he stood for some time before a smallish Ruysdael landscape. I didn't go near it myself. I hadn't that catalogue but it had had to be a Ruysdael by its sky.

I'd been so interested in Weddall that I hadn't noticed the passing of time and it was only the comparative emptiness of most of the rooms and the movement towards the sale-room that told me the sale must be already on. It was, and every seat was occupied. People were standing at the back and I found a place in a small, convenient gap. I'm six feet three and it would take an abnormally tall crowd to impede my view.

It must have been a half-hour and several pictures later when I noticed Weddall. He was behind me, trying to peer over the inter-vening spectators. I moved slightly back, managed to catch his eye and motioned for him to slip through in front of me. Now he could see and I could see over him. He gave me a grateful smile.

The sale went on. Pictures at fifty guineas, a hundred, two hundred guineas and the usual stir as the important stuff came up. The Krieghoffs made well into two thousand guineas and a Fantin-Latour over three thousand. Then came the first of the Utrillos. It made nineteen hundred and fifty guineas. Weddall looked round and up at me.

"You think Utrillo will ever get up to the really big money?"

"I hope so," I said, preening my feathers. "I've one that's very much better and cost me infinitely less."

"Really?" He seemed interested.

"And a Monet." I tried to say that with no importance at all.

Another picture was up. Ten minutes went by and in a conven-ient interval he looked round again.

"What do you make the time?"

"Ten minutes to twelve."

He nodded. He thought for a moment. Then he beckoned invitingly to me as he began making a way past me and through the crowd. He stopped just beyond, waiting for me to join him.

"I hope you won't think it an unpardonable liberty, but after all—" He smiled. "I mean—well, collectors like to show their collections, so would it be possible to see that Utrillo of yours? It's not too far away? We could make an appointment perhaps?"

"Delighted to show it to you now," I said. "It's less than a mile away. We could be at my flat in ten minutes."

"You're quite sure? I'm not dragging you away?"

"A pleasure," I said, and gently took his arm as he moved towards the stairs.

"We'll take my car," he said as we went through to King Street. "My man will probably be there. My name's Weddall, by the way, William Weddall."

"My name's Travers. Christian name the not too common one of Ludovic."

"I've met it before," he said, as I slipped round to the outside berth. "And in Chicago of all places. I think his other name was Chemitz, or something like that. An Austrian by birth. Used to be a very good client of my firm. I was an architect, by the way."

We rounded the corner. Thirty yards away Sam was giving a light going-over to the bonnet of the car. He caught sight of us and smiled as we came near. It was a smile that lighted the whole of his rugged face and made him the most likeable soul I'd seen that morning.

"Lucky you're here, Sam," Weddall said. "This is Sam Martin," he said to me, and smiled too. "Sam's been with me for years. How many is it, Sam?"

"Be about thirty years, now, sir. I was lettin' it run through my mind only a few minutes ago."

"A long while," Weddall said and shook his head. "This is Mr. Travers, Sam."

"Nice to know you, sir," Sam said, and looked a bit surprised as I held out my hand. He took off his glove and his handshake was friendly and warm.

I sat in the front and we made our way out into the traffic of Lower Regent Street. When I said we went left at Charing Cross Hospital, Sam said he knew the way. He was a good, careful driver and traffic wasn't too bad. In ten minutes we were pulling up outside the flats. Sam was out of the door almost before the brake was on to help his master out.

"Stand by, Sam," Weddall told him. "We shan't be more than a few minutes."

"Yes-*sir*," Sam said briskly. And to me, "You keep an eye on the boss, sir. Don't want him trippin' on no stairs, or nothin'."

"I like your Sam," I told Weddall as I steered him through the swing doors and towards the lifts.

"They don't come better," he said. "Sam would go through fire for me, as they say. For that matter, so would I for him."

Out in the short corridor I went ahead and had the flat door open by the time Weddall was there. We went into the living-room where the oils were hung. They were all small. The largest, the Utrillo, was only about three feet by two. He asked if he might see it closely and I took it down. He had a look at it by the window—back towards me—and I noticed that he had removed the dark glasses. He had done the same thing once or twice when he was at Christie's.

"You were right," he told me, as he handed the picture back. "I haven't seen all that number of Utrillos but this is really good. You'll sell it?"

There was an abruptness in the question. I don't suppose for a moment he was trying to browbeat me into a sale, but a lot of people might have had that impression.

"No," I said.

"Name your own price—within reason."

"No," I said again, and began rehanging the picture. "I'm still regarding it as an insurance against my senility."

"No insurance like hard cash," he told me, and then maybe he realised he was using the technique of a dealer. He gave a little laugh.

"Ah, well. There's no harm in trying. And this is the Monet?"

He liked the Monet. He agreed with me that the landscape was probably an early Cuyp and he didn't care a lot for the small Matthew Smith. Then he had a look at the drawings in the main bedroom and they included a John. He was enraptured with the miniature Queen Anne bureau-bookcase and my small collection of Chelsea-Derby.

"Amazing!" he said finally. "It just shows you the kind of thing that's tucked away in private collections. And probably doesn't get on the market." He gave a little chuckle and I think it was rather an artificial one. "Do you know, I could spend quite a lot of money with you?"

He was almost annoying by that persistence. I won't say there was a brashness about him: there definitely was just a shade too much directness, for a guest, that is, in a private house, and, when you come to think of it, he *was* a guest.

"That's nice to hear," I said. "But what about a drink? There's some sherry I can really recommend."

"That's good of you," he said, "but I doubt if I have the time."

"It's still only half-past twelve," I told him. "At what time are you meeting your people?"

At any time around one, he said. He was taking them to lunch at the Café Royal. I told him he could be there in five minutes and finally he loosened his heavy coat and I had him seated in the wing grandfather. He chose the dry sherry.

"May I give you a card?" he said. "If ever you're my way I do hope you'll call."

I just glanced at the card and slipped it into my pocket.

"Something I wanted to ask you," I said. "I've met your name somewhere and I just can't remember where it was. Something to do with collecting. Just as vague as that."

"Weddall and Borne?"

I stared.

"Good Lord, yes! That shop of theirs in Lower Oxford Street. One of the first things I ever bought was from them."

"My father's place originally," he said. "Then Borne married my eldest sister and they went into partnership."

"Curious," I said. "I haven't thought about them for years. The business still exists?"

"Not on the old premises, as you probably know. The lease expired and Joe Borne took a place in South Kensington. This is excellent sherry, by the way."

He protested, but not too strongly, as I refilled his glass.

"Well, here's to more bargains," he told me as he raised the glass. He smacked his lips when he set it down.

"You ever get landed with fakes?"

It was an abrupt sort of question, almost fired at me.

"Heavens, yes," I said. "What amateur doesn't?"

"And what are your reactions?"

"I think I just shrug my shoulders," I said, "and curse myself for being too gullible."

"Yes," he said slowly. "I suppose we *are* gullible, or people think we are. You know what my reactions are?"

"No?"

"I'm not angry at the fake. What angers me is that cheap little crooks, or big crooks, should be patting themselves on the back and thinking they're cleverer than I am."

What a mixture of moods, and even persons, he was. That pointed beard of his jutted out and he was giving a kind of sneer as if it was I who'd tried to put some smart deal across.

"And then what?"

"I have my own methods," he told me. "Give people enough rope and they'll still hang themselves. And there're few greater satisfactions than gently steering a crook into some nice little trap he's laying for you."

He took another sip of his drink and went off at a conversational tangent.

"Something I was meaning to ask you. I hope you don't think it's rude. Are you connected with the trade?"

"The antique business?" I smiled. "I'm afraid not. As a matter of fact, I'm a private detective."

His mouth gaped. He looked so utterly aghast that I had to laugh.

"Don't be alarmed. I just happen to own an agency. A very reputable one."

He still hadn't quite got over it.

"You do any detective work yourself?"

"I've done practically nothing else for a very long time," I told him. "Don't take it as boasting, but I've worked quite a lot with Scotland Yard."

"Now that's mighty interesting," he said, and his lips clamped together for a moment. Through those dark glasses I couldn't see his eyes.

"Have you a business card?" he asked. "It's more than likely I might ask you to undertake a pretty important assignment in the near future."

I always carry two kinds of cards in my wallet. I gave him the business one, and I apologised. I said I didn't like mixing business with pleasure, and it *had* been a pleasure to show an expert my humble collection.

"Not an expert," he told me. "I'm still a learner."

He finished the last of his sherry and got to his feet. I helped him to adjust the heavy coat.

"Your wife away?" he asked me.

The twin beds told him I was married. I said she was shopping and then lunching out.

"Then why not join us for lunch yourself?"

"Very good of you," I said, "but I've played hookey too long. I have to get along to the agency."

"Some other time then?"

I said I'd be delighted. And perhaps he'd lunch with me at my club the next time he was in town.

There wasn't much more talk as we walked to the lifts and went down. When I said I had no children he told me he'd had a daughter who'd been killed with her husband in a plane accident and it was her two children he was taking to lunch. I said my experience was that grandparents spoiled grandchildren, and he gave a rather satisfied smile and reckoned that I might be right.

Sam opened the door and gently went through the motions of helping him into the car. I gave Weddall a farewell smile and asked Sam if he knew the quickest way to the Café Royal. He said he knew it. He'd done quite a lot of driving in town.

"Nice meeting you, sir," he told me, and then moved the car on. Weddall gave me a wave of the hand and after a moment I went back into the entrance hall. I had a look at the lunch menu and asked the manageress to send me a tray upstairs. Then I went up to the flat.

As I was eating that rather stodgy meal I couldn't help wondering just why I'd turned down a first-class one, and it wasn't altogether because I didn't want to be thought a thruster after so short an acquaintance. I decided that the reason was Weddall himself.

I like analysing people: there are even times when I pull up short and analyse myself, and, believe me, that's a salutary experience. And that half-hour, with nothing better to do, I thought a lot about Weddall if only because he might in the near future be a client.

I decided that I didn't like him and that I didn't altogether trust him. In the age of the first Elizabeth, the most objectionable person was the Italianate Englishman. Weddall, it seemed to me, was an Englishman none too well Americanised. Don't get me wrong. I like, admire, generally trust and frequently envy Americans. Many are among my very real friends, but Weddall, it seemed to me, had acquired the wrong traits in the wrong way. It was hard to pin any definite thing down but those impressions of the man were vividly there: a wrong directness; a false assumption of real money values, a hint of power that could be ruthlessly used and, with it all, something curiously theatrical as if he were playing a part.

Much ado about nothing? Maybe, but in my line of business it pays to look before you leap. Nothing might ever come of that rather eager suggestion of an important assignment in the near future, but the possibility did remain and it was just as well to try to get as far as one could into the character of a client. And then I remembered something—Weddall's card. There was nothing much to see: just the name in plain capitals and then, in the bottom left-hand corner, as usual, the address. It was that that made my eyes pop a bit. And in the same moment I knew something else. If I wanted more information about Weddall, then I knew the man who could provide it. That was why I rang the agency.

2. SECOND ENCOUNTER

IT WAS Weddall's address which had startled me—Hinchbrook Hall, Mainford. The village of Hinchbrook was, as I well knew, only some four miles from Mainford. I'd never actually been there but I remembered the name. Mainford—not its real name, by the way—is a large, sprawling, ugly manufacturing town about an hour's non-stop run by train from town.

Some four years previously I'd had a very important job there: a job that had kept me in the town for a good many days and had ended in a pretty considerable shake-up for the heads of the police force. The client had been a man named James Landlace and he had been extraordinary grateful for what we had done, and now I was certain that he'd be only too pleased to tell me in confidence what he knew about William Weddall. Landlace, you see, was the owner of the town's biggest store, and there was what might be called an annexe for antiques attached to his modern furniture department. If, therefore, anyone should know Weddall, it was James Landlace.

That was why I rang Bertha at the agency. I reminded her of the Landlace Case and said that in the file there ought to be Landlace's telephone numbers—the store and his private address. I told Bertha to ring me back and in five minutes she gave me both numbers. I rang the store and I had about three minutes to wait.

"Is Mr. Landlace in?" I said to the quite nice voice at the other end.

"I'm afraid not, sir," she said. "Who's speaking, please?"

"A very old friend whom he'll be glad to hear from," I said. "You don't happen to know where I can get him?"

"He's at home," she said. "He's had that Asiatic 'flu. There's an awful lot of it here."

"I have his private number," I told her. "Will he be well enough to talk to me?"

She thought he would. Her information was that he was expected back in his office the coming Monday. Then she said she could put me through. There was a private line direct to Mr. Landlace's house. Another few seconds and I was hearing Landlace's voice. He spotted my voice, a bit tentatively perhaps, and seemed delighted to be talking to me. A few generalities and I got down to business. A man of his standing didn't need to swear on a stack of Bibles that he'd observe a strict secrecy. He knew what I meant by strictly private and confidential.

"I know him very well," he said. "He's quite an important person in a way. Very wealthy. He was head of a firm of architects in New York and he married money. Locally they talk of him as a millionaire, but you know what gossip is."

"You sell him much?"

"Very little. I rarely get hold of the class of stuff that would be likely to interest a man like him. I do have a standing order, though, that he's to have first view of anything we consider out of the ordinary. He has a nephew in the town, by the way—has quite a high-class antique shop almost opposite the town hall. I don't know if you remember it. Borne and Son."

"I don't know if I do," I told him. "But Weddall himself. What's your private opinion of him?"

"Hard to say," he said. "He's apt to be a bit assertive but you rather expect that from a man with his money. Actually I haven't seen him for quite a time now. His eyes are getting bad, or did you know that?"

"What is it? Cataract?"

"Frankly, I don't know. I think it was Oliver Borne, his nephew, who told me."

"The Weddalls are local people? I mean, with a local history?"

"Heavens, yes!" he said. "Hinchbrook Hall's always been their home as far back as I can go. The father had a business here before going to London. One of his sons was one of our leading lawyers. His son still is. Humphrey Weddall of Weddall, Weddall and Spurn in Church Row. The father, by the way, lived to a very great age. Old Gus Weddall. I think he was ninety."

"And William Weddall. How would you think I should regard him as a client? That's a pure assumption, of course."

He laughed quietly.

"I'd say you'd be a lucky fellow. As I told you, he's a very wealthy man."

"No snags at all—if you know what I mean?"

He seemed surprised.

"Not that I can possibly think of. You might have to see things his way, of course. There's quite a lot of toughness in him."

I didn't want to get myself in too deep, so I left it at that.

"Very good of you to let me know. And next time you're up here, send me word. It's time we had a get-together."

There hadn't been much that was helpful, but then Landlace hadn't known very much. In any case I was realising that I'd been jumping just a little too much to conclusions. Maybe Weddall's remarks about future assignments had merely been politeness. That again, as I knew, was an American trait. Folks there were so anxious to like and be liked that mere words hadn't always a true value either in themselves or in context.

In any case days went by and I heard nothing from Weddall.

I forgot all about him till Christmas had gone by. The year had only two days to go when I saw him again. He'd given me quite a few thoughtful moments the first time I'd met him. This time we didn't actually speak, but after the brief time I was in his vicinity I thought a great deal more.

It was the last Monday of the year. A valuable client from the provinces had been staying in town over the week-end at the

Stretford Hotel in Grosvenor Place and he'd asked me to have breakfast with him before he left on the boat-train from Victoria. Breakfasts of that kind are a leftover from Edwardian days but I wish there were more of them.

His train left at nine forty-five—he was going to Paris for some conference or other—so our meal began at eight-thirty. We'd finished with business on the previous Saturday so the meal was a purely social one. When the time came to leave, he and I walked the few yards to the station. The hotel was looking after his one piece of luggage.

There was no point in my going beyond the barrier so we said goodbye just before he showed his ticket and went through.

I thought of going to the bookstall and had turned that way when I saw a couple of people whom I recognised, and with them was a porter carrying a couple of bags. Weddall, dressed in what might have been the same dark clothes as when I'd last seen him, was approaching the same barrier. Sam Martin, smart as a new pin in his chauffeur's outfit, was just behind at his elbow. The porter went through first, then Weddall showed his ticket and he and Sam went through. The platform was pretty crowded and I watched them for a few yards and then went on. In a way I was glad I hadn't run full tilt into them. After all, if Weddall had wanted to make anything more out of that first brief meeting of ours, he could have done so, and it had been up to him to make the advances.

Perhaps I shouldn't have said that. I ought to have kept straight to the point instead of giving the impression of the passing of time. In fact, Weddall couldn't have been more than twenty yards along that platform when I saw something else—an operative named Mander employed by Bill Fraser of City Detection Ltd. I knew him because Bill and I often borrow operatives from each other, and Mander had done more than one job for me. He was a good man: one, in fact, of Bill's best and I couldn't help wondering if he were on a job. I watched him approach the barrier and have a quiet word or two with the ticket collector. Then he craned up and had a good look along the platform. He turned quickly back and made for the slot machine and slipped in a penny for a platform ticket.

I moved on, rather abstractedly perhaps, and when I turned the corner in the direction of the taxis I realised I hadn't gone to the bookstall after all. And then I saw something that was perfectly amazing. Weddall was making for a taxi and with him was the porter carrying the same two bags. A taxi was handy, the bags were put in the front, Weddall passed a tip to the porter who flicked a finger to his cap, and then the taxi moved off. There was no sign of Sam.

I suppose it was a kind of sleuthing instinct that made me nip back to the taxi that was coming up to the line. When the driver asked me where to, I told him to follow the taxi ahead of us, and as I settled back I saw that Rolls drawn up just ahead. What flashed through my mind was that Sam had driven from Hinchbrook to Victoria Station and would either be taking the car back or picking up his master elsewhere. Then, as we cleared the end of the long platform, I saw the train beginning to move off.

It was no trouble at all to follow the taxi ahead of us as it went straight along Victoria Street. What everything was about I had no idea, except that it was something remarkably curious. Weddall had certainly had in his possession a ticket for Dover, or Folkestone—I wasn't sure which—and yet he had never got on the train. Did Sam know what it was all about? I couldn't be sure. Maybe Weddall had actually got into a carriage and then had left it after telling Sam to get back to the car. And, if so, Sam would still be prepared to swear that Weddall had left on that boat-train.

The other taxi was still well in sight of us and where the two of us ultimately landed up was at Charing Cross Station. Another taxi was between us and Weddall. A porter took his luggage. I paid my man off and followed at a careful distance. Weddall was walking with that same erect and yet precise motion, as if mindful, as it were, of where to put his feet. He said something to the porter who set the bags down. He went into the booking-office and bought a ticket and then he and the porter set off again. The porter glanced up at the clock and said something. I didn't want to go out into the open so I tried to watch from where I was. I saw them go through the barrier on the far right to where a train was waiting and after that my view was obscured.

The porter came back through the barrier and I caught him just as he was coming through the passage to the yard.

"Excuse me"—I brought out some change as if ready for a tip—"but do you happen to have seen my uncle?"

I gave a quick description. The porter smiled.

"Just took his luggage along, sir. The Sevenoaks, Tonbridge and Hastings train. On the right there. You can't miss it. Doesn't go for ten minutes yet."

I gave him a shilling. When he'd moved on I went to the booking-office. I spun the same yam to the clerk from whom Weddall had bought his ticket. He listened impassively.

"I remember him. He'll probably be on the Hastings train."

"Do you know if he booked right through?"

"Booked to Tonbridge," he said, and went on with the job he was doing.

I went back, parked myself behind the bookstall and kept an eye on the barrier till the train moved out. Weddall wasn't playing any more games. Unless—and the thought startled me—he got out again at Waterloo or London Bridge! And after that he might be making for anywhere.

I found a taxi and went along to Broad Street and all the length of that spasmodic ride I was puzzling my wits and trying ineffectively to work out what on earth Weddall had been up to. I had a fantastic idea. Was the man and his money altogether bogus? Was he getting away from his creditors? Had he committed some gigantic fraud? And had somebody had an inkling, and got into touch with a detective agency and tried to put a man on his heels?

I, who can find almost any theory attractive, was far from satisfied about that particular one, even if it fitted so aptly the events on which I had stumbled so strangely that morning. A man who was making a getaway would surely first have realised his property and turned as much as possible into cash. And that thought gave me another idea.

As soon as I'd paid off the taxi I went into Bertha's room.

"Everything in order, Bertha?"

"A bit quiet," she said. "Mr. Norris is out but he said he'd be back in an hour. Would you like some coffee?"

I said I would, but first would she get for me the telephone number of a Mr. William Weddall, of Hinchbrook Hall, near Mainford, and put a call through. I'd take it in the office.

I had a very few minutes to wait. The voice at the end of the line was a woman's: a voice of some culture but just a bit strident. Not a youngish voice, but far from old.

"May I speak to Mr. Weddall, please?"

"Who's speaking?"

"A Mr. Charles Hare," I said. "I'm a very old friend of Mr. Weddall. We saw a great deal of each other in New York."

"I'm sorry, Mr. Hare, but Mr. Weddall is away." The voice was suddenly quite different. All the stridency had gone. "He left early this morning."

"Oh dear!" I said, and clicked my tongue. "Is there no possibility of my getting into touch with him?"

"I'm sorry, but he's now on his way to Italy. He's meeting a friend at Boulogne and they're touring Italy by car."

"That seems to settle it," I said resignedly. "When will he be back?"

"We don't actually know. Probably in five or six weeks." She gently cleared her throat. "Would you like to leave any message?"

"I'll write him from New York," I said. "I'm flying back to-night and I thought there might be just a chance of seeing him. Thank you all the same."

I hung up, put back in my pocket the handkerchief I'd been gripping with my teeth, and then let out a breath. Everything was still complicated, even if Weddall didn't seem to be fleeing the country. If he *had* been, it seemed to me he ought to have gone to Boulogne and vanished from there. But at least something in the train of events was clear. He'd given his people at Hinchbrook a perfectly good reason for being away for up to six weeks—visits with a friend to Italian museums and art dealers—and all the while, for unknown reasons, he intended to be elsewhere.

And no sooner had I got as far as that than I had another idea. Perhaps he *was* going to Italy, but had given his people the wrong date and in the meanwhile—a day, a week?—was going on some private jaunt before turning up at Boulogne. But if so—that flibbertygibbet mind of mine was off again—how did that explain Bill Fraser's operative? Then I smiled sheepishly. Why should Mander have been trailing Weddall? What proof had I? Mander might have been watching anybody on that boat-train.

And what in any case was it to do with me? That was the starkest question of all. Insatiable curiosity had once more tricked me into minding other people's business, and it was a vice, I told myself, about which I'd really have to do something by way of cure. So I settled down to forgetting Weddall. For a couple of days or so I made none too good a hand of it, and then once more he slipped my mind.

Till something else happened.

I'd like you to notice very carefully the dates. It was on December the 30th, you may recall, that the mysterious events took place at Victoria Station. It was on the morning of Wednesday, January the 29th, that I found a letter awaiting me at the office. It was marked *Personal*. Paper and the largish envelope were a grey linen and of good quality, and the letter itself was typed. A cheque was enclosed, and a sealed, unstamped letter addressed to a Mrs. Amble, Hinchbrook Hall. The letter itself was unsigned but there was no doubt as to who was the sender. There was also no address. The letter had been posted in the West End the previous evening.

Dear Mr. Travers,

You may recall that I mentioned the likelihood of employing your firm. What I am now asking you to do is only a preliminary to important work which I hope you will be able to undertake in the course of the next week or two. Will you pardon me if I impress on you the urgency for extreme secrecy. I want you, and you only, to handle the matter immediately in hand.

You will take a plane within the next two or three days and simply post the enclosed letter in Paris. That is all. The enclosed cheque should amply pay expenses. You will then write me a letter under a fictitious name addressing it to Hinchbrook Hall, Mainford, writing any gibberish you like provided you assure me this commission has been completed.

PS. I'd still like that Utrillo. But how naive and *enfantin* he so often is!

PPS. Looked you up in *Who's Who*.

I had a look at the cheque. It was for fifty pounds, payable to me personally, but it wasn't Weddall who had signed it. I couldn't quite decipher the signature even when I looked at it through a strong glass. The nearest I could get was Martin Larki and there was no name like that in the telephone directory. Even so I felt pretty sure that that cheque—drawn on a West End branch of Barclays Bank—would be honoured, and let me say at once that it was to go through my private account without a hitch.

What I thought about those instructions, what I tried to deduce and the various impasses at which I always arrived are no matter. I went to Paris early the following morning, posted the letter and stayed till the next afternoon. As Weddall had written, expenses were more than amply paid.

By the time I returned, one thing was very clear in my mind. It didn't explain everything—in fact it scarcely explained anything at all—but the one thing it did make clear was that Weddall had never gone to Italy but was convincing his people that he had, and that he had reached Paris on his way home. The rest of it I had for once the sense to leave to that week or fortnight later when Weddall would be getting into touch with me. Sufficient unto the day is the assignment thereof.

And now for something very different. It was the late afternoon of Tuesday, February the 11th: the time about 5.0 p.m. Norris was out and I was in the office alone and looking at some not-too-important reports when I had a telephone call. A Mr. Hugh Browning, Bertha said, ringing from Liverpool. Very urgent.

Mr. Browning certainly had a voice with a faint Manchester accent.

"I want you personally to do a very important job for me, Mr. Travers. Money's no object but time is. I'd like you to get busy at once. If not I'm afraid I'll have to make other arrangements."

"What *is* the job?" I said.

"Rather hush-hush. I'll tell you all about it when I see you, but some important documents are missing from our works here."

"Here being Liverpool?"

"Correct," he said tersely. "I'd like you to take the seven-twenty tonight from Euston and I'll meet you personally at Lime Street. I'm tall and rather stout and I'll be wearing a coloured handkerchief outside the breast pocket of my overcoat."

"Assuming I come, I'm very tall—"

He gave a little chuckle.

"I know that. And you're certainly not as stout as I."

"We've met?"

"You may or may not remember me. We just overlapped at Downing. But about tonight. It's very urgent: repeat, urgent. Can you make that train?"

"Probably, yes," I said, "but we'd better be clear about our terms. If the job's all that important and urgent, they may come a bit high."

"Dammit, I said terms didn't matter," he told me explosively. A moment and he quietened down. "Pardon me, but I'm a bit upset. Your terms will be met and you'll get a bonus if you clear the whole thing up."

"Right," I said. "I'll see you. At Lime Street. And what about a hotel for the night?"

"Just a moment."

He broke off, cupped the receiver, and I could just hear him snapping something at somebody.

"Sorry about that," he told me. "Everything will be arranged about the hotel. You can count on returning tomorrow."

"Right," I said again. "Be seeing you at Lime Street."

There was just time to do the usual preliminary checking on the client but I found no Hugh Browning in the trade directory for the Liverpool area. I was not surprised. The name of those works he'd mentioned might be anything. As for a Browning who'd been a contemporary of mine at Downing, Cambridge, I just couldn't recall one: in fact I couldn't remember more than half a dozen of my contemporaries by name. And he'd said *over-lapped*, which might mean that he'd gone down just as I went up, or the other way round.

Still, whoever he was, he looked like being a money-spinner for the firm. I left a guarded note for Norris, took a taxi to the flat, broke the news to Bernice, packed a small bag and said I'd have a meal on the train. I made it in good time and had a first-class compartment to myself. Almost as soon as the train moved off, dinner was on. After it—and I lingered it out—I read the evening papers, tried to doze and couldn't, and finally arrived at Lime Street. The train was only ten minutes late, which is excellent for British Railways.

I hadn't far to walk to the barrier. About half-a-dozen people were waiting there but none was tall and stout and with a coloured handkerchief leaking from a breast pocket. I decided to wait where I was. When half an hour had gone by I went to the enquiry office. I described the man I should have met and said that if he came there asking for me, would they say I'd be back in a few moments.

Then I found a telephone booth and rang the Adelphi Hotel. I managed to get a room and said I'd be there within ten minutes.

I looked through the telephone directory, but found no Hugh Browning. I went back to the enquiry office and asked them to tell Mr. Browning, if he asked for me, that I was staying at the Adelphi. I went back to the barrier but no Browning, so I took a taxi to the hotel.

I mentioned Browning at the desk and said he was to be sent up to my room. I went up myself and when another half-hour had gone by, began to find the whole thing very fishy. But all sorts of things might have happened and I managed to get a good night's rest. In the morning I enquired at the desk, but the elusive, or fictitious, Mr. Browning hadn't appeared.

But I didn't give up. Browning had mentioned important documents as missing and they might be sufficiently important as to involve Browning in some danger. So I went round to police headquarters where there were one or two people I knew. They'd heard of nothing happening to a Hugh Browning, and they knew no one of that name. And that was when I decided the whole thing was a hoax, but, luckily, not a too expensive one. And that left the big-money question unanswered—who had perpetrated it, and why?

I went straight to the office from Euston. Bertha told me confidentially that the Mr. Browning hadn't rung again. I came absolutely clean with Norris and he was as bewildered as I. A point he shrewdly made was this.

"You say, sir, that he wanted you personally to go to Liverpool, and therefore it was you personally who was got out of the way."

"Exactly," I said. "But out of the way of what?"

There was no answer. The next day he suggested that we should put the facts before the Liverpool police and ask them to make enquiries. I didn't agree. We'd been made fools of, I said, but surely there was nothing to be gained by letting anyone else know it. When he came to think it out, he said I was probably right. But whoever had been responsible for that hoax had been uncommonly clever. I told him not to rub it in. After all, it was I, not he, who'd been hoaxed.

3. A NEW CLIENT

YOU will recall that it was on Tuesday, February the 11th when that hoax was perpetrated and I went to Liverpool. That Tuesday afternoon was dull, as I remember well, and with a constant threat of rain. It did actually rain by the time I got to Euston. And it was still drizzling all the Wednesday while I was in Liverpool, though it had cleared up by the time I got back to town. The rest of the week turned dry and cold with a wind from the north-east coming straight, as the Danes used to say, from Stalin's whiskers.

I know that it was very snug in that living-room—lounge, if you prefer it—of ours on the Sunday evening. A north-east wind is about the only one we can hear and that night it was whining and howling every few minutes so eerily and so near that you almost shivered. Bernice hates the wind. I like it. When you're my age you clutch at anything that makes you part again of a poignantly far-off youth, and winds like that always bring back the first minutes in bed when I was a small boy and the shrieking of a high wind and even the slight tremor of my room only made the bed warmer and my small self somehow more secure.

It was about half-past seven and we'd just finished the Sunday evening cold supper when the telephone bell rang.

"I do hope that doesn't mean you've got to go out," Bernice said, looking up from that wing grandfather she's long since appropriated. I shrugged my shoulders.

"Glad you're in," came Jewle's voice.

"I'm glad, too," I told him. "How are you? Haven't seen you for a month at least."

"Still bearing up. You think you can stand it if I drop in for a few minutes?"

"I'll ask Bernice," I said, and I did ask her, and without cupping the receiver.

"You hear that?" I said, and he laughed and said he'd be along almost at once.

Bernice likes Jewle. If it comes to that, Bernice likes everybody. She's the sort who rarely makes an enemy and never loses a friend. And I like Jewle, too. I like him enormously. Chief-Inspectors at the Yard are important people but Jewle's as genuine and unpretentious as when I first knew him as a Detective-Sergeant. Like a lot of physically big men, he's quiet in manner and even gentle. I've worked with him several times and even under quite a lot of provocation I've rarely heard him raise his voice. And he has about him that air of utter reliability. A quarrel, however brief, with Jewle, is something that could never conceivably enter my mind.

He was in the room not five minutes after ringing and he owned up that he'd called me from Charing Cross Station. Pleasure and business, he said, and he hoped there'd be very little of the latter. And he wouldn't hear of Bernice leaving us alone.

She had made coffee for us and when Jewle had discarded his heavy overcoat we sat round the electric fire, snug as bugs in a rug. You can't hurry Jewle. When he's on a case there's nothing about him of the head-on rush. He likes to take a good look at all the angles. He's the same when he's on a purely private visit to the flat. He and I will sit there with a glass of beer and maybe nothing will be said for quite a time, and then he'll say something that's come into his mind and begin to develop it and contrive to have me airing my own views while he does the listening. And he's shrewd. He's often startled me by the things he knows.

That evening he was more direct than usual. I asked what he'd been doing with himself lately.

"Oh, this and that," he said. "You know how it is. Mostly at the Yard. Occasionally managed to get out, though. As a matter of fact I was away all Saturday. Only got back this late afternoon." He smiled quietly. "Somewhere where you're still not too popular. Mainford, to be exact."

"Mainford?" I smiled too. "I thought the police there would have loved me. Don't tell me they've taken away that statue?"

"Can't say I noticed it. Or a plaque on the wall." He smiled dryly again. "Not that it was actually in Mainford where I spent most of my time. It was a nice little village just outside it. Place called Hinchbrook. You know it?"

His eyes met mine. I felt a sort of cold shiver. There wasn't anything resembling panic but my brain was suddenly chock-a-block with ideas. And then some instinct told me to play safe.

"By name at least," I said. "After all, I was in Mainford quite a time on that Landlace affair."

"I remember you were," he sighed. "Well, it looks as if I'll be that way for a bit—I and Matthews. They've asked us to take over an inquiry there. Something bigger than they can handle."

"Murder?"

"Well, I wouldn't say that—not yet," he told us. "Mind you, I wouldn't be surprised if things began to shape that way. If they haven't already."

"And the victim?"

He was looking into the fire. I caught Bernice's eye and gave a quick shake of the head.

"A man named Weddall. William Weddall. Don't suppose you've ever heard of him."

I nodded quickly to Bernice. It so happened that we both spoke at once.

"Not that queer man you told me about—"

"I've actually met him—"

Bernice gave way to me. Jewle said it was certainly a very small world. That was both before and after I'd given him a detailed account of the morning at Christie's and the flat.

"He sounded to me like a most unpleasant man," Bernice said. "I know collectors are supposed to be rather unscrupulous people—even Ludo is sometimes—but he was really too aggressive and self-important."

"I don't know," I said mildly.

"Well, you've never heard from him since. He might at least have written you an appreciative letter."

Bernice knew nothing of that mention of his of a job of work for him. And, since it was agency business, I'd never mentioned that posting of a letter in Paris. All she'd known was that I'd gone there on business for the firm, and I'd been happy to leave it like that.

"Well, *de mortuis*," I said. "So Weddall is dead."

"Buried yesterday," Jewle added. "A very imposing funeral."

"I gathered he was a wealthy man. You don't know how much he left?"

"More than I ever will," he said wryly. "I'm assured that even after all duties are paid there'll be best part of a quarter of a million."

I whistled softly.

"No skin off my nose, but isn't that a good incentive to murder?"

"Might be," he said.

"Any relatives? And am I likely to have met them at Mainford?"

"Possibly. The new head of the family, son of Weddall's older brother, gets fifty thousand and handles the trust for two grandchildren of the old man's: a boy of eight and a girl of six. He's a lawyer."

"Wait a minute. Wasn't there a Weddall, a lawyer, in Mainford? Church Row, if I remember it."

"That's the one," he said. "Humphrey Weddall. A man of about fifty. Lives just outside the town at Castledene. A big figure in the town, he and his wife. She's much younger, about thirty something."

There was silence for quite a few seconds. I broke it.

"This possibility of murder. How's it arise?"

"It doesn't," he said, and gave that dry smile of his. "At least it oughtn't to. You notice anything funny about his eyes?"

"Only that they weren't too good."

"Well, he'd had a fall about a couple of years ago and something happened that's not too uncommon, or so I gather. The retina of his eye became detached. In fact, both eyes were affected. I expect Mrs. Travers knows all about it."

Bernice knows quite a lot about such things. She was a Red Cross Commandant in the war and she's always had connections with the hospital. "It was a question of sewing the retinas on again," she said. "If they didn't hold, then the sight was gone. Maybe I've over-simplified it but that's how it seemed to me."

"Well, Weddall had an operation and he had his eyesight, though it was badly impaired. His distance sight, I've gathered, was very bad indeed. He was very sensitive about it. and wouldn't give his family any information, but they knew his sight was getting very much worse. Then a few weeks ago he went on a tour of Italy with a friend whom we may have to trace. We know nothing whatever about him at the moment except that he was a Mr., or Signor, Perolli. The next thing that happened was about three weeks ago when his family received a letter from Paris saying he was coming home. Cutting his business a bit short, in fact. It appears his sight had practically gone and he wanted his car to meet him at Dover and bring him home, and that's what was done. When I say *his* family, I really mean a niece by marriage. A Mrs. Amble who acts as housekeeper and looks after the children. She's living apart from her husband who's had the habit of lifting his elbow too much. Don't quote me on that. I haven't got everything sorted out as yet."

He knocked out his pipe and I passed him my pouch.

"Thanks," he said. "I won't make my remark about toff's tobacco, but take it as said. And where was I?"

I passed my lighter and said Weddall was home and had virtually lost his sight.

"Yes," he said. "Well, last Tuesday afternoon he had Humphrey Weddall there and a new will was duly signed and witnessed. Humphrey left just short of ten past five and then a bit later Weddall rang down to his chauffeur, a coloured man named Sam Martin, to come up and see him. Sam came up by the lift, which Weddall had had installed when his eyes first went wrong, and when he got to the room, on the top storey by the way, no one was there. He did notice that one of the tall windows was open but paid no special attention. It was also a very dull afternoon but the light wasn't on, so Sam assumed Weddall was elsewhere. He hunted round and then went back to his quarters above the garage where there's a private telephone connecting him to Weddall's rooms in that top storey. It was about an hour later when Weddall's body was found. He'd apparently fallen from that window and his head wasn't at all a pretty sight. He must have been killed as *soon* as he hit the ground."

I grunted. I said it was a nasty business.

"But why the suspicions that everything wasn't what it appeared to be?"

He took quite a time answering that.

"Hard to say," he eventually said. "One doesn't want to rush to conclusions." Then he looked round at us and smiled a bit ruefully. "I must have been boring you with all this."

"Not a bit of it," was virtually what we both said. I added that I was extraordinarily interested.

Again there was a short silence.

"Do you know that's very fortunate?" he said to me. "Think you're interested enough to run down there with me on Tuesday morning? I've got some things to clear up tomorrow. I could ring you and make the arrangements."

"I'd like to very much," I said. "We're not too busy at the Agency. In any case I can make the time. You give me a ring late tomorrow and we'll fix it up."

We didn't mention the Weddall business again and he left about a quarter of an hour later. When he'd gone, Bernice and I chewed over what we'd heard.

"Anything really queer strike you about it all?" I finally asked her when we'd agreed it was time to be turning in.

"No—o," she said slowly. "Except that it was nice of Jewle to come and tell you about it."

"I'm not so sure," I said. "Jewle would never try to trip me up, but he didn't come here just to make a quiet evening a bit exciting."

She didn't get me.

"You and I were talking about coincidences only a day or two ago," I said, "so what about tonight? Isn't it straining credulity to think that Jewle wasn't well aware that I'd met Weddall?"

"Surely not! Weddall must have mentioned you to someone down there and somehow it got round to Jewle. What about that chauffeur you were so attracted by?"

"Sam? Could be. But somehow I don't think so. If that'd been so, wouldn't Jewle have rung me from Hinchbrook Hall and invited me to talk? And did you notice how skilfully Jewle handled the whole thing?"

Bernice smiled.

"It couldn't possibly be that you have a guilty conscience?"

I laughed.

"That'd be telling," I said, and we left it at that.

Later I was to do quite a lot of thinking. Bernice, four feet away, was already asleep, and I had her quiet, steady breathing as an accompaniment to that whirl of thought. I knew Jewle. I couldn't help knowing something about the workings of his mind. I knew beyond all doubt that he'd have handled things very differently—have come more out in the open—if Bernice hadn't been there. Somehow and somewhere he'd acquired information that made him sure that I—and possibly even the Agency—had vital information about Weddall, and the real clincher was that he'd asked me to go down with him to Hinchbrook Hall. If my association with Weddall didn't go beyond what Bernice and I had led him to assume it was, why in heaven's name was I wanted down there?

After I'd made my decision I at once fell asleep. I'd play my cards very close to the chest. I'd volunteer nothing beyond what I'd already told and I'd make Jewle himself tell me what he knew. But what it was that he knew was still a cloud at the back of my mind when I woke the next morning. What *I* knew was that there were two things he could not conceivably have discovered: the queer events at Victoria Station and the truth about a letter that had been posted in Paris.

The next morning was to bring a bigger surprise. I took my time about going to the office because I knew that Norris was having an interview with a client. In fact, I intended to look in and no more and I might have been away inside a few minutes if Bertha hadn't had a message for me.

"It was from a Mr. Martin," she said. "He wanted to know if you could see him at about ten-thirty this morning. I knew you'd be along so I said you would. I almost did ring you, though."

"Why?" I said, and just before I realised who the Mr. Martin was.

"Well, he had a curious, rough sort of voice; sort of scraping. Sounded almost like an American negro."

It is rarely that I get even faintly annoyed with Bertha but I was beginning to feel so.

"And why didn't you ring me?"

"Because he said that you'd know him. I was to tell you it was Sam."

"I do know him," I told her. "Whatever his colour he's always a client. And, pardon my telling you so, I'd be glad if you'd treat him with the same respect that I shall. Sam would appreciate that."

In the spare room where we keep the files there's just space enough to interview a client. I switched on the electric fire and soon the place looked cosy and snug. Sam was only five minutes late.

"Thank you, Miss," he said courteously to Bertha when she showed him in, and then he looked at me as if wondering how I was going to receive him.

"You remember me, sir?" he said in that husky, almost croaking voice of his.

"Indeed I do, Sam." I held out my hand. "And I'm glad to see you. I only wish you were here on more pleasant business."

I'd have known him anywhere, even though he wasn't wearing his chauffeur's clothes. The tweed suit he wore was a dark brown and the tie was black. I looked at him while he struggled for words: the faintly yellow face, the high cheekbones, the big, mobile mouth, the greying, close-cropped curly hair and the sadness in his mournful eyes.

"Sit down, Sam," I said. "Let me take your hat and coat."

I hung them on the one peg behind the door. I passed the cigarette box.

"Don't smoke, sir, and I hain't touched liquor, not for years." He smiled. With Sam, as with Dr. Johnson's acquaintance, cheerfulness couldn't help breaking through. "Reckon you might almost call me a clean-livin' man."

"Good for you, Sam. And now tell me something, or perhaps I'd better tell you something first. I've been told about Mr. Weddall, and extraordinarily sorry I was to hear it. Is it because of that you're here?"

"Yes, sir. Everybody reckon the boss fell out of that window, but I don't believe it. There've been some mighty queer doin's for quite a time now. Besides that it was his birthday— his seventieth birthday—or was to be last Saturday and he was havin' everybody down. The boss he say to me, 'Sam, we're goin' to have ourselves a real good time.' And then he fall out of a window what he knows is there. I tell that to the gentleman from Scotland Yard—"

"Inspector Jewle?"

"That's the one, sir, and he say, 'What about his eyes?' and I say the boss know his way about all them rooms of his even in the dark. Nothin's ever disturbed. I've seen him go straight to somethin' and pick it up jest like you and me."

"We'll go into that in a minute, Sam, and don't forget that whatever you say in this room gets no further. But what made you come to me?"

"Because I don't trust nobody. But that moenin' when we was at your flat, sir, the boss he say to me, 'That Mr. Travers is pretty smart,' and I thought you was a real nice gentleman, sir, so when he tell me you was a private detective, and then I found that card, I reckoned I'd take the liberty of comin' along."

He took a card from his wallet and gave it to me. It was almost certainly the one I'd given Weddall. And here I feel I ought to make something perfectly clear. Sam is someone who has to be reported as far as possible in the first person, otherwise the flavour of him and the individuality are gone. You can't shut your eyes and see him and hear him as I can even today, and yet I can't be sure that every word I think he spoke is exactly how and what he said. But maybe that doesn't matter all that much provided the meaning of what I seem to remember he said is absolutely unmissable.

"Where'd you get this card, Sam?"

"The night he sent for me, sir. I was still feelin' a bit queer when he told me to come up and when I went in his room it was pretty near dark. I see he wasn't there and then I see this card on the floor so I pick it up. The master don't tolerate no untidyness, and I reckon I was thinking about where he was and I must have put it in my pocket. Didn't tell no one about that card, sir, and when I see you really was a private detective I reckoned it wouldn't do no harm to come along."

"You were right," I said. "But let's start at the beginning, Sam. You've got plenty of time?"

He smiled.

"Yes, sir. Time's somethin' I've got plenty of. Ain't got no boss now, sir, 'cept me."

"Fine," I said. "So tell me, Sam. How'd you first meet Mr. Weddall?"

It appeared he was truck-driving in Philadelphia where at the time Weddall's firm had designed a block of flats and Sam's firm was hauling the material. There'd been some labour trouble with the men on the site and Sam didn't know a strike had just been called when he drove his truck in. He knew who Weddall was so he knew who the man was who looked as if he was being threatened by a couple of men. The bigger of the two was a real trouble-maker. Sam pulled up the truck and got out of the cab.

"I jest *hit* him, sir, and when I hit anybody them days, they stayed hit. 'What's your name, boy?' the boss say, so I told him and he say to come to his office and leave the truck be. He ask me a lot of questions about myself and then he say if I can drive a truck I can drive a car so I took the place of the one what'd just left him. Thirty years ago, that was, sir, and after that him and me was together most all the time."

"You were married?"

"No, sir. Guess I ain't the marryin' kind. Like I told the boss one day when he was talkin' about me and matrimony. 'You and me, boss,' I says, 'have been in every one of these United States and the only united state I ain't a-goin' in is that of matrimony.' The boss he laughed. He reckoned I'd got that out of a book. 'No, boss,' I said, 'I made that up out of my own head.'"

"You were almost like friends?"

He thought that over for a moment.

"Yes, sir. I reckon in a way we was. When folks was present it was always 'yes, sir' and 'no sir', but when we was together I always called him boss. First time I did it I was plumb scared. I thought he'd say, 'Sam, quit callin' me boss,' but he never did. Guess he kinda liked it. There was never no liberties but we used to do a powerful lot o' talkin'. Sometimes he'd even ask my advice. And he never let no one take no liberties with me. The boss wouldn't tolerate nothin' about colour."

"You knew all the family?"

He smiled.

"Yes, sir, and I guess they knew me. Mrs. Weddall—a rare nice lady she was. And Miss Evelyn. I remember the day she was born. And we was at her weddin'. Used to come over here a lot, sir. Old Mr. Weddall was at the Hall and Miss Evelyn was there, too, when she wasn't with her husband. He was a military man and a lot o' time he had to go abroad. And them two grandchildren, they was born at the Hall. Reckon there weren't nobody I didn't know."

"Mr. Weddall thought of you in his will?"

"He left me five thousand pounds, sir, so Mr. Humphrey tell me. He always say to me, 'Sam, if anythin' happen to me you won't never have to work no more.'" He gave a slow shake of the head. "Reckon I'd give more'n that five thousand pounds if he weren't dead."

"Yes," I said, "I think you would."

I had a lot of background and it was time I began to insinuate a few questions about Weddall and the last few weeks.

"Something I ought to tell you," I said, and told him that Jewle and I were old friends and that he'd seen me and given me a rough idea of the happenings at the Hall. I said that I was puzzled in a way since he couldn't have known that I'd ever met Mr. Weddall. Sam looked puzzled, too.

"He didn't say nothin' about the letter?"

4. HINCHBROOK HALL

THIS was Sam's story, and no wonder Jewle could hint at possibilities of murder. I'd like, by the way, for you to notice the times. It was at twenty to five that Tuesday when Sam was rung and told to come up to the study on the top floor. Humphrey Weddall arrived with the new will at five to five and almost at once the two witnesses came in: the under-gardener, Walter Horless, and the housemaid, Daisy Higman. Humphrey, as later enquiries and witness showed, left the Hall shortly after ten past five.

But to return to Sam. He took the lift and when he came into the study Weddall gave him a letter. "See that's mailed at once, Sam. Make sure it's properly posted and don't mention it to a soul."

Sam put the letter in his inside breast pocket and went down to the garage to put on his cap and overcoat. Humphrey Weddall was just arriving at the front door in his car and Sam had a word with him. It looked like rain—indeed there was already a fine drizzle—and then Sam went on to the garage. And that's all he knew. Someone coshed him and when he came to a few minutes later, the letter was gone. But he'd been aware that the letter had been addressed to me at the Agency, and that "Personal" had been in the top left-hand corner of the envelope.

And Sam had told all that to Jewle. Jewle had seen the mark of the coshing on Sam's skull. He hadn't had any doubts about Sam's veracity, so there was no wonder that he'd rung me on the Sunday night. If Bernice hadn't been there, he'd doubtless have told me the whole story. Even if he had, I'd have had a good answer. Sam, by the way, hadn't the faintest idea who or what had hit him.

"You spoke of some queer doings at the Hall, Sam. Can you tell me about some of them?"

"Yes, sir. There was Mrs. Amble: Miss Grace as we used to call her—"

"She's the housekeeper?"

"Yes, sir." Sam seemed to take it for granted that I knew the lay-out of the Hall rooms. "I did a powerful deal o' thinkin' before I said anything to the boss, and then I reckoned he ought to know: I mean about her bein' in the workroom and listenin' at the study door; I ketched her twice though she didn't ketch me. The boss had me tell him all about it. He told me to keep it under my hat. Reckoned he knew a powerful lot more than anyone give him credit for and I wasn't to do nothin'."

"I see. And anything else?"

"Yes, sir. That day we see you, the boss said somethin' mighty peculiar. He said, 'You noticed anyone followin' us around?' I told him I hadn't seen nothin'. 'Got no time to watch nothin' but the traffic,' I told him. Then when I went up that night as I always did to see if there was anything he wanted, he said the same thing again and I told him I hadn't seen no one. Then he reckoned he'd seen someone in Christie's when he was there and he'd seen him again when he come out with you and got into the car. Reckon he was sittin' in a taxi that was parked jest along the block. 'Didn't see nothin', boss,' I told him. 'Got to keep my eyes on the road if we don't want no accident. And why should anyone be followin' you, boss?' 'Can't tell you, Sam,' the boss say. Reckoned, though, he could think of a powerful lot o' reasons."

"And was that the last time you went to town before Mr. Weddall went to Italy?"

"The last time, sir."

"Tell me about that morning—if it *was* a morning when he left for Italy."

Everything fitted in. Sam had driven to Victoria. He had wanted to pick up the bags but Weddall said the porter could do it. Weddall, by the way, was supposed to be joined in the train by another friend who'd accompany 'him' to Boulogne where the Italian friend would take over. Weddall told the porter to leave the bags on the platform for a minute and to stand by and Sam thought it was something to do with the friend he was meeting. At any rate, Weddall told Sam not to wait. He'd better get back to the parked Rolls.

There were a dozen more questions I'd have liked to ask, but they could wait. Sam wasn't going to vanish and I was going to Hinchbrook Hall.

"Right, Sam," I said. "And now the important question. Just what do you want me to do?"

He looked surprised.

"Want you to find out all about it, sir. The boss never fell out of no window."

"But employing me will cost you money—"

He didn't give me time to finish but was lugging a thick wad of notes out of his inner pocket.

"Tain't no question about money. I been a careful man all my life and gone easy on spendin'. Hain't had no cause to spend."

"It isn't that," I told him. "Just hold on to that wad for a minute, Sam. What you want me to do the police will do and it won't cost you a cent."

He shook his head.

"No, sir! That Mr. Jewle was a real nice man but I hain't no faith in cops. Never did have. And I hain't never tangled with no cops, not in my whole life. Don't want to begin now, sir."

"Very well, Sam," I said. "I'll take your money and I'll try to give you good value. Fifty pounds. Twenty-five as what we call a retainer and twenty-five for expenses. When I want more I'll let you know."

Sam counted the notes—all fivers. He said it didn't seem much. It was peanuts compared with what he'd brought with him. I said he might ultimately have to pay more, though I hoped it wouldn't be as much as another fifty pounds. Even that seemed to be peanuts. Before the contracts came in I had to make various things absolutely clear and I made him more or less swear on each. Nobody was to know that he'd ever seen me except on a certain Friday. Under whatever pressure he was not to mention that he was my client. If he had a bank account—and he had—the contract was to be kept safely in the bank and he was to see to that at the earliest opportunity.

"Nobody knows you're in London?"

"No, sir. Supposed to be treatin' myself to a day in Mainford."

"Then that's where you've been," I said. But when the contract was in his pocket I didn't let him leave till I'd had a look outside. I even walked to both ends of the street.

"Everything clear, Sam." I held out my hand. "May see you tomorrow at the Hall. And play it dumb. You've only seen me once in your life and after that you've never heard my name mentioned."

"Don't you fret none about me, sir," he assured me. "I'm goin' to be jest the dumbest man that ever was. Yes-*sir*."

It had been a miserable Sam Martin who'd entered that room that morning, but a comparatively cheerful one who'd left it. It had been not much more than an inquisitive Travers who'd received him but it was quite a thoughtful one who'd just let him out. It looked once more as if I'd soon be playing a remarkably tricky game if I weren't to get into trouble all round. But I'd secured at least my lines of communication by swearing Sam to secrecy and, whether he believed it or not, Jewle would have to accept what I'd implied about Weddall—that my only contact with him had been that personal one of a certain Friday morning.

But there was more to it than that. I had to own up to the fact, for instance, that it was only sheer curiosity about Weddall that had made me accept Sam as a client. But for that I'd have sent him away with the assurance that Jewle was much more competent than I to discover the truth about Weddall's death but that I, nevertheless, would do anything I thought might help. And now I was in possession of facts about which Jewle knew nothing—that business card that Sam had picked up in Weddall's study, for instance, and the eavesdropping of Grace Amble and, above all, certain inconsistencies in Weddall's words and actions even as reported by Sam, let alone such things as the mysterious happenings at Victoria Station and the posting of that letter in Paris. And so to the really big question. I'd taken Sam as a client but how was I to be able to operate at Hinchbrook and give him value for what he'd paid? He hadn't paid much, that was true, but that was partly due to a kind of easing of my conscience and because any work that was done would be by me personally and wouldn't appear in the books.

Two courses were at least open to me, and the fact remained that I *was* going to Hinchbrook, and at Jewle's invitation. I could therefore do what I'd sometimes done in the past—hand out to Jewle in driblets facts that I'd already discovered and so make myself both omniscient and indispensable. But that was something I didn't quite like. Maybe I was getting squeamish, but there was something about that course of action that left a not-too-pleasant taste in the mouth. So I might have to adopt another plan—tell him in confidence that I was working for a client who was merely an onlooker. That'd be no business of Jewle's, nor would it be any kind of betrayal of Sam.

I saw Norris later that morning. After I'd told him just a few of the facts he agreed that the Case, from our point of view, was more exploratory than anything else and that any subsequent charges would depend on what we were able to do. Later, when I began thinking over the trickier aspects of that Case again, something else came as a relief. Why not let events shape themselves? Why cross bridges before coming to them? Why not, in fact, listen to what Jewle had to tell me on that journey to Hinchbrook, and then make plans accordingly?

And that listening and planning began much sooner than I'd thought. We left Trafalgar Square, Jewle driving, at half-past one the next afternoon, and as soon as we were clear of the suburbs, Jewle began telling me about the coshing of Sam.

"Doesn't seem to surprise you much?" he said.

"But it does," I told him. "Hitting Sam on the head, I mean. But the letter—no. Why shouldn't Weddall write to me?"

"What about?"

"Good Lord, man—think! Wasn't he anxious to buy one of my pictures?"

He grunted.

"And impress on Sam the necessity of posting it safely?"

"Why not?" I said airily. "If I'd been prepared to sell that picture I'd have asked fifteen hundred pounds."

That shook him.

"Big money. So why didn't he get Sam to register the letter?" He grunted again. "And why write to the Agency and not to your private address? You'll admit that he'd been there."

"He'd asked me for a card and I'd given him the one I had handy—a business one."

"And that's another curious thing," he said. "Matthews is down there and the way I saw things was how you'd been putting them—that he must have had one of your cards. But Matthews hasn't been able to find one."

"All trivialities," I told him. "You can find a dozen explanations of that. What about the real question? Who was it that didn't want that letter to get to me? And was even prepared to knock out Weddall's chauffeur to get hold of it? And why?"

"I know all that," he said obstinately. "But why you? Why should a letter to *you* be dangerous?"

I nipped through that opening in a flash.

"That's what I want to find out. It might even affect the Agency. If I'm not going to be too much bother to you, I think I'll put in a day or two down there."

I'd taken a bag with me, intending to spend the night at a Mainford hotel. Now he said there might be room for me at the Hen and Chickens at Hinchbrook where he and Matthews had fixed up rooms. And that going out of his way to be helpful wasn't all it seemed to be, or I didn't know him. Jewle wasn't altogether satisfied about me, and for a day or two at least he wanted me parked somewhere handy.

"Suits me down to the ground," I said. "I'll be working for no one but myself. Or I can be in your hands and you can put me wise to what you pick up."

I went back to that matter of the coshing of Sam and who might have done it. It was from the subsequent talk, and from what I picked up in the course of the next day or two, that I was able to compile that little genealogical tree of the Weddalls that you've seen at the beginning of this book. Some of it should already be familiar but a second glance should fix everything firmly in your mind. Add these few facts and you'll know far more than I did when we got to Hinchbrook.

Old Gus Weddall was, as you may remember, an art dealer. He had four children—Augustus, William, Lucy and Mabel. Young Gus became a lawyer; William joined the firm of a cousin in America, Lucy married Joe Borne, the art dealer with whom Old Gus founded the firm of Weddall and Borne in Lower Oxford Street. Mabel was the problem child. She ran away from home and married an actor named Arthur Delver. Delver left her or she left him, and finally he drank himself to death. Such a veil was thrown over what happened to Mabel that one could only assume that she had brought up her son Jeffrey on the proceeds of what was known as a "life of sin". Jeffrey became an actor and he too had alcoholic bouts. During the war, when he was in ENSA, he met and married Grace Amble, who was a nurse. Jeffrey's name was not even mentioned under the breath of the Weddalls and that was, I was told, because of a perfectly scurrilous letter he wrote to Old Gus. Gus, then almost ninety, had ideas of reconciliation and wrote to Jeffrey accordingly. What Jeffrey wrote back about the Weddalls generally and the treatment that had been given to his dead mother, was sufficient to make his name anathema. It so happened, however, that just when William Weddall wanted someone to act as housekeeper and look after the two grandchildren, Grace finally left her husband. Borne's son Oliver, recommended her, as did his father; William Weddall apparently liked her, and also Grace resumed her maiden name. That was in 1955.

There was one other thing about which Jewle enlightened me as we were nearing Hinchbrook. I'd asked him why Weddall had never become an American citizen. After all, his wife was American and his money had been made there. Jewle smiled in that dry way of his.

"After all there *are* still some people who prefer to stay British. And he was always backwards and forwards, you know. And I think he looked forward to retiring to his old home."

"Know what actually made him retire?"

"His wife's death," he said. "I had quite a dossier from Matthews this morning and if I remember rightly he had quite a packet of trouble all at once. As his wife died in the spring of '53, so his father died that early summer, not that that was unexpected. Another couple of years and the daughter, Evelyn, and her husband were killed in a flying accident." He gave another dry smile. "I think I'd like to have met old Gus Weddall. He seems to have been quite a character."

"Joe Borne, his old partner and son-in-law is still alive," I said as I remembered a certain happening. Jewle seemed in quite a good humour and I wanted to keep him that way. "I had an amusing reminder the other day of that business of theirs in Lower Oxford Street—Weddall and Borne—one of the first places I'd patronised when I was a very young and callow collector. It was at Christie's when I was hoping to pick up something for Bernice and I happened a bit later to be looking at a set of twelve Cromwellian chairs. A certain Bond Street dealer whom I happen to know was looking at them, too, and I asked him what he thought of them. 'Three right and the rest Weddall and Borne,' was what he said. 'Pre-First World War Vintage.'"

"Fakes?"

"More or less. Three right ones made up to a set of twelve. And I don't mind telling you that I couldn't have picked out even one of the three right ones."

We were just coming into Hinchbrook. It was a cold, frosty February day with a thin sun that was only enough to make light and faint shadow, but in what sun there was, Hinchbrook looked a remarkably pretty village. Ahead of us I could see a church tower. Hinchbrook seemed all trees and in the summer there would never be such a view.

"The Hall is just across from the church," Jewle told me. "The pub's here, just in the green."

The green was like hundreds of others, four or five acres roughly in a square and, fronting it all round, cottages and a shop or two. At the moment the centre was a football pitch and in the summer there'd doubtless be cricket. Jewle drove right round so that the car was heading for the Hall.

It was a largeish, clean and apparently well-conducted pub and Jewle arranged for a room for me—Matthews's room. He and Jewle would have a couple of beds in the larger room.

"The food's simple but good," he told me as he moved the car on. "Humphrey Weddall has put his uncle's study at our disposal, by the way, which is very handy. There's quite a youngish rector at the church there. His wife used to be a secretary and she used to slip across most mornings and work for Weddall. The name's Gray. They've a daughter who goes to the same high-class little school as Weddall's grandchildren. But here we are."

Along its frontage to the road, Hinchbrook Hall had a high brick wall. It curved inwards to opened iron gates on tall pillars. A weedless private road, bordered by shrubs and trees, curved right for about fifty yards and then the Hall and its ornamental gardens were in full view.

"Nice place," Jewle said as he let the car come to a halt. "That and five thousand a year'd suit me fine."

It was a Queen Anne house, and the tinkerings and additions through many years had not altogether destroyed its character. Two wings had been added and I could see only the nearer one, and the architect had given it the same lofty windows. In the front a Georgian porch had been added, and there was a smaller replica of it in the front of the further wing. Away to the right I could see greenhouses and a cottage: in the summer the trees would make them invisible.

"The kitchen garden's there," Jewle said. "The head gardener and his wife live in the cottage. An under gardener lives in the village. What d'you think of the place?"

There was only one thing to say, that it was a magnificent place and that Weddall had spent a fortune on it. A lot of the landscape gardening looked recent and a small swimming pool was definitely new.

"Wait till you see inside," Jewle said. "That's where the money is. I'm no collector but I know that."

Just short of the house he turned into the drive that led back to the garage and outbuildings. It was a large, two-storeyed garage and I saw the Rolls there and a station-waggon. Matthews suddenly appeared from a back door and joined us.

"Saw your car," he told Jewle, and gave me a grin as he held out his hand. I've known Matthews since the time when he was walking a beat. He always did imagine himself as a bit of a wit, but there's no more malice in Matthews than in a month-old kitten.

"So you had to come, sir," he said. "Thought we'd be having a nice cosy month down here and now it looks as if we'll be pushing off again."

Jewle cut in. "Was there anything new?"

"Yes," Matthews said. "Might be something interesting. A Mr. Pepson, Mainford town clerk. Wouldn't say what it was all about but he seemed pretty agitated. I said you'd probably see him here at about five and I'd give him a ring."

"We'll go right up," Jewle said, "and you can ring him from there. Might as well take the back door."

We went into and through a small cloakroom and along a corridor to the front of the house. There was quite a big hall from which a couple of doors led to our right. There was a fine staircase and by it was the automatic lift that Weddall had had installed. I'd just time to get a general impression of period furniture and quantities of pictures before the lift door closed. We stepped out on the second storey landing and went through a door almost opposite—a tall, panelled door that opened into a tall, handsome room—Weddall's study.

It was a warm room—the whole Hall was centrally heated— but in a false fireplace an electric fire was on. The carpet was plain but on it were two lovely Bokhara rugs. The writing desk was Queen Anne as was the bureau-bookcase. Books were everywhere, and a cabinet by the far wall was full of white and pink china that looked like Swansea. There were no pictures except two portraits in oils which Jewle said were of Weddall's wife and daughter. The two easy chairs and the chesterfield were reasonably modern. The walnut chair at the writing-desk was one of a set of six, the rest standing round the walls.

"Wish I'd brought a pantechnicon," I told Jewle.

"You've seen nothing yet," he told me. "Better do that telephoning," he told Mathews, "and then rustle us up some tea. Ask if that chauffeur can bring it up."

We went through the door on the left into what Jewle said was Weddall's workroom. It was plainly carpeted. Various pictures, some obviously good, were on the walls and several more were stacked round it. The centre of the room—two large bedrooms that had been thrown into one—was occupied by a long, plain deal table, half of which was covered in green baize. There were drawing materials, instruments, and a couple of drawing-boards; brushes—a score of them—in a jar, and two paintboxes. The room had a faint smell of turpentine. Around the table were four perfectly plain, late Victorian chairs.

"He used to do a lot of what I'd call architectural designing when he was first here," Jewle said. "When his eyes went he dropped it or didn't do so much. The drawers of that table are full of designs and plans and things. None made very much sense to me."

He was moving towards the door at the far end of the room.

"Take a peep out," he told me, "and you'll see just where we are. Mrs. Amble's bedroom is the first in the corridor. The cook and maid are farther along. One of the later wings, of course."

I had a look. A narrowish staircase led down from the corridor from my left. That meant there were two staircases: the one we could have taken instead of the lift and this other one that was probably in the old days for the use of the staff. But the position of Mrs. Amble's room showed how easy it was to eavesdrop at the door between workroom and study.

We went back to the study. Jewle pointed to the left-hand window as we came in.

"That's the one that Weddall fell from. Like to look down?"

It was, as I said, a very lofty room and the windows tall, but I should say it was not much more than a couple of feet from the floor to the interior sill. I know that that sill wasn't much above my knees. In fact, when I'd pushed the lower half up, I held well on to the frame as I looked down. From where I was it looked the very devil of a drop.

"The easiest thing in the world to fall from here," was what I said to Jewle. "As for anyone with Weddall's eyes . . ." I shrugged my shoulders and left it at that. And then Matthews came in.

"He'll be here at five," he told Jewle. "And he insists on Humphrey Weddall being here, too. Says he'll arrange it himself. Tea's on the way up."

Before he finished speaking there was the sound of the lift and then the rattle of crockery. Just a few seconds and Sam was tapping at the door.

5. Man With a Grievance

"Good evening, gentlemen," Sam said and manoeuvred the trolley into the room. He was wearing a white coat with the suit he'd had on when he came to Broad Street, and the tie was still black.

"Thank you," Jewle said. "Travers, this is Sam Martin. I think you've met before."

Sam looked at me, head slightly on one side. Then he grinned broadly.

"Yes, sir. This gentleman and me are acquainted. This is the gentleman who was with the boss at Christie's and then they went along to this gentleman's flat."

"How're you keeping, Sam?" I asked.

"Pretty well, sir. I ain't doin' no grumblin'."

"You had your tea, Sam?" Jewle asked him. Matthews found a side table and began setting out the tea-things. It looked quite a high-class tea: two kinds of sandwiches and a lot of small cakes.

"Never have no tea, sir. Always make myself a cup o' coffee. Don't eat nothin', though."

"Then we're not keeping you," Jewle said. "I wonder if you'd mind telling Mr. Travers about what happened to you last Tuesday night. That business of the letter. Start at the beginning."

Sam's face was dead-pan. Nobody would have guessed that I'd heard the whole thing before. But not the whole thing. There were additions. When Sam came back to consciousness that evening on the garage floor it was in time to hear the bell, and he just managed to get up the stairs before the ringing stopped. He said he'd thought things out and it was then almost twenty-past five. Weddall said, "Sam, get up here, will you. I want to see you." It was then that Sam realised his hands were dirty on account of falling on the garage floor and he'd also bust a knee of his trousers. It must have taken him quite five minutes to make himself presentable and even then he didn't feel in too hurrying a mood. It must have been at least five-twenty-five when he went into the study.

"And Mr. Humphrey Weddall's car had gone?"

Sam said there wasn't any car there. He seemed to have heard a car move off much earlier. Just when he couldn't say. His head felt a bit muzzy but he thought it was while the bell was ringing.

We'd begun our meal. Jewle said Sam might as well sit down. He had a few more questions to put which he wanted me to hear. I'd done quite a lot of thinking about Sam. I guessed he was in a way a lonely sort of man if only because of his colour and living away from the house in those quarters above the garage. I guessed, too, that Sam did quite a lot of thinking. You could tell that by the careful way he put his words together. In my mind's eye I could see him and Weddall in that study: not master and man but master and trusted sharer of many long years in the past and doing what Sam called a powerful lot o' talkin'.

"What's been worrying me," Jewle said, "is why Mr. Weddall should write to Mr. Travers. Did he ever mention writing?"

"No, sir. He never mentioned no writin' to me."

"But did he mention Mr. Travers?"

"Yes, sir. When we was comin' away from the gentleman's house, the boss he reckoned Mr. Travers was a mighty smart man."

Jewle laughed, though he must have heard it all before.

"Did he say why?"

"No, sir. I told him I ain't doin' no listenin'. Can't do no listenin' in traffic."

"And very sensible, too. And Mr. Weddall never mentioned Mr. Travers again?"

I could tell by Jewle's face that what Sam told him was something new. Sam, it appeared, had found a parking place after dropping Weddall at the Café Royal. Later the party had walked with Sam to where the car was parked and for the homeward journey Mrs. Amble and the two children had sat behind and Weddall had sat in the front with Sam. During the journey there were plenty of occasions when it was quite safe to talk and it was during one of these that my name had cropped up again. Weddall had chuckled to himself.

"Somethin' amusin' you, boss?"

"Yes, Sam. If ever you get into trouble, you go and see that Mr. Travers."

"He's a real gentleman, boss."

"He's a private detective."

Sam hardly believed him.

"Didn't look like no detective to me, boss. Looked like a real nice gentleman."

"You'd come across plenty of detectives in your time?" Jewle said, and Sam said he sure had: hotel detectives, detectives employed on big construction jobs—private security police, I imagined. At any rate, that was the last time my name had been mentioned to Sam.

"Mind if I ask a question?" I cut in. "When did you and Mr. Weddall do most of your talking? And was it up here?"

Every night of his life when Weddall was at home, Sam had come up at about half-past nine to see if there was anything his master wanted before retiring. Weddall nearly always told him to sit down and then they'd talk, mostly, Sam said, about old times.

"Did he ever ask you questions about anyone in the house or on the staff?"

"No, sir. He never asked me to tell no tales."

"And his eyes, Sam. When he got back from Italy, I mean. How were they? Was he virtually blind?"

"No, sir. He could just see to eat his meals. Used to have all his meals up here. Most always did. And he could read. Used to hold the book right up to his face and sorta squint."

"He could get about from room to room?"

"Yes, sir. Used to have a stick like a blind man do. Didn't like no one to touch him 'cept me."

These were all the questions. We'd finished our meal. Matthews helped stack the debris on the trolley and Sam left.

I stoked my pipe.

"A real nice gentleman and smart," Jewle said, and chuckled. "Well, I wouldn't quarrel with that. I might add a few more adjectives, though. But what were you getting at with those questions?"

"Trying to get the lie of the land," I told him. "But I'm coming round to the murder point of view. You're not going to convince me that at quarter-past five last Tuesday night Weddall decided to throw the bottom of that window right up and look out. What could he see? Or what could he be trying to hear?"

"All right," Jewle said. "If someone hit him on the head and then pushed him through, who was the someone? Far as we know, only the staff was on the premises, if you count Mrs. Amble as staff. Humphrey Weddall had gone long before Sam was rung."

"What did he do when he left this room? You've never told me what his alibi is. I take it he's got one?"

"There was nothing to discuss, he says. He checked the will with Weddall in the morning and almost as soon as the signing was done he said goodnight and left. He hadn't seen the children for some time so he went through the workroom there and down the other stairs to what's still called the nursery. Mrs. Amble heard him having a word with the children and she came in just as he was leaving. She went down with him because she was going to the kitchen and she heard his car drive off. That was still short of a quarter past and Weddall was not yet even in the process of ringing Sam. And we know that Humphrey drove straight back to his office. And there's something else to add. Where's his motive?"

"Fifty thousand pounds and the management of a big trust fund. Who gets the house and chattels?"

"He does. And why not? He's the head of the family."

"You're right," I said. "He'd only to wait and the money was his. No need to anticipate things. His reputation's good?"

"A very old-established firm. Handles all the best people. You can take it from me that Humphrey Weddall's in the absolute clear." He glanced at the bracket clock that stood by the telephone on the desk and got to his feet. "Better have a polish. He and that town clerk are due in a few minutes."

*

There was a cloakroom and lavatory on the landing near the lift, and when we left it we heard the sound of the lift on its way up. Jewle glanced at his watch.

"Only five to. They're a bit early."

It wasn't they: it was he. James Pepson admitted he was a bit early and said he had rather over-estimated the time. He looked a dry, dour sort of character: nearly six feet, spare and slightly stooped. His hair was greying and there wasn't much of it except round his ears. He wore thin-rimmed glasses that had made a red kind of furrow on the bridge of his generous nose. Two deep grooves led from the wide nostrils past his deeply dimpled chin. I put his age at sixty.

We talked generalities till Humphrey Weddall appeared, and he was five minutes late. He gave Pepson almost a glare.

"I called at your place and they told me you'd gone," he said testily. "I made sure you'd wait for me."

"I didn't say so," Pepson told him curtly.

I guessed there wasn't a lot of love lost between the two. Certainly they were vastly dissimilar. Weddall was of Pepson's height but stout and florid: in fact he was something of a cross between Harold Macmillan and Arnold Bennett. There was something of the country squire about him. His hair was fair with the merest trace of grey and he had an untidy moustache below which one couldn't help noticing the slightly protuberant teeth. His manner was what I'd call ample, with just a touch of the over-bearing. He looked a bit older than his forty-nine years.

At that first faint clash of personalities, Jewle had jumped in with introductions, which meant myself—a Mr. Travers associated with himself on the Case. The name obviously conveyed nothing to Weddall. We got ourselves seated.

"You keep talking about a Case," Weddall said, and tried to make it not too serious. "Surely you're not still of the opinion that my uncle's unfortunate death was anything but an accident?"

I was watching Pepson. His lip curled slightly.

"Now don't you worry about us, sir," Jewle said mildly. "Nothing like making sure. We'll probably be away and gone in less than no time. But you, Mr. Pepson. You say you've got something to tell us that might be important?"

He certainly had. It was something that had been damped down and now he was opening the flue and everything was coming out at full blast. His harsh, dry voice had a perpetually bitter emphasis, and he refused to be put off by Weddall's incipient interruptions. Put into chronological order and somewhat pruned of those interruptions and the brief flashes of anger or pique that accompanied them, his story was this.

Old Gus Weddall had always wanted, after his arthritis got bad and he retired from business, to do something about the Mainford Museum and Art Gallery. It was an almost squalid, gimcrack affair—I quote Pepson there—that nobody patronised and had to be supported by the rates. Old Gus wouldn't do anything unless the city collaborated. If they did, then he'd spring-clean the place, weed out rubbish, donate his own collection of pictures and see the place was modernised and put on a paying basis. Admittedly the site was unfortunate, tucked away in Mill Street, but Gus Weddall thought that with his suggestions carried out and a certain amount of regular publicity, the town would have something of which it might be proud rather than ashamed. The Council dillied, dallied and pottered about: Old Gus finally lost his temper and virtually told them to go to hell. That was about a year before his death and he hadn't included Pepson in his maledictions. Pepson was about the only man connected with the Council for whom he still had any regard.

And now one of the interruptions, leaving out the by-play. Humphrey—I'd better call him that to avoid confusion with his late uncle—said Pepson must have had an exaggerated idea of what Old Gus wanted to do. Gus had been a spender and had left under five thousand when he died. Everybody knew that it was William Weddall who was subsidising Hinchbrook Hall, and had done for years. That was why Old Gus had left the Hall and its contents to him.

Be that as it may, Pepson went on, that didn't affect what had happened about a year ago. William Weddall had sent for him and had told him, in the very strictest confidence, that he knew about and respected his father's intentions, and it was he who was going to carry them out. His plans were almost ready to be embodied in a deed of trust, and what he proposed to do made Pepson's eyes almost pop out of his head. He was actually going to build and endow an entirely new gallery on a new site and give it the nucleus of what might become in time an important collection and put Mainford on the artistic map. But everything was to be strictly secret. Nothing would be known till after his death. The new museum and art gallery, by the way, would bear the Weddall name. What he wanted Pepson to do was to make the most careful soundings of Council opinion and also to have in mind a site. If the Council was still hostile or unenthusiastic, then Pepson would notify him accordingly and the plan would be dropped.

"How could you keep such a thing secret?" Humphrey asked a bit scornfully.

"The answer is that I did," Pepson told him, "otherwise *you'd* have heard about it long ago. My method was to suggest to various members of the Council that the Council itself ought to do something and that there were plenty of public-spirited people in the town and district who'd be prepared to help. In fact, I was in a position about two months ago to tell Mr. Weddall that I was sure the whole thing would go through without a hitch. That was when he showed me the plans. The first year or two he was here, he worked on those plans and he had them completed to his satisfaction. I'm no architect but the building he'd designed struck me as something that'd be unique for this town and be an inspiration for any future development."

"Just a moment," Humphrey said. "Was that why you informed me that you thought you might be an interested party and asked to be present on Saturday when the will was read?"

"It was," Pepson told him curtly.

"Then you must have felt a bit of a fool. I was instructed to draw that will just before my uncle left for Italy and to have it ready when he returned—"

"You did it yourself or did Spurn do it?" Spurn, I remembered, was the other member of Humphrey's firm.

"I was specifically asked to do it myself. There were certain new bequests—Mrs. Amble's five thousand, for example—and alterations to the trust deed on the grandchildren's behalf. At any rate, he wanted a new will. He signed it, it was duly witnessed and you heard it read." His face was getting even more red. "So much for this museum."

"And I tell you"—Pepson was almost shouting—"that I saw the plans and that Weddall was enthusiastic. And nothing has occurred that'd have made him change his mind."

"Where *were* those plans?" Jewle asked quietly, and the room had a queer silence after Pepson's outburst.

They'd been in a drawer of the workroom table. Jewle proposed that we should go and have a look at them, so in we filed. There were special lights above the table and Matthews switched them on. There were drawers on both sides of that long table but there wasn't a lot in them: more instruments, drawing and painting apparatus, mostly, but half a dozen plans as well. They were all smallish. One was for additions to the gardener's cottage, and another for a kind of folly that Weddall had thought of erecting at the far corner of the grounds to break the contour. The rest were in embryo: merely rough ground-plans or sketches. Of the plans for the Weddall Museum there was no sign. Pepson was looking incredulous. Humphrey had the modest quietness of a man who's proved a case.

"Something else was here," Pepson said. "There was a small book in which were details of all his pictures. Prices and where he bought them, and so on. Where's *that*?"

Jewle shrugged his shoulders. "It's not in the study and it's obviously not here."

"Nothing in his bedroom," Matthews said.

Pepson shook his head with a kind of helplessness as we filed back to the study.

"If I may venture to say something—" That was Humphrey. He cleared his throat. "It should be obvious to all that my uncle definitely changed his mind. I don't doubt you, Pepson, for a bit, but my uncle could be a very secretive man. Also, of course, there's the possibility that he was intending to give the project—if I may call it that—more thought and that he'd subsequently have made another will. But for his eyes he was in excellent health. He had a very good expectation of life."

For Humphrey that struck me as a reasonable and even generous statement but I don't think Pepson was altogether satisfied. And, by the way he moved away from him later when they were taking the lift, there didn't seem to me to be any sudden urge for friendship. Jewle, who'd politely accompanied them, said much the same thing when he came back.

"Pepson's a man with a grievance," he told us. "He's certain there's been some underhand work. What d'you think?"

"Looks to me like a question of fact," Matthews said. "Weddall gave Humphrey instructions and they were carried out. And the clincher, as I see it, is this. Weddall wanted Humphrey to see to things personally; in other words, to keep the will confidential. He didn't want Pepson to know he'd changed his mind about that art gallery stunt. If all and sundry had seen that will, you bet your life something would have got round to Pepson and he'd have been here wanting to know why."

That seemed an excellent point. I didn't know Spurn, Humphrey's partner, but for all I knew he might have been a bosom pal of Pepson's. Jewle knew about him, though. It was amazing what he and Matthews had gleaned in so short a time. Spurn, they said, had been managing clerk to the Weddalls and had been made a partner when the elder Weddall died.

"The missing plans," Jewle said. "That seem normal to you?"

I didn't know. We humans act in all sorts of ways, and react, too. I would have thought that, having spent a very long while over getting out the plans, Weddall would have kept them somewhere, especially if Humphrey's suggestions had any validity. If Weddall were likely to change his mind again, then the plans should have been kept.

"But that's not the vital point," I said. "Why is the book missing that had all the information about Weddall's own pictures? Why should Weddall have destroyed that? The plans—possibly: if he'd discarded the idea. But he still *had* the pictures."

"Yes," Jewle said. "Might be a good idea, Jack, if you had another hunt round. Try his bedroom again. We'll push along to the pub."

The Hen and Chickens was a democratic pub: it had no saloon bar. What had once been a saloon bar was now the main bar since it was the only room big enough for darts. The bar itself was double, with the landlord in the middle ready to deal with orders both ways. We went into the old bar, as they called it, and I asked Jewle what he'd have. We both had bitters— pints. A darts game was on in the other room so I suggested we should go through. I did go through, and I expected Jewle at any minute to be joining me. There was a good fire and I made myself comfortable and the darts players were so good that I forgot all about Jewle. When I looked for him some time later, I saw him and Matthews in the other room talking at a table in the far corner with a middle-aged man who had something of the farmer about him. A pint of bitter was enough for me so I went back to my chair and watched a new game starting. Before it was over, Jewle looked in and called me. It was time for the evening meal.

A room upstairs had been put at our disposal as dining and sitting-room. The food was to be plain but good: a hot meal at mid-day and a cold one in the evening. Cold meat, potatoes baked in their jackets and cheese with celery to end with was the menu that night. Even before we sat down to it, Jewle began telling me about something that had just happened. The man with whom he'd been talking was Harry Gribling, head gardener at the Hall. Jewle had stood him a pint and had directed the talk to things generally at the Hall. The something had come out. With the diffidence of the countryman, Gribling had mentioned something which Jewle knew was important. It was something that Gribling's wife had seen—two things, in fact. And since Weddall's death had been assumed to be an accident, she'd attached no importance to them.

I keep back what they were because to anticipate what the three of us did after supper would make for repetition, but as soon as the meal was over we went back to the Hall. Gribling's cottage was nearer the pub, and the wall that fronted the Hall grounds ended there. Entry to the cottage was by a narrow side road, and just beyond the cottage gate was a private way to the green-houses and the kitchen gardens. Matthews went on to the Hall and the three of us had synchronised our watches. Jewle knocked at the cottage door. Gribling's wife was a rosy-faced woman of sixty; stoutish, pleasant-mannered and quite well-spoken. Jewle introduced himself but apparently she knew all about him. We went through to the living-room. Her husband would have come with us, Jewle told her, except that a darts match was on at eight o'clock, as she probably knew, and he was playing.

Five minutes later we went up the narrow stairs to a bedroom. When she'd drawn back the window curtain Jewle switched off the light.

"Here's where I was, sir," she said. "Usually Harry's in at five for his tea but he was a bit late so I thought I'd turn down the bed. The room faces west, as you see, and it wasn't quite dark. You can see the Hall quite plain from here in the winter, and usually when I come up to do the beds, about six, I have a look. Mr. Weddall's light was always on. Even if the curtains were drawn you could still see the light through. Sort of a dull light, if you know what I mean." She gave a start. "There, sir: look! Someone's just switched the light on."

The study windows were indeed a faint orange in the darkness. There was no real shape but only a suggestion of height. The folds at the curtain sides forced the light inwards, as it were.

"Just a moment, Mrs. Gribling."

Jewle struck a match, let it burn for a second or two and blew it out. Another second or two and there was nothing but blackness across at the Hall.

"That's what you saw, Mrs. Gribling?"

"That's it, sir. I saw the light and then it went out. I wondered why. The master spent all his time in the study since his eyes got so bad and I never knew the light to be put off till he went to bed. Then when I'd done the bed I had another look and the lights went on again, and just then I heard Harry coming in. And that's when I saw the man. He was running towards the road—"

"The private road from the greenhouses?"

"That's it, sir. He came round by the greenhouses and I saw him almost clear. He had on a lightish overcoat and hat— a soft hat— and he was fairly tall and he looked about—well, say forty or so."

"How long did you have him in view?" Jewle said, as he switched on the light.

She smiled.

"Couldn't have been any time. I just saw him as he crossed over the grass and then he was through the gate."

"And the time by that alarm clock there was then twenty-five past five?"

"Yes, sir. And that clock's always kept right by wireless. And the one in the downstairs room was the same. 'Wherever have you been?' I said to Harry and we both looked at the clock and he said he didn't think it was so late. He'd waited for a word with Walter—that's the under-gardener—who'd been doing something for Mr. Weddall."

"That's right," Jewle told her. "He and the housemaid had been witnessing Mr. Weddall's will."

We went back downstairs. Jewle said we were grateful, and as a prelude to putting, apparently off-handedly, the usual last-minute questions.

"You know young Mr. Borne, the antique dealer at Mainford?"

"Oh, yes, sir. I've seen him more than once at the Hall."

"Strictly between ourselves—and I mean that—could the man you saw running have been Mr. Borne?"

She smiled.

"Oh, no, sir. Mr. Borne is much shorter. Besides, he's a bit lame. He was wounded in the war."

"May I ask a question?"

There was almost an apprehension as she looked at me. It was natural. She'd heard my name but I was still a stranger and up till then I hadn't uttered a word.

"The man was running, Mrs. Gribling, so he must have had some reason to run. Could it have been to catch a bus? Is there a bus at that time? Say, to Mainford?"

Her face lighted.

"Yes, sir, there is. Five-thirty at the Green."

"And you haven't a timetable of trains from Mainford?"

She had one. Every three months one was given away by the *Mainford Gazette*. I had a look at it and showed something to Jewle. There was a non-stop from Mainford to town at six o'clock and the bus would easily catch it.

Two or three minutes later we joined Matthews on the main road.

"A job for you right away." Jewle gave him the description of the running man. "Take the car and get along to the bus depot and see what you can unearth. If the same conductor's on duty, try and get a fuller description."

We walked on towards the pub and the car.

"Everything fits," Jewle said. "Tomorrow morning I'll get an official statement from Mrs. Gribling if only as justification for hanging on here. You saw it all?" he asked me.

"Yes," I said. "But I'm not so happy about it as you are."

"And why's that?" he asked me sharply.

"Well, take what one might call the bright side first. We now know just when Weddall fell from that window. At between five-fifteen and five-twenty the light went out and that was just after he'd rung down to Sam. When the light went on again it was Sam who switched it on."

"Well, what's wrong with that?"

"Nothing," I said. "We can even assume that someone lurking near by—in the workroom, for instance—knew he had to act before Sam got up there, so he cracked Weddall on the skull, switched off the light, pitched him out of the window and made his getaway. We know he was in a hurry because he did something else he shouldn't have done—he drew the curtains of the window."

"Dead right," Jewle said. "That's how I see it. It's how I've *got* to see it."

"But Mr. Travers said something was wrong with it," Matthews cut in.

"Not exactly wrong," I said, "but what we've got is another factor—the running man. Why shouldn't Weddall have heard on the concrete below his window the steps of that running man? The times fit perfectly. If he did he switched off the light, threw up the window and just drew the curtains back enough so that he could look out. Not to look perhaps: his eyes weren't good enough for that, but to listen. That's when he might have fallen and if he did, then the curtains would fall back in place."

You could have cut the silence with a knife. Then Jewle grunted.

"If you were betting, which theory would be the favourite?"

"I won't commit myself," I said. "But tell me this. At the post-mortem, was any bruise found on Weddall's skull?"

Jewle sniffed.

"The top of his head was like pulp."

"Then I still won't commit myself," I said. "I take it that what we're all hoping is that Matthews here will find out something about that running man. Once we know about him, we may have some of the answers."

6. THE BUSY BEE

THE bed was hard and I took a long time to go to sleep. I wasn't worrying: I like a hard bed and when I got used to it I knew I'd sleep just as well as at home. And it wasn't only the bed that kept me awake.

Already I had plenty of ideas about Weddall's death, always provided it was murder, and what I'd also fitted in was another queer happening which I'd never even associated with his death. I kept asking myself if it would be sound business to mention it to Jewle and I decided that it would. It would be another admirable excuse for staying on at Hinchbrook. When I woke in the morning I still thought it a good idea to tell him and Matthews about that hoax.

What woke me was Jewle himself hammering on the door and coming in with a cup of tea. I put on my hornrims and looked at my watch. It was only seven o'clock.

"What's biting you?" I said. "I thought breakfast was at eight."

He and Matthews had been up over an hour.

"Trying to knock a hole in that theory of yours," he said. "Went along to the Hall and tried to find out if Weddall could have heard anything up in that study with the windows closed. The answer is he couldn't. He might have heard a brass band but he couldn't have heard any running feet. Matthews had to make the very devil of a clatter before I could hear, even with windows partly open."

I'd thought he'd looked cock-a-hoop.

"Any luck last night with our friend the running man?"

"Couldn't have had better," he said. "He did take that bus. They're double-deckers and he went on top. About six feet, grey hat and grey tweed overcoat. The bus was fairly full—people going to the pictures and so on—but he got a seat right up front. Kept his collar well round his ears. When he got off at the railway station the conductor happened to notice he had a little scar by the side of his chin."

"And what now?"

"Matthews is taking the eight o'clock bus to Mainford and trying to make sure he went on that train. If he took another, then where'd he book to. If he did take the train, then we'll try and pick up the trail at Euston."

In about twenty minutes I was ready for breakfast. It came in at once: bacon and sausage, toast, marmalade and coffee. As soon as we'd settled down to it I made my disclosure. Naturally it was all in confidence.

"That's an amazing thing," Jewle said. "Someone rang you about going to Liverpool. And just before five on that Tuesday night! There must be a connection."

I said I was inclined to agree. Both Norris and I had worried our wits as to why anyone should play such a trick, and now it looked as if there was an answer.

"I gave Weddall a business card. Also we know from Sam that he'd alluded to me as a private detective, so we can assume that the letter he wrote to me wasn't about pictures but about something far different—"

"You mean suggesting some enquiry for him?"

"Well, why not? After all, if he was murdered it was for somebody's very good reason. And somebody heard him give Sam that letter."

"Wait a minute," Jewle said. "Let me think."

He muttered to himself for a bit, then gave himself a nod. "The telephone call to you could have come from the Hall?"

"It almost certainly did. And, if so, you might be able to check."

"But how did the caller know so much about you?"

"Because my name, as a detective, had been mentioned in the hearing of at least one person—Mrs. Amble. In the car that day. Also the caller could have got everything he used for that call from *Who's Who*. And the caller pretended to be in such a tremendous hurry and flurry that he gave me no time to ask any questions."

"It's the very devil," Jewle said, and clicked his tongue. "It alters the whole complexion of things. Someone has to get that letter even if Sam has to be knocked on the head. The letter is read and, from what's in it, somebody knows you've got to be got out of the way for best part of a day. And meanwhile Weddall was murdered. It would look like an accident. It wouldn't appear in any national papers so you wouldn't see it. You'd still go on wondering why you'd been made a fool of."

Matthews wanted to know how timings fitted. I said they fitted pretty well. If the hoaxer was the one who killed Weddall, he had to work on a tight schedule but it could have been done. He'd finished with me by ten-past five so there was time to go to the study. Humphrey Weddall had left by then.

"We're assuming the devil of a lot," Jewle told us. "All this is based on the assumption that the hoaxer rang you from the Hall. As I said before, that narrows things down to Mrs. Amble and I don't see her hitting Weddall on the head and getting him through the window."

"There's always the running man. For all we know he might have been someone Weddall knew well. The two might even have talked before Weddall decided to ring for Sam."

"Yes," Jewle said. "One thing at a time is the safe play. We'll concentrate on that running man."

"Just one other thing," I said, and I had to change my informant. "Don't I remember Weddall telling me that he was about to have some sort of celebration on his seventieth birthday?"

"That's right. He was having his relatives down for a special do. Last Saturday week—the day he was buried. They were all to be there: Humphrey and his wife, his brother-in-law Joe Borne and Joe's son and his wife and you can count in Mrs. Amble who's on the spot. The only one left out was Mrs. Amble's husband, Jeffrey Delver. He's been cut off even without the usual shilling."

I said that what I was thinking was that that special occasion at the Hall might also have had in it some question of urgency.

"You mean," Matthews said, "was he having them here for a celebration pure and simple or to spring something on them? Something he'd discovered?"

"That was the general idea. And he had to be got out of the way before it came to light."

"Wait a minute," Jewle said. "That's problematic. We can't get our teeth into it. But this running man. He's a fact. We know a bit about him and we ought soon to know more. So let's give it twenty-four hours before we start casting the net any wider."

It was almost time for Matthews to catch his bus. Jewle said he himself would be taking the car and calling on the Mainford police. There was a bit of a twinkle in his eye when he asked if I'd like to go with him.

"I'll stay where I'm safe," I said. "I'll ring the Agency and Bernice and say I'm staying on for a bit, and then I think I'd like to look over the Hall. Purely as a collector."

"Yes," Jewle said ironically. "Purely as a collector. You wouldn't be wanting to run your eye over Mrs. Amble?"

"That's an idea," I told him. "If it's included in the price of admission."

As I rang the bell at the front door of the Hall I could hear the red-lacquered grandfather clock in the hall striking nine. I had to wait a minute or two before the door was opened, and by Mrs. Gribling. She remembered me at once from the previous night. I didn't know that she worked at the Hall every morning except Saturday and Sunday. She told me that, and that her husband and Sam always had their lunch in the kitchen with the rest of the staff. I learned that as we went through from the Hall to the long dining-room. It occupied most of the width of the original building.

"If you'll wait here, sir, I'll find Mrs. Amble. The children have gone to school so I think I know where she is."

There was plenty of good stuff in that room. I couldn't have said if the long dining-table was right but I thought the Chippendale chairs were definitely Weddall and Borne. There was hardly a blank space between the oils on the walls. The bracket clock on the fine old mantelpiece was right and so were the *famille rose* vases that flanked it. Just as I was about to look at the sideboard, Grace Amble came in.

"Mrs. Amble?" I said, and smiled as I held out my hand. "My name's Travers. I knew the late Mr. Weddall and he'd given me a standing invitation to inspect his collections, so as I was here I thought I'd ask your permission to take advantage of his offer. Very sad about his unfortunate death."

That rigmarole had given me a chance to inspect her. She was in the middle thirties: a tallish brunette with rather a sharp, almost pinched face; thinnish lips but remarkably expressive eyes. But for those eyes, and her smile, she would have looked quite plain. She was wearing a bright tweed skirt and a greenish blouse, and round her rather long neck was a string of amber beads. The whole get-up looked a bit exotic.

"I'm sure we'd be very pleased for you to look round," she told me, and I wondered whom she meant by *we*. But I knew her voice: it was the somewhat strident one I'd heard that day when I'd rung the Hall. "Would you like me to come with you?"

"I don't think I need bother you," I said, and smiled. "I think I'm reasonably honest."

She smiled, too, but the smile didn't look too genuine to me.

"I'm sure you are. I was wondering if you'd know your way about."

We compromised. The only rooms that might interest me were the drawing-room on the first floor and the room where I was, and she'd come along later and see how I was progressing. The study, I'd told her, I already partly knew. So she went out to what a later peep through the door told me was a small lobby with the kitchens beyond it and the back stairs leading up from it, and I began looking at the pictures: the ones, no doubt, that

Old Gus had once intended to present to the Mainford Museum and Art Gallery when the spring-cleaning was over.

Let me say straight away that I'm no expert. I know a little about a lot of things and a lot about a very few. Even the study of one Italian school can be a man's lifework and I'm the merest amateur, but I did recognise quite a lot of old Victorian and Edwardian friends of my callow youth. But even if I hadn't spotted, for instance, Poynter's bit of Roman history, Albert Moore's draped reclining girls or the Leader landscape, the little plaques at the bottom of each frame would have told me both artists and subject.

Pictures may bore you, but even if they don't you're not to be taken on a conducted tour. It's enough to say that some of those pictures, unless he'd acquired them much later when values had steeply dived, had cost old Weddall a fair amount of money. There were also artists of whose names I'd never even heard and which I wouldn't have hung in my flat if I'd been given them. There were also eight pictures with what I might call a permanent value: pictures worth a lot of money and sure one day to be worth far more: pictures, in fact, almost too good for a Mainford gallery.

I give the list in case you should happen to be interested: Reynolds—*Admiral Davis*, Turner—*Thames at Gravesend*; Gabriel Matsu—*Interior*; Cuyp—*Horsemen with Cattle*; Gainsborough—*Lane Near Sudbury*; Murillo—*Peasant Boys*; Guido Reni—*Head of a Man* and Poussin—*Temple of Neptune*. But when I began to examine them—it was a clear morning and the tall windows gave ample light—I suddenly remembered something. Somewhere in America I'd seen that Matsu, and I couldn't be sure if it were New York, at the Metropolitan, or Chicago. And then I noticed something else. The frames of all those eight pictures weren't original.

At the risk of boring you still more, let me explain. A period frame, to put it briefly, is either carved and possibly gilded wood or wood ornamented with *gesso* work—which is plaster— especially at the corners where the joins are concealed by various designs. Or it may be of, say, ebony or walnut, with the joins at the corners quite invisible because of the excellence of the work. But suppose you acquire an unframed old master that isn't too valuable. Old frames are tremendously dear and the older, the dearer. They're also very scarce, so what a frame-maker or dealer would almost certainly suggest is this. Use a frame from some old but far from valuable picture that wasn't of the same period, perhaps—that'd be expecting too much—but not too much out of keeping, and then cut it down to the size of your picture. But unless you want to spend a lot of money on pretty-pretty stuff to conceal the joins, those corner joins would certainly be detected by anyone who was seriously looking for them.

So there it was. Those eight pictures were all copies. I'd gathered that Old Gus was a bit of a rascal and I couldn't help chuckling at his idea of foisting those pictures on Mainford as originals. Sooner or later someone would spot the fact but that was something with which he'd probably been prepared to cope when the situation arose and by that time he might be pushing up the daisies.

The chuckles suddenly ceased. My mouth gaped a bit.

"Wait a minute," I said to myself. "What about William Weddall? Would he have tolerated fakes in his house?"

It was then that I realised that I hadn't the faintest idea just how much of an art expert William Weddall had been. He had talked about Utrillo but did that make him an expert? He'd been a busy man all his life, so where had he found the time to become an expert? It was true that the very nature of his work must have made him familiar with many interiors and possibly collections, but that was remote indeed from making him competent to distinguish a fine copy from an original. That was something that sometimes caused squabbles among even those supposed to be the last word in pronouncements.

I was just thinking I might do worse than have a word with Sam when the door opened.

"Oh, you're still here!" Grace Amble said.

"Just going up to the drawing-room. You'll come with me?"

"Yes, I'd like to."

"That'll save searching me when I leave," I said, and she laughed.

Grace Amble wasn't off the top shelf. It wasn't so much the thin, rather piercing quality of her voice—I once knew a duchess who literally shrieked—as its suburban quality and the preciousness that covered it with the thinnest of veneers. We chattered gaily as we went up the stairs and I stopped once or twice to look at the pictures that covered not only the walls of the hall but went up with the wall to the first floor. There was nothing of quality among them, though I did see a couple of Dendy Sadlers, and they've been fetching quite fair prices lately in the sale-rooms.

She opened the first door as we turned from the landing.

"Mr. Weddall's bedroom. So handy for the lift, especially when his eyes got so bad."

It was a beautiful, airy room with one four-foot bed. The walls had a few prints and some personal photographs. We went on to the drawing-room and my mouth drooled with envy. It had everything: fine period pieces, porcelain including two superb groups of pre-Marcolini Dresden, some wonderful early Staffordshire, colour prints and watercolours of the early English school. I could have spent a whole morning in that room.

"I always think it's a lovely room," she said. "Evelyn had a lot to do with it, I believe. She was Mr. Weddall's daughter who was killed in an accident."

We went back by the main stairs. I thanked her and said what a pleasure it had been and I certainly hoped we should see each other again. When the door closed on me I wondered just what I should do. Then I thought I'd drop in on Sam. I found him in the garage, washing down the station waggon. He grinned when he saw me and quickly turned off the hose. I gave him the greeting I'd often heard in Montana.

"How're you doin'?"

"Doin' fine, sir. How're you doin'?"

"Can't grumble," I said. "You're pretty busy."

He'd had the station waggon out to take the children to school and the roads had been wet.

"You're staying on here, Sam? I mean after you get your legacy?"

"Don't know, sir," he said, and his face fell. "Me and the boss sorta made two. Don't want to go back to New York and don't want to stay here—not now." A smile came slowly through. "Guess I'm one o' them displaced persons."

"It'll come to you," I said. "But tell me something. Since how long did Mr. Weddall take up pictures? You know, collecting them and so on."

You could almost see his mind working as he shaped the words.

"He was always interested in them kind of things but it weren't till we came here for good that he took it up. Reckon it was a sort o' bug that bit him. You know about old Mr. Weddall, sir, and what he was goin' to do?"

"Yes," I said. "He was going to put the Mainford Museum in order and give it some of his pictures."

"Yeah," Sam said, and smiled again at something. "Couldn't hear nothin' much else one time when we was here. The boss he used to laugh. Then when old Mr. Weddall died the boss he say to me one day, 'Sam, we ought to do somethin' about that Museum,' and I guess that was when he got bit by that bug."

"Mr. Weddall bought pictures himself or through an agent?"

I had to explain what I meant by that, and then he told me that Mr. Joe Borne bought some and the boss bought the rest. It was most of those in the workroom he meant. There weren't many as far as he knew. The boss, he said, would talk about them some nights before he went to bed. He'd take Sam through to the workroom and Sam smiled again as he told me about it.

"He'd show me somethin' he'd just bought and he'd say, 'What do you think about it, Sam?' and me, I'd do a powerful deal o' thinkin' and then I'd say, 'That's a mighty fine picture, boss. *Yes-sir!* a might fine picture.'"

I laughed.

"Well, I must be pushing along, Sam. Might perhaps slip in for a private talk with you tonight. You'll be in?"

"Yes, sir. Come in about eight and I'll make you a cup o' coffee."

I went out to the main road. Short of the gates I stopped.

I went back, skirted the garage and went along a path that bordered the kitchen garden. Gribling and his assistant were spraying fruit trees well to the left of the greenhouses, but I kept to the lee side and cut across the grass to the side road in the steps of the running man. When I came to the main road again I saw a bus approaching. I nipped across the road, waved, and it stopped for me. I'd intended nothing of the sort but I took a ticket for Mainford.

The conductor put me off at the nearest stop to Mill Street and I made my way to the museum. The door was open and I walked in. There was a charge of sixpence on Wednesdays and Saturdays but there was nobody at the desk. I'd walked round two of the rooms—and I was the only one there—when an elderly man came in and asked me if he could give me a ticket. I gave him a sixpence and he peeled one from a roll.

In under half an hour I was out in the street again. That museum was a hotch-potch of everything, with almost nothing that interested me. There were not more than a couple of pictures in the quite large collection that I'd have had as a gift. A lot of them were local and most of the rest those heavily-varnished oils that clutter up the walls of most of the small provincial collections. And the place had a musty smell. One thing I will say for it, it was quite well lighted.

It was nearly half-past twelve so I walked the few hundred yards to the Homeways Hotel and had lunch. A couple of the old waiters were still there but no one whom I knew.

When I came out I was at a loose end and then it struck me that I might as well take a bus ride to Castledene and have a look at Humphrey Weddall's house. I had a quarter of an hour to wait and there weren't more than ten people on the bus. I went on top and asked the conductor where the house was. He said it was the first big one on the left as we came into the village.

It was only a ten-minute run and I remembered almost each yard of the *route*. Castledene's as much a high-class residential suburb as a village in its own right. Weddall's house was a large red-bricked one—Victorian Tudor—in quite large grounds, and no sooner were we nearing it when the bus suddenly pulled up with such a jerk that I was shot forward in my seat. I was in the one furthest front and I only saved myself from a crack on the skull by instinctively shooting out my hands in front of me.

A woman was the cause, and I had a good look at her. I guessed she was Humphrey's wife—a smartly-dressed woman in the thirties with a made-up face and a look of money about her. The car was a fairly new Jaguar coupé. She'd come too far out into the narrowish road in order to have a good view. A lorry had been coming the other way and, if our bus had tried to pass her, there would certainly have been trouble.

The lorry went by. The road was ours and we went on. The lady wasn't pleased. She gave the driver a look that should have dropped him over the wheel.

"Who's she think she is?" a woman a seat or two behind me asked her companion.

Five minutes later I got off the bus at the church. There was a return one in five minutes so I took it. I got off at Mainford Town Hall and thought of enquiring about a bus to Hinchbrook, and then I happened to catch sight of an antique shop. It had two fairly big display windows and over the door was BORNE & SON. I looked in the windows and then went into the shop.

It was the usual clutter of a fairly high-class provincial shop: the quite good and the not so good in almost everything: furniture, china, pottery, copper-ware, clocks, miniatures, brass-ware, prints and all the rest of it. The only pictures were the very small ones that were blood brothers of some in the museum.

A bell had tinkled, and almost at once a man came in from a side room. He was about five-feet eight, stoutish and walked with a slight limp.

"Pardon me, but are you Mr. Borne?"

"Yes, sir."

"Then, pardon me again," I said, "but your name's not too common and when I saw it I wondered if you were by any chance related to the firm of Weddall and Borne? I knew them in Lower Oxford Street more years ago than I care to remember."

Something told me he knew who I was.

"Very interesting, sir. As a matter of fact that Mr. Borne was my father. He still has a shop you know. Quite a biggish place in South Kensington."

"I think I know it," I said. "I must make a note to drop in."

"And your name, sir, if I may ask?"

I told him, and I was surer than ever that he knew it already. When you've spent half a lifetime examining witnesses and suspects, there's not much that passes you by.

"You've come to live here, sir?"

"A very temporary visitor. I live in town."

"Indeed, sir? And anything you're specially interested in?"

"A lot," I said, and smiled. "The trouble is finding the money."

"Oh, no, sir," he said, and laughed. "Prices have gone up, and don't I know it, but there's always something somewhere. We've more rooms upstairs, by the way."

"Some other time," I said. "Sorry to have disturbed you but I was interested in the name. And I'll certainly have a look at your father's place. Does he keep a general stock or specialise?"

"Pictures, sir. Nothing nowadays but pictures."

I'd been edging towards the door, so I just nodded at that and smiled a goodbye. As I walked back towards a bus-stop I wondered if he'd be watching from the door.

I GOT off the bus at a convenient stop and walked the short distance to the Hall. Jewle would almost certainly be there and, while I had nothing exciting to report, I wondered how Matthews had progressed on the trail of the running man and if there was anything that Jewle himself had unearthed.

Away to the left I heard the noise of children and when I was clear of the shrubberies that bordered the drive I saw three children by the swimming pool. A windbreak of polled poplars had been planted round the pool but now the leaves had gone I could see concrete strips and the little covered shelter at the far end. A girl, school satchel over her shoulder, was standing at the open end: interested apparently in the noisy game of tag the two other children were playing round the shelter—a much younger girl and a boy. The girls were wearing the same school uniform, or so I judged by the hats, and the boy had a similarly coloured blazer and what looked like the same badge on his cap.

I guessed who the three were and I made my way across to them, and not with any thought of what I might call business but because I like children and usually get on pretty well with them. As I neared I saw that the pool was now empty. It was about forty feet long and fifteen wide; three feet deep at the far end and about eighteen inches at the nearer, and that meant that Weddall had had it made especially for the grandchildren.

My feet were making no sound on the grass and I was quite near to the elder girl before I spoke.

"Hallo!" I said. "What's going on here?"

She gave me a cool, poised look. She was about nine: a rather thin girl with a slightly freckled face. She had fair hair worn in two pigtails tied with ribbon that matched the green of her hat and she was wearing glasses, and but for them I think she would have been almost pretty. My first impression was that she was a very assured young person.

"They're awfully silly," she told me in a highly superior way, but maybe she had some cause.

"They're awfully young," I pointed out. "They'll quieten down when they're as old as you and I."

She gave me that cool look, saw that I was smiling and gave a shy smile that all at once made her far less assured.

"Perhaps you can tell me something," I said. "Why is it that little boys always have to shout and little girls have to scream?"

"It's just showing off," she said, and was all superior again.

"Yes," I said judicially. "I think you're right. What's your name?"

"Brenda. Brenda Hortensia Gray."

"My name's Travers," I said, and before I could say anything else the other two children were running towards us. If I hadn't caught the girl she would have run into me.

"Steady," I said. "You might have hurt yourself if you'd fallen in the pool."

She was plump, and rosy-cheeked from all that running. I asked her name.

"Jean," she said, and giggled.

"She's Jean Weddall Holt," Brenda informed me. "And that's Paul Weddall Holt."

Paul was the image of his sister, a good-looking, well-grown boy of eight. He, too, was somewhat self-assured. Still, it's a poor cock that can't crow, as they say, on its own dunghill.

"Gribling's going to put a little water in the pool when there's another frost," he told me, "and then we're going to slide."

"That'll be fine," I said.

"I can slide," Jean told me.

"You tell the most dreadful stories," Brenda said coolly. "You know you can't slide."

"Oh yes she can," Paul said. "Not very well, though, but she *can* slide."

"Now children, time for tea."

Grace Amble's voice was suddenly so near that I must have given a jump.

"I hope they're not annoying you, Mr. Travers."

"Not a bit of it," I said. "I was going to the Hall and saw some fun and games going on so I thought I'd come and investigate."

"They're very noisy sometimes," she told me. "And Jean, you'd better be very careful now Mr. Travers is here, and you, too, Paul. Mr. Travers is a policeman."

I looked at her. She was looking at the two children and the look had more than the irony of some shared joke. Paul grinned sheepishly and looked away. Jean's face flushed an even more fiery red. She stared at me for a moment and then she literally took to her heels and ran wildly towards the house.

"You've frightened her," I said, just a bit annoyed.

"She probably has a guilty conscience," she told me, and with that same smile of secret amusement. "Tea-time, Paul. Are you coming, too, Brenda?"

"Thank you, Mrs. Amble, but I have my lessons to do," Brenda told her primly. "And something to do for Mummy."

"Well, some other time," Grace Amble told her. "You coming this way, Mr. Travers?"

She and Paul were apparently making for the east wing. "Going up to the study," I said. "Inspector Jewle has given me a spare key so as not to disturb the household."

Brenda and I walked on. Nothing was said for the first few seconds, and then she asked, in the same cool way, if I were really a policeman.

"Only a sort of special kind of one," I said. "That's why I don't wear uniform. But tell me something: why was Jean so scared?"

Her lip curled.

"She's very stupid, really, and she's always doing stupid things. She thinks they're clever."

"Ah, well," I said. "I do stupid things myself. And now I must leave you. Have a good tea and don't work too hard." She just smiled as she moved away. Then she broke into a run and she was out of sight by the time I reached the front door.

Jewle was in the study, just finishing his tea. I said I'd had a cup and a cake at Mainford.

"So you went there after all," he said. "Anything particular in mind?"

I gave him a perfectly full and honest account of my day. He laughed at my revelation of Old Gus's donation of faked masterpieces to the Mainford Museum.

"He was quite a character, that old boy. I heard one or two things about him today, and the funny thing is that nobody bears him a grudge. The old story, perhaps. Everybody likes a rogue. And what did you think of Mrs. Amble?"

"I didn't like her at all," I told him. "A hard, calculating woman, and I like her even less when she puts on the charm."

"Yes," he said. "She may have had a lot to put up with from her husband but I can't help being on his side."

He pushed the trolley out to the landing.

"I looked in at the museum, too," he said. "Just getting the general background after what Pepson told us. Like you. A pretty grim place, I thought. Oh, and here's something else. All Weddall's glasses I could find. The local police took them away so as to get an expert report on his eyes."

There were no less than five sets. Those in red cases were of high magnification.

"I'm no oculist," Jewle said, "but his eyes were pretty bad. These two in the blue cases were merely dark glasses to keep the light from his eyes when he didn't want to use them. No particular astigmatism or anything like that, simply that the retinas only reflected partially and had to be assisted."

"And what was he wearing when he was killed?"

"None at all. He'd evidently taken them off and laid them by while he rang down to Sam."

"Seems in keeping," I said. "Also there were times—before he had that trip to Italy—when he preferred to use no glasses at all. At Christie's that morning and at the flat when he was looking at a picture, for instance, and wanted to rely on what natural sight he still had. Anything else happen? Anything from Matthews?"

Matthews was in town and wouldn't be back till the next day. He was organising the hunt for the running man who'd been traced as far as Euston. I looked at my watch.

"Something I'd like to do," I said, "and we can get it over before supper. I'd like to have a look at all those pictures in the workroom there."

"Good," he said, and got to his feet at once. "I'd like to see the old maestro at work."

"So would I," I said. "As it is, you'll have to be content with me." We went in.

"Shut that door, will you? We don't want to be disturbed."

He opened the door and had a quick look along the corridor. "There's no key."

"Well, bolt it."

A moment and he was saying there weren't any bolts.

"Come here a minute. This is extraordinary."

He had another glance along the corridor and his voice lowered.

"See this, and this? Here's where the bolts were. See this almost new paint?"

He was right. There *had* been bolts, but quite recently they'd been removed and everything made good.

"What was the idea?" he wanted to know. "Someone wanted to get in and out of here just when they liked?"

I grunted.

"That's what it looks like. Maybe they wanted to listen at the study door there. That may be how it was known that Weddall was giving an important letter to Sam. Still, we can make all fast now. I'll get a chair and wedge it against the door handle."

A minute or two and I was at work with Jewle as head assistant. The pictures on the wall looked unimportant, so I began with those on the floor. I moved a picture round—all had been placed with their backs to the room—and made a quick note, when I was able, and he did the replacing. Again I don't want to bore you with the details of that hour and a half's work. Every picture there was good enough for most art galleries, the prices ranging, in my judgment, from less than three figures to up to four. A couple of Fragonards, for instance, the minor Dutch school, the school of Canaletto, a couple of early Italians, a fair Barker of Bath, two which I thought were seventeenth-century German, and a few which I liked but couldn't identify. The total was enough to fill any reasonably-sized room of a gallery.

But, and it was a very big but, again there were pictures that were very different, and Jewle found Weddall's glass in the study so that I could have a real good look at them. All were unmistakably French, and of various schools: a Courbet, a Manet, a Bonnard, two Cézannes and, later, a Matisse, a Gauguin sketch, and a comparatively realistic Braque. All those pictures were practically together.

"Something's wrong," I told Jewle.

"They're fakes?"

"Frankly, I don't know enough to be sure. But think. Do you realise what this small collection would be worth if they're genuine? Might be anything between fifty and a hundred thousand pounds."

He stared.

"How could even a wealthy man like Weddall collect on that scale?" I asked him. "This sort of stuff is for the super-millionaires."

We put the pictures back against the wall. Jewle removed the chair and we went back to the study. We hadn't reached it when the workroom door opened and Grace Amble looked in.

"Sorry," she said. "It's you, Inspector. I thought I heard someone."

"It's all right, Mrs. Amble. We were just having a look round."

She closed the door again. We went on to the study and I switched off the workroom lights.

"Damnation!" Jewle said. "We weren't keeping our voices down. For all we know she might have been listening in the corridor." He shook his head glumly. "I suppose in a way we were trespassing."

It was a pity, but there it was. Jewle wanted to know how those special pictures affected the Case—as if he didn't know.

"Someone—maybe his brother-in-law Joe—has simply been taking advantage of his loss of sight to switch some fakes on him," I said. "If that's so, there're a couple of new suspects— Joe and his son. And it explains why that book was taken from the table drawer where Pepson saw it."

"Yes," he said, "but what about probate? Weddall's bank is the executor so wouldn't they have an assessor to work out an agreed value on the contents of the house for tax purposes?"

"Suppose the executors did. The assessor for the art objects would be an expert. He'd know the pictures were fakes and they'd be priced at virtually nil. If anything was pinned on, say, either of the Bornes, all they'd have to say was that Weddall couldn't afford originals and wanted them to find him some first-class copies."

"Where are the originals?"

"Lord knows," I said. "I don't know enough about it for that. But there needn't be originals. Remember that famous Dutchman who took in all the experts with his fakes, which included one or two Vermeers? His were originals, not copies. They just had to be originals. He painted an original picture in the style and manner of Vermeer and used the same pigments and so on. That's what may have been done here. I just don't know."

"Wait a minute," Jewle said. "Let's suppose something. Let's suppose Weddall had had an expert in surreptitiously and discovered they were fakes. Might that be one of the reasons he was having all his relatives here for that birthday celebration? To show up Joe Borne and his son?"

"Could be," I said.

"Then Mrs. Amble could tell us if there were any special visitors." He shook his head. "But, no, we can't do that. We don't want to let anyone know we're wise."

I'd never had a look at any of the books in that room and when I began taking them out I thought I knew how the comparative novice, Weddall, had got most of his knowledge. There was volume after volume, some of them most expensive, on schools and individual artists. Every one had been read. Some, like a couple of volumes on the French Impressionists, were dog-eared, and most had pencilled margins. In that room were at least a couple of hundred pounds' worth of books on art.

Jewle had been browsing on his own.

"Here's a *Who's Who*," he told me. "Didn't you say that hoaxer who got you to Liverpool could have got his information about you from *Who's Who*?"

I had a look at it. It was the latest edition and the few lines about me were there. I also happened to see the time by the bracket clock. We'd have to get a move on if we weren't to be late for supper.

I remembered something as we were walking to the pub—the telephone call the hoaxer had made. Jewle said the checking was a long business but he'd asked the local police to check if a call to me had been made through the local exchange. As a matter of fact there was a message for us when we got to the pub. The landlord had taken it down.

Call, answering your requirements, made from Hall.

We had a quick drink for the good of the house and went up to supper. Jewle told me there were two independent lines at the Hall: one to the study and one in Mrs. Amble's room. There were extensions from Mrs. Amble to the study and three from the study— to Mrs. Amble, the kitchen and Sam. As to the hoaxer, he must have rung me either from the study or from Mrs. Amble's room.

"Weddall couldn't have been the hoaxer, or could he?" Jewle said.

It was easy to say no, but how could it be disproved? All we could do was think it most unlikely. The running man, with Mrs.

Amble's connivance, seemed far more probable. This was as far as we were prepared to go.

"No use tackling her," Jewle said. "She'd only deny anything and we'd do far more harm by giving things away."

Everything seemed to depend on getting hold of that running man. In the meanwhile, I'd thought of something I'd like to do—have the next day in town for the purpose of dropping in on Joe Borne. It was too much to hope I'd find anything out, but if I'd been right in thinking that Oliver Borne had recognised me, then Joe might recognise me, too, and it wouldn't do any harm to note his reactions. And I wanted to know the kind of trade that Joe did.

I rang the Hall and Mrs. Amble answered. I said would she be so good as to let Sam Martin know that I couldn't, after all, accept his kind invitation to drop in that night for a cup of coffee. I tried to put just a touch of snobbery into it as if it had been a bit presumptuous on the part of Sam and I was taking a polite way out. She said she understood.

Next morning I took the eight o'clock bus and then the nine o'clock train. I had a cup of coffee in Regent Street and then hopped a bus that would drop me near City Detection Limited. What Jewle didn't know would cause him no worry, but what I was to find out was to make that surreptitious visit about as lucky a one as I'd ever made in my life.

Bill Fraser was busy at the moment, his receptionist told me, but I didn't have to wait more than ten minutes before he was free.

"Hallo, there," he said. "Haven't seen you for quite a time. How are you?"

I said I was fine and I hoped he was. He asked if I'd have some coffee and I said I'd just had a cup and after a little more chit-chat he asked what was on my mind.

"As a matter of fact, Bill, I've come here to save you what might be an awful lot of trouble. I'm in it up to the neck myself but with a little private co-operation I might keep you out of it."

That was portentous enough in all conscience and it had him worried.

"What's up then? What's the trouble?"

"I'll tell you, but in the strictest confidence. That all right?"

"It's all right with me."

"You recently had a client who gave you the job of keeping an eye on a certain William Weddall?"

"William Weddall." He frowned to gain time. "I think we did. Why?"

"Again strictly between ourselves, the police think Weddall's been murdered. I'm involved, too, and I think murder is practically a certainty. My proposition is this: you tell me about it, always in the strictest confidence, and I'll practically guarantee to keep the police away from your door."

He bit his lip. He grunted.

"This isn't some sort of a catch, is it?"

"You know me," I said. "I don't go in for catches, Bill. I had business with Weddall and that's why I was roped in. He lived near Mainford and the police have had me down there. As a matter of fact I've got to go down there again tonight. And I can tell you this. The police have a description of Bob Mander whom you had following Weddall, and unless I can head them off—and with your co-operation I can—they'll be here asking questions. There might be the sort of publicity you and I don't like."

Bill's a fat man and the chair creaked as he leaned back in thought.

"Nothing doing," he said. "Unless you can guarantee I'm not going to be bothered. You've got influence. Plenty of influence."

I did some thinking, and some fidgeting. As a performance it was far from bad.

"Right," I said. "I may have to stick my neck out a good deal further, but I'll keep you out of it. I'm not happy about it but I will."

He unlocked a filing cabinet, riffled through the files and brought one back to the desk. He kept pursing his lips and making little noises as he read.

"Yes," he said, "three jobs. The first picked him up at Euston and he was followed to Sotheby's to a sale, and he took a taxi back from there to Euston at about half-past two. The second time he was picked up in his car at Wm. Whiteley's and then on to Christie's and—"

"I know," I said ruefully. "And then on to my flat. And from there to the Café Royal, out again after lunch with a woman and two children and on to the car and home."

"And that's where you come in?"

"That's it," I said. "That's where the raven starts croaking."

"Raven? What raven?"

"Forget it," I said. "What was the third time?"

He turned over the page.

"The third one. Oh, yes. Picked up at Christie's, lunch at Short's and home. All we had to do was pick him up, see what he did, describe anyone he met, and see him on the way home. That last job was about a week after the second one."

"And nothing since?"

"Nothing since."

"And the name of your client?"

"You know I can't tell you that. Would you tell me?"

"If it were murder—yes. And if you were trying to save me a lot of trouble."

"Yes," he said, and with a finger eased the tight collar round his neck. "And what if I don't know the client's name?"

"All the more reason to tell me," I said. "You don't know: I won't know. Was it one of those telephoned communications?"

"Something of the sort," he said. "A telephone message giving all particulars and saying cash would be sent the following morning, which it was."

"But the report," I said. "Where did that have to go?"

It was like squeezing blood out of a flint. It took a couple of minutes of argument and assurances before he oozed out what I wanted. The reports had to be sent within twenty-four hours in a sealed envelope addressed to a Mr. S. O'Brien, c/o Borne & Son, 1 Willow Street, South Kensington.

I hope I didn't move a muscle.

"Well, we can keep the client out of it," I told him. "Was the procedure the same for the next two times?"

"Yes," he said. "Except that we knew we could rely on getting paid."

"Right," I said, and rose from the chair. "I'm not interested in what you did, Bill. I rather hoped there might be a lead to someone who might have killed Weddall. And I'm dead sure now I can keep you in the clear. But wasn't there a fourth assignment? If there's not, then we both may be in the soup. You dead sure there wasn't a fourth?"

"Silly of me," he said. "Must have got two pages stuck. As a matter of fact there was a fourth, now I come to look at it. To be picked up at Victoria one morning and be sure he got on the boat train."

"Good lord!" I said. "That's more like what I want. And did he take that train?"

"He did. Strictly between ourselves, he was going to Italy."

"Fine," I said. "Just what I want. You know what. Bill? I'll lay you ten to one in pounds you hear no more about it."

I shook his hand with quite an enthusiasm. He went with me to the outer door, and when I left him I wondered how long it would be before he saw that the whole thing somehow didn't make sense. From his personal point of view, that is. From my own it made quite a lot.

8. BRIEF ENCOUNTER

IN THE taxi that was taking me towards South Kensington I was thinking about a whole lot of things. There was Bill Fraser, for instance, who'd been rushed off his feet with a spate of ambiguous words. I didn't hold it against him that he'd held back that fourth assignment. After all, if he could get immunity from police questioning by revealing three, why produce a fourth?

It was the fourth that had been the most interesting, since it not only fitted in with a theory that I was beginning to shape, but it showed that Weddall had been a whole lot smarter than certain people had imagined. He'd spotted Bill Fraser's man and he'd outwitted him. He'd had some luck, of course. If Mander hadn't gone to buy a platform ticket, Weddall might have been spotted making his getaway.

It was pretty good, too, to know the name of Bill Fraser's client. That O'Brien character to whom reports had been sent was almost certainly non-existent. Joe Borne was the man who'd had Weddall watched, and almost certainly because of those fakes in the workroom at Hinchbrook Hall. The fact that all four assignments had been crowded into a very few weeks showed that things had been working up to a crisis.

I wondered who had tipped Borne off on those occasions when Weddall had come to town. I thought it could only be Mrs. Amble. But another queer thing was that on each occasion, except on that leaving for Italy, Weddall had merely come to attend a sale. And then I had another idea. Weddall should have had no need to inform Mrs. Amble where he was going. All he'd had to say was that he and Sam wouldn't be in for lunch. Had Weddall deliberately told Mrs. Amble exactly where he was going, and because he was playing cat and mouse? I thought it might be so.

The taxi slowed down. I was apparently at Willow Street and a second or two later I was having a look at the shop over which was the name BORNE & SON. It was immediately off the main street: a one-windowed place whose three storeys seemed to belong to the one business. In the window was one picture flanked by two smaller ones. I crossed over and had a look at them. The centre one was a Stubbs: a horse held by a groom, and a background of trees and a distant house. The smaller farmyard scenes were by some early nineteenth-century artist named Edelmann.

I went into the shop and I was pleasantly surprised. There was quite a spacious lobby with rooms leading back from it, and quite wide-carpeted stairs that ran up to the first floor. Pictures were carefully placed and, as the rooms had been given a furnished look with period furniture along the walls and even an occasional mirror, the effect was one of intimacy and class. A man in a dark suit, an assistant almost certainly, came towards me from nowhere, feet silent on the thick carpet.

"Good morning, sir. Can I help you?"

"Just looking round," I said. "May I do that?"

"Of course, sir." The suave voice was very apologetic. "We like people to look round. If you want me, sir, I shall be in the office." He waved a hand towards another room.

I looked round and I had the same feeling I always had when I browsed in picture shops of the best class—the hope of finding something that I knew and liked and the gradual certainty that compared with the dealers I was little more than an ignoramus. If I knew an artist it was either because his signature was plain or because the usual little wooden plaque at the bottom of a picture gave name and title. And practically all the names conveyed nothing to me.

I was running a quick eye over an abstract—a queer sort of dissolving pattern of scrawls in hectic colours—when I saw something in the rococo mirror that was hanging near it. A man was coming down the stairs and he was either a workman or an artist: a tall, stooping man of about forty. He was wearing a beret but it wasn't only that, and the straggling moustache, that gave him a foreign look. The white, working coat he wore was paint-stained and the sleeves were too short and revealed more stains that ran well below his wrists. He disappeared in the direction of the office. A minute and I heard voices; no words, merely sound. A voice was angrily raised. Almost at once the man came into sight again in the mirror. He was looking annoyed and his hands went out in an angry gesture as he went back up the stairs.

I suppose it wasn't surprising. Upstairs there would be a man or two whose jobs were to restore both frames and pictures. Quite a few of the pictures that I'd seen had obviously been cleaned. I was thinking no more about it and was moving on to another abstract when I heard a faint sound and I looked round to see another man approaching me. I guessed he was Joseph Borne.

"Good-morning, sir."

Our eyes met and I was dead sure he recognised me. The whole man seemed to stay still for a moment before the smile reappeared and the slightly deferential bow. He was a shortish man, probably Scandinavian in origin: hair so fair that you could hardly discern where the grey began, and his eyes were a startling blue. He looked about seventy and good for many more years.

"Mr. Borne?"

"Yes, sir." He was still so deferential that I almost expected him to add: "Joseph Borne, at your service."

I put a lot of my cards on the table. I told him who I was, that I'd been in Mainford, had been attracted by the name, and so on and so on. A minute or two and we were chatting very pleasantly about the state of the trade compared with the old days in Lower Oxford Street. We discussed the abstracts. He mentioned the artist's name and said that in his judgment it was one day going to be a very big one. I said bluntly that in my opinion the abstract business was largely a racket. He smiled.

"Maybe in some cases," he told me. "But Galileo and Wagner—didn't people think they were running a sort of racket? And Stravinsky. And Klee, Braque"—he reeled off a lot of names—"What about them? Would you have risked your money on them twenty years ago?"

We had been moving slowly along almost in a circle and were virtually in the entrance lobby again.

"Excuse me a moment," Borne said hurriedly, and I saw that a man was coming through the door. Borne was moving ahead to meet him. The man smiled and looked as if he were about to hold out his hand. Borne's hand went up to his shoulder and he almost whipped the man round. Borne was talking quickly, but so softly that I couldn't hear a word. The man looked back towards me and suddenly I knew who he was. The grey hat, the grey overcoat, the height of him and that whitish scar by his chin.

I moved forward but the man had gone hurriedly through the door. Borne seemed to be cleverly blocking my way.

"I think I've seen that man somewhere. Who is he?"

Borne spread his palms. He was moving round, directly between me and the door.

"Just a pest," he said. "Always supposing to have information about some picture or other. Just a crank. His name's Brown. I think it's Brown. . . ."

I'd moved round him and his voice was an agitated diminuendo as I went through the door. I strode out the few yards to the main street and just caught a glimpse of the running man on the far side. And before I could nip across myself, the traffic lights were against me and the traffic was surging past. When the lights changed and I did cross, there was never a sign of him. And I was suddenly angry: angry with myself for having let Borne delay me: angry at what I might have done and the time I might have saved. But it didn't last long. I waited there by the kerb till I could stop a taxi.

I got off at Northumberland Avenue and walked the short distance to the Yard. Matthews wasn't in but I managed to contact someone I knew, and wrote a longish note for Matthews.

I stressed the urgency and said he was to have that note the minute he came in. It was then half-past twelve so I hopped a bus that was going near my club.

I had lunch there and kept the thoughts dammed back till I found an unoccupied corner of the smoke-room and the steward had brought me coffee. But thinking got me nowhere beyond the obvious—that the running man and Borne were old friends; that Borne had recognised me and didn't want me to come into any contact with the man, and it complicated matters because the quick backward look the man had given me hadn't seemed to have in it any recognition. Another thing that was obvious was that if the running man had killed Weddall, then Borne was aware of it; and it seemed to follow that Borne must have been in some way the organiser of the crime or else there wouldn't have been that clumsy but frantic attempt to keep me in the shop till the man had made his getaway.

I left the club earlier than I'd intended and because the thoughts were circling round and round and getting me nowhere. And I had one more job to do before taking a train back to Mainford. It arose out of what Jewle and I had been discussing the previous night.

I'd thought it might be a good idea to let an expert have a look at the pictures at Hinchbrook Hall. Jewle said the visit needn't be surreptitious. He was seeing Humphrey Weddall in any case and could say that a friend of his—Jewle's—had expressed a wish to see the collection and Humphrey couldn't do other than give permission. Jewle was having a busy day. Not only was he seeing Humphrey—he wouldn't tell me precisely why—but he was going to the Mainford bank that had handled William Weddall's business. There was no need to ask why he was doing that. What he'd been wanting was to trace the prices that had been paid for pictures, and to whom.

I walked from the club to Pall Mall and the offices of Wilber, Forbes & Co. They're insurance people and high-class valuers for insurance and probate, and they'd done a fairly recent valuation for me. It's a wise thing and I can't understand why far more people don't do it. Firms like Wilber, Forbes have experts who make a valuation of everything you own in the way of chattels. If there's a fire, then the insurance company accepts without question the valuation they've made. If you die, the income-tax people do the same. No argument, no bother. You have a bound inventory, there's one for safety at your bank, Wilber, Forbes have one in their safes and the insurance company—whose business in your case is handled by Wilber, Forbes—have a fourth, and what's in those inventories is accepted as a true valuation. If you sell anything or acquire anything new, you notify Wilber, Forbes and the necessary adjustments are made to the inventories and the premium.

Ten minutes after entering the doors I was admitted to the office of Mr. Frank Wilber. We had never met but he'd obviously looked me up in the firm's files. I told him I had the chance of buying some pictures and I'd like the use of a really good expert, just for the following morning. He'd be met by me at Mainford Station, and I'd like him to travel by the nine o'clock from Euston.

"I see by our files that our Mr. Colgate did your own last valuation," Wilber said. "Would you like him? Always better, we think, to have someone with whom you're acquainted, and he happens to be available."

I said I'd be delighted to have Colgate.

"There's not a better expert working for any company, or with his experience." He gave me a quizzical look. "Mind you, he comes pretty expensive."

"Don't get a wrong impression," I said. "All I want is this. I tell him what I can buy a picture for and he just nods or shakes his head and says buy it or don't buy it. He can be where I want him at half-past ten and he can be back here in town for a late lunch."

Wilber thought for a moment.

"Well, you're a client of quite long standing and I'm sure we shan't overcharge you. A maximum of fifty guineas ought to cover it." He saw my raised eyebrows. "It might be considerably less."

That was how we left things, and I had just the time to catch the four o'clock from Euston. I bought some evening papers and they shortened the journey pretty well. By the time I'd gone through them we were not a great distance from Mainford.

I was to have another surprise. As I came through the barrier whom should I see standing there but Brenda Gray. She was apparently waiting for someone. She caught sight of me and gave a shy smile.

"Hallo, Brenda," I said. "What're you doing here?"

"Meeting Mummy," she said, and her face lighted as she looked beyond me. "Hallo, Mummy!"

A woman was with us. She stooped and kissed her small daughter.

"Hallo, darling. You got here all right then?"

"Of course!" Brenda told her importantly. And then Mrs. Gray caught sight of me. She gave me a quick look and then she smiled.

"Am I wrong or are you what Brenda called the funny police-man?"

"I expect I am," I said. "I met Brenda yesterday at the Hall." I held out a hand. "How are you, Mrs. Gray?"

She'd intended going home by bus but I said I was taking a taxi and I hoped she and Brenda would come with me. She had a couple of parcels and I took the larger one, and we managed to get the taxi. On the ride to Hinchbrook we had quite a gossip. She was obviously a woman of considerable culture: quite plain, like her young daughter, but very charming in manner. I put her age at forty, so she'd probably married fairly late. She told me she'd been a secretary before marriage: personal secretary to a well-known industrial magnate.

"What did you actually do for Mr. Weddall?" I wanted to know, and she said that when he was at the Hall she came along most mornings at about ten o'clock and looked through his corres-pondence and then he'd dictate any answers and she'd type them on her portable.

"Nothing a great deal different from what I'd always been used to," she told me, "except there were usually sales catalogues and letters from art dealers which I wasn't so familiar with."

"When did you first start working with him?"

It was just about a year after his father's death: in fact when she and her husband came to Hinchbrook. After his eyesight failed he began to rely on her more and more.

"But he was always very good," she said. "If I wanted to go anywhere he'd always have Sam take me in the car. Do you know Sam? He's a great character."

I said I certainly did.

"Yes, *ma'am*," I said, and she laughed.

"Sam's nice," Brenda told us. "And strict. He won't let the children act silly in the car."

Mrs. Gray gave me a look.

"Darling, you mustn't be too grown up," she told her daughter, and picked up the thread again. Yes, she said, Mr. Weddall was one of the kindest people she'd ever known.

"It was queer," she said. "In a way he was very English and yet he was somehow more American. Very democratic. The way, for instance, he and Sam were more like friends."

"Did you handle his financial business?"

"Only to the extent of enclosing his cheques when it was necessary. But he was a charming man and so easy to get on with. His daughter, they tell me, was also a very charming person. Very sad about her death—she and her husband. He was quite wealthy, by the way. I believe there's a very substantial trust fund for the children. You've been in the drawing-room?"

"A lovely room."

She sighed.

"Isn't it? That was Evelyn's creation. Everything in it was hers and when she died Mr. Weddall wouldn't have it disturbed. It was valued for the purposes of the trust fund but it's just as it was when she was alive. It was she who was in charge of everything at the Hall even before her marriage." She laughed as the cab began to slow. "Heavens! Here we are already. Doesn't the time fly when you're talking!"

I paid the driver. Brenda took the smaller parcel and ran off down the rectory drive. Mrs. Gray thanked me and apologised for the absence of Brenda's thanks.

"She's excited at what's in the parcel," she said, and with a slight lowering of a voice by way of imparting a confidence— "Mr. Weddall left me a nice little legacy. I've been shopping in town on the strength of it."

We both said we'd like to see each other again. She went down the drive and I walked on to the pub. I thought Jewle would be there but he wasn't. When I'd had a bit of a polish I went down to the bar for a drink and I'd been there only some ten minutes when Jewle looked in. We went through to the darts room. It was early and we had the room to ourselves. He'd had a call from Matthews so he knew about my encounter with the running man. Later that evening, when Matthews got back, he thought we should come to one or two decisions.

Jewle had had one of those patient, exploratory days trying to fit this to that. Jewle had grown up, as it were, in the Yard and the Yard can afford to be patient. Half the things that Jewle had been doing I'd either forgotten or else I hadn't thought of them. The man Perolli, for instance, with whom Weddall was supposed to have spent that recent holiday in Italy: he was someone I'd forgotten, but the Italian authorities were trying to find him.

There was the matter of insurances. Humphrey Weddall's firm, like a lot of solicitors, handled a considerable deal of insurance work through their chief clerk, and they'd handled the insurances on the Hall. Jewle had seen both the former clerk, Spurn, and his successor and he'd learned one or two interesting things.

"If it wasn't a racket I don't know what else you can call it," he told me. "Old Gus is Humphrey's grandfather? Right. Must keep in with Grandpa, so what do you do? You suggest a valuer for insurance purposes and you handle the insurance for the company and the contents of the building get quoted at a lump sum. No check, in other words, on individual items. Then Gus dies and his son William takes over. He leaves all his business to Humphrey and the insurances go on in the same sweet way— with two exceptions. He insured separately all the new pictures he bought and there was a special valuation of the drawing-room and the insurances on that were a charge on the trust. The Holts left about fifty thousand pounds which went to the two children. Humphrey and a brother officer of the late Major Holt are the trustees, and when I tell you that this officer is a serving one and at present's in Malaya, you can see that Humphrey is virtually in control."

"And what's Spurn like?"

"Pretty old. Highly competent, no doubt, but I can't see him as much more than a routine sort of partner."

That was interesting. Jewel didn't know just how interesting it was. Or did he?

"William Weddall's will," I said. "Would you mind refreshing my memory about it?"

He knew all the provisions. The quarter of a million that Weddall had left including house, contents and certain American investments. A biggish chunk had been left to the Architects' Institute of America for such charitable purposes as they might determine. Fifty thousand went to Humphrey, and five thousand each to Mrs. Amble and Sam. The Bornes got a thousand each, Mrs. Gray five hundred and there were smaller legacies to the head gardener and the cook. When everything was finally settled it looked as if the new trust for the children would amount to between sixty-five and seventy thousand pounds.

Now I couldn't tell Jewle what Sam had told me, that Mrs. Amble had been a listener at doors, that Weddall had known it and that he'd told Sam he knew a whole lot more than anyone suspected. And why then had Weddall left Grace Amble five thousand pounds? But I could mention the new trust. Wasn't it strange that Weddall had added a very big sum to another big sum? Weren't the children rather too well provided for? And wasn't Humphrey taking on another big responsibility?

"Oh, yes," he said. "I've thought that out but I don't see how it helps. Some people like power—"

"And money."

"Yes, and money. Humphrey's almost certainly fond of both. But he didn't kill his uncle. By the way there was something else I was going to tell you about those insurances. Those fakes, or not fakes, in the workroom, weren't insured. And they weren't paid for. I've traced payments—nearly all to Joseph Borne—for practically all the others. And do you know what I guessed about that? That those pictures hadn't been in the Hall long enough. And Sam verified it. He remembers Weddall's excitement when they arrived. *How* he doesn't know, but it was two or three days after Weddall got back from Italy." Everything fitted in so snugly that I think I must have chuckled. Weddall announces the Italy trip, and the fakes are got ready for his return. Joe receives the all clear. Weddall's eyes are very much worse when the pictures arrive.

"If we can pin all that on Joe Borne, we might put the screws on him and make him talk: I mean if we can't pick up that running man," Jewle said. "But to get back to Humphrey. I had lunch with him today at the Homeways Hotel and he told me his house at Castledene is in the market and the contents are being sold. I think he'll be moving into the Hall before the end of the month. I met his wife, by the way. She'd been busy at some women's committee meeting or other in the town and dropped in at the hotel for coffee with us." He gave his old dry smile. "Struck me as very conveniently arranged."

I told him where and when I'd seen her.

"Oh, yes," Jewle said. "She wears the trousers. Humphrey was all 'Yes, my dear,' and 'If you think so, my dear.' Not that she didn't go out of her way to be very charming with me."

He waved a hand. I looked around and saw Matthews. The room had begun to fill up during that long palaver and it was as near as nothing to supper time, so we went upstairs. Matthews was as optimistic as ever. The shop in Willow Street was being watched and Joe Borne would have a man on his tail from then on.

"What'd Borne tell you?"

"Much the same as he did you," he said, "and he had it corroborated by that shop-walker chap. The man's name was Brown. 'Sure it wasn't Smith?' I said, giving him the old sarcastic touch, but he didn't turn a hair. No, it was Brown. A sort of dealer's tout who'd bothered him before. And he added a nice little touch about thinking Brown wasn't quite all there."

After supper we sat as usual round the fire, and no matter how much we tried to avoid talking shop, we always got back to it, and it got us no further. As for the morning, I said I'd like to meet Colgate in Jewle's car. Jewle said I'd better go alone and he'd join us at the Hall. What Matthews was going to do he didn't say.

COLGATE was a man of very near seventy. He'd spent best part of a day at the flat when he was drawing up the inventory and, in case you think that's a pretty long time, let me say that it's the smaller *objets d'art* and the less valuable individual pieces that account for the time. At any rate he'd had lunch with us and we'd liked him very much, and I think he had a reasonably good opinion of us. His father had been an antique dealer in Bath and he'd carried on the business later, with always a partiality for pictures. Later he'd become a free-lance dealer, buying only what he knew he could place. Then he came to the notice of Wilber, Forbes, and they made him a good offer. He'd been with them for about seven years.

I picked him up at the station and he seemed pleased to see me again, and he asked after Bernice. I quizzed him about when he was going to retire but he only laughed. He was one of those thin but wiry men who go on living for ever.

His dry, cold hands had had a grip that left my own hand tingling.

But it was a ticklish business coming out into the open and telling him so much and no more. He listened but made no comments except that he thought everything might be interesting. We went straight up to the study where Jewle did some more explaining. Ostensibly Colgate was at the Hall for the reasons I'd stated: in reality he was there to say whether certain pictures were genuine or not, and maybe to throw a kind of general light on things. Jewle, by the way, had already seen Mrs. Amble. She knew that a friend of his was looking round the Hall with Humphrey's permission.

"She didn't like it a bit," Jewle told me. "Didn't like being by-passed. However, here we are and that's that. Where shall we begin?"

We began at the bottom and worked up. I steered Colgate straight towards the first of those eight pictures in the dining-room and, in case you've forgotten them, here is the list again: a

Reynolds, a Turner, a Gabriel Matsu, a Cuyp, a Gainsborough, a Murillo, a Guido Reni and a Poussin, all in comparatively modern or reproduction frames. Colgate didn't say a thing till he'd seen the whole eight, but he seemed to me to be getting more and more agitated.

"All copies," he said and began wiping his glasses. "And all painted during the last ten years. Do you know anything more about them?"

We didn't—for the purposes of that inspection.

"Mind if I have another look?" he said. "And a quick one at the rest of them?"

In five minutes or so he was saying there was nothing of any great importance. Three or four were quite interesting but—well, might we go back to the study? There was something rather confidential he'd like to mention to us. So back to the study we went, via the lift.

"When I stepped into that room," he told us, "I never expected to see what I did. It was almost like seeing a ghost."

It was an extraordinary story he told us, but first let me make something perfectly clear. If I've given the impression that Hinchbrook Hall was some great house open to the public on certain days on payment of a fee, then I was wrong. It was a quite large and partly old private house with no grandeur and no pretensions. The general public had no more chance of entering its doors that it has of entering your house or mine.

This was the story and it was told frankly because the parties concerned were all dead. It was, in fact, a minor scandal dating back to the early twenties. All over England there are private collections in houses as unpretentious as Hinchbrook Hall, and one such collection was at a certain Ablington Court, some thirty miles from Mainford. The owner was a very old lady, senile if not actually dim in her wits, and she was very much of a recluse. When she died it was found that certain pictures were missing. Gus Weddall was traced as the purchaser, at least to the satisfaction of her heirs, assigns and solicitors. An action was threatened on the grounds that the old lady hadn't been of sound mind. Gus said she had. She had even insisted on being paid cash, and he produced receipts for some three or four thousand pounds. No trace could be found of the cash said to have been paid but, if any action was brought, then Colgate had never heard of it.

"Tell me if I'm right," I said, "but we know the reputation of Gus Weddall and what he was capable of, so did he acquire those pictures and cache them and only bring them out years later when the whole thing had been forgotten?"

"That I wouldn't know," he said. "But that isn't half the story. I'm pretty certain that at least some of those pictures were on sale in New York a very few years ago."

"Just a minute," I said. "That fake Matsu. I'm dead sure I saw the original in New York a few months ago."

"Yes," he said. "I think it's in the Metropolitan. But what I can't understand is why the pictures were copied. It might have been some sort of insurance against that old scandal being raked up. On the other hand, if it were and the pictures became evidence, then he'd have had to explain the fakes."

"Look," I said. "Could you make a personal and private enquiry into the whole thing? The New York sales, for instance, and the date?"

"I could," he said, "When I'm not actually employed by Wilber, Forbes, I'm my own master."

"It's urgent and you'll be working for me personally," I said.

"Not necessarily," Jewle cut in. "If it turns out to be closely connected with what we're here for, then I'll be responsible. But you go ahead, Mr. Colgate. You'll certainly get paid. And now what about those other pictures? Mr. Colgate knows about them?"

I said he knew what they were, or were supposed to be: a mixed collection of French schools from realists to expressionists. That was when we were going into the workroom.

"They're all together, over here," I said, and led the way to the far corner.

And then I stopped short. Jewle looked flabbergasted too. Those pictures had gone. As far as we were concerned they'd vanished as if into thin air.

It took about five minutes to get Mrs. Amble and she was looking remarkably wary when she entered the study. Jewle didn't bother about introducing Colgate, he just went right ahead.

"But it's impossible!" Grace Amble said. "Who on earth could come up here and take away pictures?"

"It wasn't the mice," Jewle told her grimly. "They were there two nights ago and now they've gone. Seven or eight framed pictures that were in the workroom. Someone had to get up here and get them down in the lift. And you heard nothing?"

"If I had heard anyone, then I'd have thought it was you. But if you're imputing—"

"Now, now," Jewle told her quietly. "I'm imputing nothing. All you've been asked is if you can throw any light on a most extraordinary happening. And you can't."

"I certainly can't."

"Well, we're grateful to you in any case," he told her. "And now will you do us a favour? Send Sam up here if he's available."

She was still looking aggrieved. Jewle shrugged his shoulders as he made for the telephone. He rang Humphrey Weddall. He didn't say why he wanted him but he wanted him urgently. There was evidently some expostulation but Jewle was firm.

"He'll be here inside half-an-hour," he told us, and then there was a tap at the door and Sam came in. He gave a slow look round.

"Mornin', gentlemen."

"This is Mr. Colgate, Sam," Jewle told him and Sam bobbed his head. "Think you can take him to Mainford Station in a minute or two? Or anywhere else in Mainford he wants to go?"

Sam said he certainly could and he'd be in time to collect the children on the way back.

"Something else, first, Sam, and I'd like this gentleman here to listen. Do you remember quite a big batch of pictures coming here soon after Mr. Weddall got back from Italy? Mr. Weddall would have been quite excited about them."

"Sure do, sir. It was when you just said. The boss he took me in there same as he often did and man! was he excited."

"Another thing, Sam. Last night or the night before did you see or hear a private car coming down the drive or up to the house?"

Sam frowned and shook his head. You wouldn't hear much back there above the garage, and with the wireless maybe going and the windows shut on a cold night.

"No, sir: never heard nothin'," Sam said emphatically.

The three of us went down in the lift together. I explained to Sam why I hadn't been able to accept that kind invitation of his and I said I'd certainly drop in on him some night soon. While he was fetching the car I settled everything with Colgate. Anything he had to send us was to go to Jewle or myself at the pub, and if there was any change of plans I'd notify him at once. He gave me his private address and telephone number.

When I got back to the study, two women were there, Mrs. Larkwell, the cook, was about sixty: short, inclined to stoutness and with hair drawn tightly back to an old-fashioned bun.

Daisy Higman, the housemaid, was of medium height, quite good-looking but obviously very shy. Compared with Mrs. Larkwell she was inarticulate.

"Neither of these ladies heard anything," Jewle told me when they'd been introduced. "Unfortunately, from our point of view, they're very good sleepers."

"You have to be," Mrs. Larkwell said. "We go to bed about half-past ten and it's up next morning at half-past six, winter or summer." She smiled. "Even so it ain't like the old days."

"You've been here long?" I asked her.

"All my days," she said complacently. "I come here as scullery maid when I was thirteen and I've been here ever since."

"And you, Daisy?"

Her smile was a shy one.

"Almost two years."

"And what about the new ownership?" Jewle said. "Are you carrying on, Mrs. Larkwell?"

"Well"—she frowned. "I wouldn't like to say. It all depends."

Jewle must have scented disclosures. "I think you can go now, Daisy: thank you very much. Just a last word with you, Mrs. Larkwell."

"And now," he said, when there were just the three of us, "perhaps you can give me a little more information. You like it here?"

"Well," she said, "if I hadn't liked it I wouldn't have been here so long. My husband was under-gardener here and when he was killed in the war I was glad to stay on. It's comes to be like home."

"That was under old Mr. Weddall?"

"That's right." She smiled. "He was a rare one, was old Mr. Weddall. Kind-hearted, though. Used to holler and shout sometimes but never meant nothing by it. Not really."

"And the late Mr. Weddall was different?"

Again she smiled.

"All the difference in the world. A real gentleman, Mr. William was. Kept himself more to himself, though. That was on account of his eyes."

"What about holidays here?"

"One full day off a week," she said, "and take it in turns to have half days Sundays. I have Wednesdays and Daisy Thursdays. Mrs. Amble, she almost always had Tuesdays, only we always had it arranged so that someone was here to look after Master Paul and Miss Jean. Mrs. Amble liked going to London. She come from there."

"This is strictly between ourselves, but you get on all right with her?"

"Oh yes," she said, though it wasn't too enthusiastically. "She never interferes a lot, not now. We know her place and we keep ours."

"Of course. And what's this about not staying on?"

That was a different question. She seemed to be wondering just how to answer it.

"Everything said here is in strict confidence," Jewle told her. "You needn't be afraid of speaking your mind with us."

"Well then, I don't like Mrs. Humphrey." The nod said her mind was made up. "I've worked under one nice housekeeper here and of course there was Miss Evelyn. She was a real lady if ever there was one. And Mrs. Amble who isn't so bad, but I'm not working for Mrs. Humphrey."

"You don't like her?"

"I don't like her and that's a fact. And she can never keep anyone in her own house. Far too bossy, they tell me. Don't treat people right. Servants aren't going to put up with what they had to in the old days."

"You're quite right," Jewle told her. "And we're grateful to you, Mrs. Larkwell, for your help. And you needn't worry about anything being repeated."

"I know that, sir."

She seemed to have difficulty making her exit. She hesitated, even at the door.

"Something else you've remembered?" Jewle asked quietly.

"Well, yes, sir. Though I don't know if I ought to tell you about it."

"Tell me in any case," Jewle said. He looked out on the landing and closed the door again.

He had to wheedle the words out of her. It was true, he said, that the police weren't yet satisfied about Mr. Weddall's death. And yes: Mrs. Gribling *had* told us about the man she'd seen that night.

"Well, that's what I think I ought to tell you," she said, "only I don't want nothing to get out." She moistened her lips. "There's been a man in the house, in Mrs. Amble's room."

"How do you know?"

"Well, Daisy once thought she heard someone talking. A man. And another time there was a smell of tobacco, and Mrs. Amble, she don't smoke. I smelt it myself."

"I see," Jewle said. "Well, we won't question Daisy. We want to keep this between the three of us. And thank you for telling us. It might be a great help."

He waited till she was out of sight at the turning to the stairs. He looked at his watch.

"Humphrey ought to be here now. Probably hanging about just to show his independence. A profitable few minutes, don't you think?"

"Very much so," I said. "I liked that bit about Grace Amble's Tuesday trips to town. You know what I'm beginning to think? That she's a kind of liaison here."

"For the Bornes?"

"Doesn't everything point to it? She knew we'd had a look at those pictures in the workroom. And if the two Bornes knew about me, it could only have been because she told them."

I broke off. There was the sound of the lift and almost at once Humphrey Weddall was coming in. Jewle had anticipated him and had opened the door.

"Thank you," he said brusquely, and gave me a somewhat curt nod. "I hope it's something important you've got me out here for, Inspector. I'm a pretty busy man."

He didn't attempt to sit down. He didn't remove his hat and he didn't even loosen his overcoat. His face was red as if he'd worked himself up into some sort of temper. Even the blond moustache was more straggly.

"You must give us credit for *some* things, sir," Jewle told him mildly. "But to come to the point. This is your house, sir?"

Humphrey stared.

"Of course it's my house! You didn't bring me here to ask me that? And if it comes to that, I still don't see what you're still here for."

"Plenty of reasons," Jewle said quietly. "Your uncle was having a seventieth birthday, for one thing, and he'd arranged a family reunion, and he was looking forward to it. That precludes suicide.

Those windows were never open at night and as his eyes were too bad for him to see anything, why should he suddenly decide to look out? Then—"

"A score of reasons why he might have opened a window."

"Maybe, maybe not. Then there was that attack at about the same time on Sam Martin. And—this is news to you—a strange man was seen under suspicious circumstances in the grounds a few moments after your uncle's death."

Humphrey stared. He was biting that moustache of his.

"What man?"

"We're trying to find out, and that's why we're still here. If you withdraw permission, then of course we'll go elsewhere, but that won't stop us going on with enquiries till we're satisfied. But to go back. It's your house and everything in it is yours, except the drawing-room contents, and that's why I asked you to come here. There's been a theft."

"A theft? What sort of a theft?"

Jewle waved a hand at me and I told Humphrey all about those pictures, and the curious thing to me was that he didn't seem so much annoyed as highly uneasy. Jewle took over with the enquiries already made.

"I know nothing about pictures," Humphrey told us, "but even if they *were* fakes, they were the property of the estate. Don't take me the wrong way, but isn't there something rather ridiculous about the whole thing? Fakes! Who'd want to take away fakes? Or wouldn't they know they were fakes?"

His tone was quite different, almost conciliatory.

"Look, sir, would you mind sitting down," Jewle said. "I'd like to talk this over. You'd like some coffee? I can ring down for some."

"Thank you, but I just haven't the time."

There was some fussing as he drew the chair back from the fire. Jewle waited.

"We're going to take you into our confidence, sir. It's almost a certainty that those missing pictures were supplied to Mr. Weddall by the firm of Borne and Son. They were his buying agents and virtually all the payments we've been able to trace were made to them. I admit that the missing pictures don't appear to have been paid for . . . Just a minute, sir."

The telephone bell had rung. Jewle picked up the receiver. He didn't say much except *yes* and *right* before replacing it.

"About what I was saying, sir," he went on. "The pictures were almost certainly recently delivered and no payment had been made. And that brings me to something extremely confidential. You were here with Mr. Pepson and you know your uncle's original intention was to build an art gallery and present a nucleus of a collection, and the missing pictures were delivered to him, we think, as part of that nucleus. If they were genuine, then they were worth many thousands of pounds. So there's the question, sir, and I'll come right out with it. Your uncle's eyes were very bad indeed, so did Borne and Son take advantage of the fact to try to sell him fakes?"

"Preposterous!" He waved a hand as if to dismiss the whole thing. "Joseph Borne would never be guilty of anything like that. And, wait a moment! The pictures weren't paid for?"

"We think not."

Humphrey smiled.

"Then if they came from Borne and Son they were still their property. You've found no indication to the contrary?"

"No."

"Then wouldn't he have a certain right to remove them?"

"Come, come, sir." Jewle looked positively hurt. "You're a lawyer. And Mr. Borne isn't a fool. He'd know he couldn't touch anything here without the express sanction of the executors. And they'd just as certainly have consulted you before they gave such permission."

"Don't forget he was a relative by marriage."

Jewle let out a breath.

"Joseph Borne didn't apply for permission. That telephone call told me so just now. And he obviously didn't apply to you for permission."

Humphrey shrugged his shoulders.

"Let's get to the real point," Jewle went on. "Are you going to mention the matter to Borne? Or are we to do it?"

Humphrey took a second or two to make up his mind.

"Personally I think the whole thing's more or less of a mare's-nest—no reflection on you, Inspector. It's just a matter of some valueless fakes. Nevertheless, I will have a private word with Joseph, but understand this: he's a member of the family and I won't stand for any scandal."

"I'd prefer you to ring him now, sir. I have the number of his place in Kensington. I'll ring him for you and you can speak to him."

He'd already picked up the receiver and was dialling Exchange. Nothing was said while he waited, and then: "May I speak to Mr. Borne? . . . Mr. Humphrey Weddall, speaking from Hinchbrook Hall. . . . Yes, I'll wait."

He motioned to Humphrey and handed him the receiver. In less than a minute the talk was in full swing, and it was all very hearty. Some pictures supposed to be missing. French pictures, and it was thought that Joseph had had them sent to the Hall. Fakes, or so it was said.

A period of listening, with an occasional grunt from Humphrey and the conversation was virtually over.

"My dear fellow, I was perfectly sure you hadn't . . . Of course not . . . When will you be down this way? . . . I see. Well, be sure to look me up. Goodbye."

He turned to Jewle. The slight smile was definitely ironical.

"Just as I thought. He knows nothing whatever about those pictures. As he said, fakes are not in his line."

He picked up his hat from the chair.

"I trust you'll let the matter end there. You were right to send for me, of course, and I'm very glad the whole thing has been cleared up. Very glad indeed."

Jewle, at the door, couldn't keep back a last word.

"That doesn't alter the fact, sir, that the pictures are gone, and as I told someone else, the mice didn't take them."

"No, I guess not," said Humphrey amiably as Jewle went with him to the lift.

10. VANISHING LADY

JEWLE didn't say a word when he came back. I'd never seen him look so angry.

"Might as well say it," I told him.

He grunted.

"Say it?" He grunted again. "If I'd told him just what I thought we'd have come to blows. Did you ever hear such damn nonsense? What's he think we are? Fools? And him a lawyer!"

"Better ring for that coffee," I said, and the words were hardly out of my mouth when Matthews came in with a tray and three cups.

"Saw Humphrey off the premises," he told us, "and then thought I'd like some coffee. Saw Daisy and she said you hadn't had any so I made it three cups. What happened with Humphrey?"

I told him. Jewle wasn't exactly in the mood.

"Damn queer," Matthews said. "What's his idea? What's he doing? Covering up for old Borne?"

Jewle chipped in. The coffee had made him feel better.

"He was covering up as soon as the pictures were mentioned. Mind you, from the way he listened while he was being told about them, I don't think he knew a thing. What I'll bet he did know, as soon as Mr. Travers had even mentioned pictures, was that Borne was in it. That's when he began covering up. Butter wouldn't have melted in his mouth when he was talking to him on the phone. He was virtually inviting him to disown everything."

"And virtually inviting him to run down here and have a private chat about it all," I said.

"What's the idea?" Matthews wanted to know. "Has Borne got some hold over him, or what? Or was he in the swindle?"

"Don't think so," I said. "But I agree that there's something fishy between him and Borne. And there's one thing we *shall* know, and that's if Borne comes down here. Depends on whether he can slip the tail you've put on him."

"You'd better get in touch," Jewle told Matthews. "Do it from the pub. I might want to ring the Yard myself."

"What've you got in mind?" I asked him when Matthews had gone.

"Damned if I know," he said. "This whole business is simply lousy with things and you can't tie them up. Take old Borne. Would he want Weddall dead?"

"The last thing he'd want," I said. "A dead Weddall couldn't pay for those pictures. Weddall's death blew sky-high a very profitable scheme."

"Yes. And the pictures were removed so's we wouldn't be able to prove a thing. Wonder where they are now? Wouldn't mind betting they're in some dark spot in young Borne's shop in Mainford. He'd be the one who collected them from here. The old man couldn't do it."

"Neither could young Borne, without collusion."

"And that brings us back to Grace Amble. She's the kingpin. Wonder why she used to go regularly up to town."

"She hasn't while we've been here."

"Didn't need to," he said. "Not if it was our friend the running man who was in her room. He brought the news of the instructions for once. And according to what that cook told us, he'd been here before." He gave himself a nod. "He certainly knew the short-cut from the back door past the greenhouses to the road."

Interesting enough as far as deductions went, but what could be done? We knew a little, guessed at a lot and could prove practically nothing. Grace Amble would deny everything, just as old Borne had denied. What it all boiled down to was clapping a hand on the shoulder of the running man. He was someone who'd simply have to talk.

Jewle got to his feet. His mind was made up, he said. He'd see his superiors at the Yard and lay all the cards on the table. They'd have to make the decisions: things that he couldn't do without express authority, like grilling the Bornes and Mrs. Amble. I waited while he rang and got the all-clear from Whitehall 1212. There was a handy train at mid-day that he could just catch, so we went back to the pub. Matthews drove him to Mainford and he'd be having lunch on the train. And he was hoping to be back some time that night.

Matthews and I had our meal. He was proposing to sit at the telephone extension we'd had rigged up in our room. I'd read the newspaper and had nothing much to do, and when I began wondering just how I'd pass the time, I had an idea. I'd drop in on Sam.

February's about the queerest month for weather. You get days when you're sure winter's over and then, almost before you can get out your heavy overcoat again, the ground may be under a foot of snow. That afternoon was overcast and a bitter north-easter was blowing and, as I didn't know the local weather signs, I couldn't tell if snow were coming or if it'd be merely a long, cold spell. Or, for all I knew, I might wake up next morning to sunshine and a balmy spring air.

Sam wasn't making any forecasts. He'd dug himself in. I had to give a couple of calls from the foot of the stairs before he appeared. He gave a huge grin at the sight of me. It was a cosy place he had, and he certainly knew how to make himself comfortable. The electric fire was full on in his smallish living-room, a well-sprung easy chair was plumb in front of it and on the low table was the paperback he'd been reading. Three or four framed photographs were on the walls, and there was a little dining-table and a book-case crammed with more paperbacks.

"You don't do yourself too badly here, Sam," I said as he took my hat and overcoat, and he gave the same broad grin.

"Yes, sir. The boss reckoned I was to have everything jest as I wanted it. Didn't matter what it cost."

He showed me the small bedroom with bathroom attached. There was also a tiny kitchen, nicely fitted up and with a mini-ature electric cooker. And the whole flat was so spotless that I doubted if I could have marked a finger on a speck of dust. He looked pleased when I told him so.

"Don't allow no women up here, sir. Women can get you in a heap of trouble. Yes—*sir*."

"There's something in that," I told him as he drew another chair to the fire. "Won't you find it cold when you have to go out to fetch the children?"

He wasn't going out. Mrs. Amble had gone into Mainford and she was calling for the children on her way back.

"Don't often happen but I'm on duty to-night. Baby-sittin'."

"How come, Sam?"

It was going to be a big night. The finals for a competition for the best dramatic performance by local societies was being held in the town hall at Mainford. Mrs. Humphrey Weddall was President and she'd sent tickets for all the Hall staff except Sam. He didn't seem the least put out about being omitted. As he said, someone had to be in the nursery in case anything happened to the children, and it was a job he'd done once or twice before.

"Where do all these books come from?" I asked him. "Never saw so many paperbacks in my life, unless it was in a second-hand bookshop on Broadway at 12th."

"The boss used to be a big reader before his eyes went so bad," he told me. "Always used to give 'em to me when he'd done readin' 'em. Right an armful sometimes."

I had a look at them.

"Wouldn't have thought he'd have had a taste for detective stories. Mostly American, too."

"Yes, sir. The boss used to do a powerful lot o' readin'. Reckoned he wanted somethin' to keep him awake, not to send him to sleep." He grinned. "Most always when I start readin', my eyes start a-shuttin'. Can't keep 'em open noways. Reckon I was dozin' off when you give that holler."

I picked up the book he'd been reading and I had a pleasant surprise. It was a book I'd enjoyed years and years ago—*Seven Keys to Baldpate*. I remembered seeing a picture that had been made of it. Sam said it was a good book. Weddall's death had interrupted his first reading so he was now reading it a second time.

"The last book he ever give me," he said. "Jest after he got back from Italy. Reckoned he wanted me to read it, real particular. Reckoned as how he was goin' to ask me what I thought of it." The animation went from his face. "Never did, though. Never had time to finish it afore he was dead."

He was quiet for a moment. I broke the silence.

"Mind if we talk business, Sam?"

"Business?" he said. He gave me a quick look and then his face lightened. "Yes, sir. You go right ahead."

I told him he was the best client I'd ever had. He'd never bothered me with questions and he'd taken it for granted that I was carrying out my part of the contract. But now I thought we ought to have a chat.

"I can't say we've settled the matter of just how Mr. Weddall died," I told him, "but we're making progress. All sorts of things have happened which makes me sure you were right in coming to see me. I can't say more than that at the moment. Feel like answering a few questions?"

These were some of the things I learned. When Mrs. Amble went to town she always drove herself to Mainford and left the station-waggon in the station yard. You could park there for a shilling. She usually went early and got back late. The staff thought she went to see old friends or a theatre matinée, and that was from things she had let fall. That was all Sam knew.

He knew nothing about any pictures in the dining-room or any reframing. I re-explored that question of when Weddall had first taken an interest in pictures, and Sam was still sure it wasn't till about a year after his coming to the Hall, and that made it 1955. I didn't tell him so but I had a check on that. Those books on art in the big case in the study were of two kinds: out-of-date ones that had belonged to Old Gus and had been his reference books, and highly modern ones dating from about the time on which Sam insisted.

Sam knew both the Bornes. Both had come occasionally to the Hall, and the elder had come at least once after Weddall's return from Italy. Sam could pass no opinion on either. To him they were connections of the family and no more. I gathered that the little he knew was picked up from gossip at the lunch table in the Hall kitchen.

No one liked Mrs. Humphrey, he told me. The cook's word for her was *stuck-up*.

"Reckoned her folks didn't have no money though they was class," Sam said, "only she couldn't have been real class. The real class is like the boss. Treat ever'body as if they was somebody. Same with Mrs. Amble. She ain't no class. Soon as she started bossin' round, Mrs. Larkwell she upped and told her. Any more bossin' and she was goin' to speak to the boss." He grinned. "Didn't have no more trouble after that. Didn't affect me none, though. The boss, he was the one give me orders. Didn't take no orders from no one else."

He saw me glance at my watch and he hopped up at once. I said a cup of coffee would be fine. As he went into the little kitchen I heard the children's voices and then the sound of a car. I peered from behind the window curtain and saw Mrs. Amble coming round the side of the Hall with the station-waggon. She garaged it and I had a good view of her back as she went towards the rear door. She was carrying a parcel. The fur coat she was wearing looked good, even from that distance away. Still, Weddall must have given her quite a good allowance and quite a fat legacy was practically in her bank.

It was grand coffee: made in Sam's electric percolator and topped with good cream. I hadn't had coffee like it since I was in the States, however hard Bernice had tried. Sam didn't eat anything but there was a slice of cake for me. Mrs. Larkwell made him one every week. Mentioning America got Sam going on reminiscence. We talked about places we knew, and when I got up to go it was well after five o'clock.

"Haven't enjoyed an afternoon so much in years," I told him.

"Come again, sir. Ain't nobody more welcome."

He gave me a wave of the hand from the open door. I looked round the garage corner but there was no one in sight. There was nobody by the swimming pool and I wondered if Gribling would throw a pail of water down that night to make a slide. And that made me think of those three children as I walked briskly back to the pub: the almost precocious poise and self-possession of Brenda, the mischief in Paul's eyes and that look of utter terror that flared with the red across Jean's face just before she ran frightenedly towards the house. And there'd been that queer amused look on Grace Amble's face: a look that had had in it even something cruel: a secret satisfaction at the frightening of a small girl.

I opened the door gently and, sure enough, Matthews was asleep, the telephone just behind him and a ruined tea-tray at his elbow. He was cat-napping, he said, and stirred at the faint sound of the door. Nothing, he said, about Joe Borne, but he'd had a call from Jewle who'd be taking the six o'clock from town.

I met the train in the car. Jewle told me that the Powers-that-Be, as my old friend Wharton used to call them, had been kind enough to express their confidence in his handling of things so far, but it might be as well if we vacated the Hall and made the pub our headquarters. They, too, saw the importance of the running man. Intensified enquiries were being made, and Joseph Borne wouldn't exactly be overlooked. If there was anything suspicious in that report that Colgate was furnishing, then Borne would definitely be questioned.

The meal had been put off to suit Jewle's arrival. As soon as it was over, he rang Humphrey Weddall. A courtesy call, as he said, to thank him for the use of the study and to tell him we were vacating it in the morning. But no one seemed to be in the house. I suddenly remembered why. If his wife was the big noise at that dramatic show, then Humphrey would certainly have to be there. Jewle said it wasn't all that urgent. Humphrey could be rung from the Hall in the morning.

"Might as well go downstairs," he told us. "You never know what you might pick up in that bar."

I said I'd stay by the telephone. I was having a nice little nap before the fire when they came up again at ten. Maybe I'd had a clear conscience. I had rung Bernice.

In the morning we all took it easy: a latish breakfast, a look through the newspapers and Jewle's casual remark to me that we might as well get along to the Hall and telephone Humphrey. Just as we were leaving the room a call came. We waited till Matthews had taken it.

"Joe Borne," he told us. "He's just been seen off on the nine o'clock from Euston. Heading for Mainford."

"Who'll pick him up there?"

"I can't," Matthews said. "He's already seen me."

"Right," Jewle said. "You let the locals do it and keep well out of sight."

Matthews left in the car. Jewle arranged with the landlady to take any messages, and he and I set off for the Hall. It was the same kind of morning. The bitter wind was swirling the dry leaves and the roadside verges had a whitish sheen from the night's frost. It was warm in the study but Jewle switched on the fire just for the look of it.

"Nothing of ours here," he said. "Anything you want to have a last look at?"

I went into the workroom, just on chance, but the pictures still weren't there. I had a good look through those art books and only confirmed what I'd known before. Everything seemed to prove that Sam was right. Weddall had settled down in his old home, and that was in 1953. His daughter was in charge of the house and Jean was little more than a toddler. The daughter, Evelyn, joined her husband in Kenya for a short holiday before flying home, and it was on that flight that both were killed. It must have been a cruel blow to Weddall, and the Hall for a time must have been an oppressive place. There was a demand for something to fill in his days and he recalled his father's old idea of modernising the Mainford Art Gallery, and at once he began designing something far different—a new, up-to-date gallery. And it'd be when those plans were practically completed that, as Sam put it, he'd been bitten by the picture bug. And that meant that Weddall had been dabbling in pictures for only about two years. No wonder he'd been like putty in Joe Borne's hands. And add to that the weakening of Weddall's eyesight, and Joe saw prospects of profits beyond all dreams.

But Joe was a shrewd man. As I saw it, he'd never overplayed his hand. He'd bought or supplied from stock quite reputable pictures at reasonable prices and all the time he was getting ready for the big coup. Maybe it was he, or his son, who got Weddall interested in French schools and the fabulous prices they were fetching. And my guess was that Joe had told him one day— and probably when he got wind of that trip to Italy—that he'd unearthed in a private house some pictures to make the mouth water. The owner didn't know their real value and they could be picked up for maybe a quarter of what they were worth. And when Weddall got back from Italy, or wherever he'd been, there the pictures were.

Jewle was speaking. I'd heard him talking on the phone to Humphrey but I'd been so taken up with those ideas of mine that I hadn't heard what he'd actually said.

"Well that's settled," he told me. "Humphrey tried not to sound too pleased but you bet your life he's glad to see the back of us here. You finished?"

Something came to me: something I'd thought of almost the first moment I'd ever entered the room.

"I've been meaning to ask you this and somehow it always slipped my mind. If Weddall was hit on the head, what was it with? There doesn't seem anything suitable in the room?"

"I thought you knew," he said. "There used to be a heavy paper-weight here: one of those glass balls with a flat base. Heavy enough to knock anyone out. Daisy remembers it up to almost the last moment. That's another one of the reasons why we've been hanging on here." His hand went out to the telephone again. "Sure you've finished? I ought to tell Mrs. Amble we're going and give her the keys. Just a matter of courtesy."

Something strange seemed to be happening at the other end. "Really?" he said, and, "It's certainly odd. . . . She isn't with any other friends?"

A minute or two and he was hanging up.

"Something unusual seems to have happened. Mrs. Amble didn't come home last night. Mrs. Larkwell has already rung Mrs. Humphrey and she isn't there. One or two other things seem to've been happening, too."

We took the lift down and went through to the far wing. Through the open door of the kitchen I could see Mrs. Gribling mopping the tiled floor. Mrs. Larkwell, wiping her hands on her apron, came out of another room just by the stairs. I hadn't been in that entrance hall before. It was much smaller than the one in the other wing and comparatively bare. A white-faced grandfather clock with a movement of a mowing man stood by the wall at the stair angle and there were two nice eighteenth-century hall chairs by the telephone stand.

"Would you gentlemen like to come into our room," Mrs. Larkwell said, and that would be the staff sitting-room from which she'd just emerged. Jewle said he liked kitchens. I like them, too. It's some carry-over from childhood when, wherever else was cold, a kitchen had warmth, and things to eat.

Bella Gribling gave us a smile. Daisy blushed—I don't know why—and got up from a chair by a drive window. It was warm there and somehow there were the very same smells of years and years ago—furniture polish and hot roast beef.

"I wouldn't like my wife to see this kitchen," Jewle told the company. "She'd never do another stroke of work in her own till I'd done something about it. It's a regular palace. And now, what's all this about Mrs. Amble?"

Mrs. Larkwell was spokesman and every few words she'd look at the other two women for confirmation. It was certainly a queer story. Sam had brought the station-waggon to the door and the party had set off at about ten past seven, Mrs. Amble driving. Harry Gribling sat in front with her and the three women in the back. When they reached the big municipal car park just back of the town hall, Mrs. Amble told them to go on ahead and she'd see to the car.

"And that was the last we see of her, sir," Elizabeth Larkwell said. "When we came out we looked for her and she wasn't there so we went and looked for the car and none of us couldn't see a sign of it nowhere. We spoke to the attendant and he didn't know anything about it neither, so after a bit we decided to come home on our own. Lucky there was buses running. Then when we got back we all had a cup o' tea and a mite to eat and then Harry and Bella went home and I said to Daisy, 'T'aint no good waiting up no longer,' and we was both a bit tired so we went up to bed. Then this morning the children come rushing down here wanting to know where Aunt Grace was. That's what they always had to call her, so I said was she in her room and she wasn't. I had a look for myself and her bed hadn't been slept in."

"She'd never done this before?"

"Never. She might have come in late but she was never away all night."

"I see," Jewle said. "And later on you thought of ringing Mrs. Humphrey and she knew nothing?"

A bell rang. Mrs. Larkwell looked up at the indicator.

"The front door. Wonder who that is. Couldn't be her, though. You go, Daisy."

The story was left for a moment in the air. A woman's voice was heard. The door from the dining-room opened and Daisy was ushering Mrs. Humphrey in to the lobby, and she seemed to be casting shrewd eyes about her as if to spot a speck of dust or Mrs. Amble herself emerging from under the stairs. The look switched to us. Jewle introduced me. She gave a gracious bow. Jewle explained that we'd just at that moment been leaving the

Hall and Mrs. Amble's name came up because he'd wished to hand her the keys.

She loosened her heavy fur coat. She was quite a tall woman and but for that hard, imperious look she might have been quite handsome. She certainly looked older than her thirty-six years. I had an excellent chance to run an eye over her while Mrs. Larkwell went over the whole story again.

Mrs. Humphrey gave an exasperated click of the tongue. "Mrs. Amble must be spoken to. She'd no right to leave the children like that. As for last night, the whole thing was spoilt for me when you rang me this morning." The tongue clicked exasperatedly again. "I suppose there's nothing to do but wait till she comes back. Perhaps you'll ring me, Elizabeth."

"Yes, ma'am."

"May I say something?" That was Jewle. "I don't like the look of things, Mrs. Weddall. I don't like that business last night of not being in the car park to bring the staff home. I'm wondering, in fact, if you'd do something for us and it's very lucky in a way that you're here. Would you have a look in Mrs. Amble's room? If she intended to be away she must have taken extra clothes or something with her. Mrs. Larkwell will probably know something about her wardrobe."

Mrs. Humphrey thought it a most sensible suggestion. Bella Gribling asked if we'd like a cup of tea and Jewle said we would. Daisy went out and I had a chance of a quiet word with Jewle.

"You think she's bolted?"

"Too big a stroke of luck," he said. "It's something bigger than that. What I can't get over is that business of last night. And why there was no phone call from her this morning."

The kettle had been on the boil. We'd drunk our tea and eaten a slice of cake well before Mrs. Humphrey sailed in again.

"Elizabeth says there's nothing missing," she told us. "And I must say I'm beginning to agree with you, Inspector. It's most unusual."

Jewle thought the local police should be informed. Even if Mrs. Amble did turn up with some reasonable explanation, no harm would have been done. Perhaps Mrs. Larkwell could give a description of the clothes she'd been wearing. Mrs. Larkwell could mention only the brown hat with the yellow feather, the fur coat and a new pair of brown shoes. They'd probably been in that parcel I'd seen her carrying the previous afternoon.

The station-waggon was missing, too. Jewle said he'd get the registration number from Sam.

"About last night, Mrs. Weddall: did you actually see Mrs. Amble in the town hall?"

She certainly didn't, or that was what the look implied. As President, she'd been in the front row with various distinguished visitors. She mentioned the Lord-Lieutenant and his wife. And afterwards she and her husband had entertained those visitors to a small buffet supper in one of the annexes.

"Well, I'll get to work," Jewle told her. "You've been more than helpful. Would you mind if I used the study?"

She was most gracious. Certainly we could use the study. And she hoped we'd ring her the moment we had any news. She walked with us through the dining-room, and Jewle opened the door and watched till the car had disappeared at the bend of the drive.

"A Jaguar," he said. "The one you saw her with the other day. And if that coat wasn't mink, then I'm a rabbit. Humphrey must be doing pretty well."

"Every man to his taste," I said. "She must have some extraordinary virtues somewhere or he'd have strangled her long ago. Shall I get the car number from Sam?"

When I got back he had almost finished telephoning. A minute or two later he was switching the fire on.

"Might as well be comfortable while we're here."

"They're ringing here if anything turns up?"

He said they were and we might as well take advantage of the chance of a little more luxury. If nothing came through by mid-day, he'd ring again and have any calls switched to the pub.

"Perhaps you heard me but I told them they ought to concentrate on that station-waggon," he said. "If they find it and she isn't in it, they might get a clue from its whereabouts."

"In it?" I said. "You think she's dead?"

He begged the question.

"She certainly knew a whole lot more than she ever told us. Still, no use speculating till we know something."

We lighted our pipes. We looked at some of the books. I wandered restlessly off to the workroom and opened drawers and had another look at the pictures. I came back and looked at some more books. An hour and a half had crawled by and Jewle looked at his watch.

"Might as well have that call switched to the pub."

He'd spoken quietly. Just as he rose the telephone bell shrilled and in the silence of the room it was as if it were at my very ear.

11. THE LADY REAPPEARS

SAM drove us in the Rolls. It was a Saturday morning and there was a lot of traffic, but we did the four miles in well under ten minutes. At the town hall we went left, skirting the main car park and then through to another just by the cattle market. A uniformed man was on the look-out for us.

"You needn't wait, Sam," Jewle said. "And you might go to the pub for us and explain about lunch. Say we'll have it for supper. Just the two of us. Mr. Travers won't be there."

The constable showed us the spot where the car stood. A frosty night, as we knew, and no sign even of tyres, let alone footprints.

"Quite a few cars stay all night," he told us, "and that's why it wasn't anything unusual. No one minds it as long as they pay up, and that's why the attendant didn't pay any particular attention. Then when they started making enquiries, there it was."

"She was in the back?"

"That's right, sir, and with a rug over her. If anyone'd looked in they wouldn't have noticed anything particular."

We walked on towards the police headquarters, a stone's-throw from the town hall, and that wasn't more than a couple of hundred yards away.

"She wasn't killed there," Jewle said. "Someone parked the car there and her in it. Waited till the attendant was engaged elsewhere and then parked it and nipped off."

The station-waggon was in the police garage. Meers, the Chief-Constable, was there, and his Chief-Inspector, a lean, red-faced, loose-limbed man named Ansen. The chief gave me a warm shake of the hand. Maybe he knew that it was I who'd really got him his job.

Nothing had been touched except a door handle. The car had been locked and there'd been no keys. Ansen gently drew back the rug. I'm pretty squeamish but there was nothing much to see; just a dead woman with protruding eyes.

"Manual strangulation," Ansen said. "You could have told that even if you couldn't have seen the marks."

"No ideas? No nothing?"

"Nothing," Meers said. "We bust a door to get the handbrake off and towed the car here. We haven't even printed it. All we know is the little you told us."

"Mind if I suggest something before we have a talk? Get it printed and get her on the slab as quick as you can. You don't mind my interfering?"

"No interference," Meers said. "If she's to do with that other business, then she's all yours and we'll do anything to help."

"We think she was in it up to the ears," Jewle told him. "So will you get her opened as soon as you can. Time of death might be important. The stomach content ought to give us it."

We went up to Meers's spacious, business-like room and chatted a bit till Ansen joined us.

"Mind if I phone?" Jewle said.

He had a three-minute talk with Mrs. Larkwell. I knew it because her voice came through so loud.

"Better get this down," he told Ansen, "and let your surgeon have it. At twenty to seven she ate some cold chicken and potato salad, followed by some hot treacle tart. She brought the tray down with her from her room at just before ten-past-seven."

Ansen rang through. We settled down again. Jewle said he'd be putting quite a lot of cards on the table and he certainly did. There was nothing we knew about Grace Amble that he kept back. Meers kept chewing his upper lip and Ansen kept frowning and nodding.

"And as far as you know, old Mr. Borne might be in his son's shop at the moment," Ansen said. "There looks like a connection."

"Don't let's jump too far ahead," Jewle told him. "All I know is that Joe Borne's probably in Mainford. After all, he and his son are both Borne and Son. He probably comes here regularly. But what you might do is try to trace a call from Oliver Borne to his father some time yesterday. If we can find that out we might know if the visit was special. We can prove no definite connection between Grace Amble and either of the Bornes. No use seeing either of them till we've got something we can really get our teeth into. And she wasn't a close relation. Only a distant connection."

"What about her husband?" I said. "Oughtn't he to be informed?"

"They've been separated for years," Jewle said. "Still I suppose we ought to do it. We can ring from here?"

Meers said we certainly could. The room was our own. He looked up at the clock. It was half-past one and could he send us in something from the canteen?

In five minutes we had the room to ourselves and were attacking a hot meal. Jewle got the first edge off his appetite and then rang Humphrey Weddall at his private address. It was Mrs. H. who answered. Mrs. Larkwell had wheezed and bellowed: Rachel Weddall's voice was stridency itself. From where I sat I heard almost as much as Jewle.

He cupped the receiver.

"The lady knows all about it. A pity we told Mrs. Larkwell. Just fetching her husband."

Humphrey came on the line. His voice was more of a boom and I could catch hardly a word. He went on and on. Jewle was wishing he'd get off the line, if that's what the face meant he made at me. And he let out a breath when he finally hung up.

"Neither of them knows a thing about Grace Amble's husband except that he was some sort of an actor. Humphrey wanted to come here but I headed him off. So where do we go now?" He set to work again on his almost cold meal. "What about the War Office? No?"

He knew that I'd promised Bernice to get home for the week-end, so I said if he'd leave Jeffrey Delver to me, I'd make some enquiries.

"Didn't want to give anything away to Meers," he said, "but Delver's the one man we want to see. Anything occur to you?"

I had to smile.

"Only what's occurred to you. If Grace is dead, Jeffrey Delver gets five thousand pounds."

"Yes," Jewle said and pushed back his plate. Mine had been clean long since. Then Ansen came in with a couple of cups of coffee.

"Seems as if I've timed it pretty well," he said. "Some news already from downstairs, by the way. She had the usual crack on the skull before she was strangled. Nothing in her nails and no signs of a struggle. Must have gone off nice and peaceful."

At the door he said they were working on that telephone call. And it'd be about another hour before there was anything definite from the stomach content.

"I don't want *him* at my funeral," I told Jewle as we lighted our pipes. "Even with orchids. And what do we do now. Just wait?"

That seemed about all. Meers came back and we talked about Hinchbrook Hall for a bit. Ansen rang to say no call could be traced from Oliver Borne to London, and if it had been the other way, then only a stroke of luck could give a check. A detective-sergeant came up to report a whole lot of prints in the car, and Jewle gave him the full list to be checked at the Hall. The interesting things were the handles and steering column. They had smudged prints, which looked as if the driver of the death waggon had worn gloves.

"Gloves," Jewle said. He left the word suspended, as it were. His mind was searching for something and almost at once he had it.

"She wasn't wearing gloves," he said, and it was obvious whom he meant. "Isn't that right. Chief?"

"She wasn't," Meers said. "None in the car and none where we found it."

"Get the Hall for me, will you? Ask for Mrs. Larkwell. She's the cook."

A couple of minutes and Meers had her on the line. Grace Amble had definitely been wearing gloves—fur-backed, fur-lined gauntlets. Beautiful, expensive gloves, according to Mrs. Larkwell.

"You might get a full description of them when you're at the Hall," Jewle told the sergeant. "What was in her handbag, Chief?"

"Nothing but what you'd expect," Meers said. "Your wife and mine'd probably have the same things. Nobody's prints on it but hers."

The sergeant left. Jewle shifted restlessly in his chair. Something else was on his mind.

"How does this strike you?" he said to us. "When she was found she wasn't wearing gloves. Right. Therefore she wasn't killed in the car itself. She was killed somewhere where she'd take the gloves off and that means indoors."

I said it completed a sequence. There'd been no need for Grace Amble to let the other occupants of the car go on ahead. Where she could have parked the car was only a few yards from the town hall entrance and they could all have gone in together. Also, those other occupants would have known where to find the car in case they left the building first when the show was over. She'd had it planned. As soon as they'd gone she drove the car elsewhere and that was where she'd been killed. And whoever had killed her had overlooked the gloves.

"Which means they were found later and are probably ashes," Jewle said.

He saw me looking up at the clock.

"What train do you want to take to town?"

I said it didn't particularly matter. The four-fifteen would do. The trouble was I had to go back to the pub to collect my things. I think Meers was about to say he'd see to that, when Matthews came in.

"Heard the news," he said, "but I didn't think I ought to leave the other job. Nothing much to report."

"Joe Borne's still in town?"

"Just left on the three o'clock," Matthews said. "He went straight to his son's place this morning and stayed there till nearly one. Then he went out to the son's house and straight from there to the station."

Jewle grunted.

"A pity we couldn't have had the place wired for sound."

The buzzer interrupted him. Meers picked up the receiver. A minute or two and we had the information we wanted. Grace Amble had been killed at as near eight o'clock the previous night as made no difference.

"And that seems to make it sure," Jewle said, "that she was killed here in Mainford."

There was no point in my staying any longer. I wasn't official anyway. Matthews said he'd drive me to the pub and back to the station, and I told Jewle again that I'd try to find Grace Amble's husband, Jeffrey Delver. Everyone agreed that if I could, that'd be better than putting out any kind of public appeal. I also said that with luck I'd be back on the Sunday night.

Matthews and I talked about the murder. He's an ebullient sort of chap and I think that in that apparently callous way the police often seem to have, he was rather glad. It was, for one thing, a change from the Yard and town, though he didn't say so. What did he think, and who didn't, was that a real honest-to-God murder left no doubts that Weddall had been murdered, too. And when we were on our way back he told me a secret.

"I didn't let it out in front of the chief," he said, "but the Bornes had another visitor this morning. The two men we had on the job meeting Joe at the station didn't know it but I had an idea, too. I hadn't said anything about a back way to Oliver's shop so I had a hunch I'd stay round there myself. And a good job I did. Even before Joe arrived—I know because I checked the times later— who should come in by that back way but our friend Humphrey. Must have walked from his office. And he was inside for half an hour and then came out the back way again."

I was almost wishing I hadn't to go to town. Even then, I guessed there'd be plenty to hear when I got back. And that was to be later than I'd intended.

I offered to take Bernice out to dinner but she said she'd rather stay in the flat. As soon as I'd had a bath and a change, I rang Tom Holberg at his private address. Tom has one of the biggest theatrical agencies in town and he's been a friend of mine for years. His daughter Miriam answered the phone. She's been acting lately as his secretary. Her father was out, she said, but they expected him in fairly early. She's married to Franz Weinberg, the violinist, and I asked after her two children, and that wasn't a kind of preliminary soft-soaping. I like Miriam. She's a fine woman.

"Maybe you can help me," I told her, and gave her a confidential tip that the whole thing was most urgent.

"Jeffrey Delver," she said, "I seem faintly to remember the name. You know nothing else about him?"

"With ENSA during the war and then married a nurse named Grace Amble. Started lifting his elbow too much and finally she left him. He may not even be in the business any longer."

"I think he is," she said. "There's something about him at the back of my mind, and recently. I'll ask Daddy and get him to ring you. That all right?"

I said it'd be fine. I rang off and almost at once a service dinner was coming up, and then the Traverses settled down to a domestic evening. Bernice can be implicitly trusted. She never asks questions but if business is mentioned she's always ready to help. When I'd rung her during the week I'd just mentioned complications over Weddall's death and that evening, when I'd brought her more up to date, she mentioned something that had entirely slipped my mind. More than once lately I've begun to think that something is going wrong with my memory. Either that or I go rushing so far ahead that I forget to go far enough back.

"When you told me about Weddall coming here that day," she said, "do you remember you said he had a most peculiar look on his face? It was when he was asking you about fakes."

It came back to me so clearly that I could almost see him in the room, and almost instinctively I glanced up at the Utrillo.

"Yes," I said. "And I told him that what knowledge I had had been gained by some rather dear experience. And then he said he didn't mind so much being swindled. What annoyed him was that a swindler should be congratulating himself on having far more brains than his victim. And the best way to treat a swindler was to lure him on and then expose him."

My fingers went instinctively to my glasses.

"You're right!" I told her. "You've got something there. Weddall did know he was being swindled!"

It fitted. It explained why Weddall hadn't paid for those French pictures. He'd made some excuse not to pay until he'd had those pictures vetted by an expert. My fingers moved again. *I* was to be that expert. That was what had been in that letter which had been taken from Sam. And if I'd pronounced those pictures as fakes, then Weddall would have blown the whole thing sky-high at that birthday gathering when all the family was at Hinchbrook. And that was true because I remembered something else: something that had been told me by Sam. I couldn't recall the exact words, but Weddall had told Sam—and was I right in thinking it had been confidentially and yet jubilantly?—that he and Sam were going to have themselves a mighty fine time.

The telephone went. Tom Holberg was ringing me. A few purely personal words and he came to the point.

"That Jeffrey Delver. Miriam ought to've remembered him. We don't handle him but we do some work for Harry Milstein. Delver was with one of his companies, playing the suburbs in an American musical. They're doing a week at Croydon, starting last Monday, and this Delver rings up on the Saturday evening and says he's sick or something."

"A week ago today?"

"That's it, and we had to find a replacement."

"He's still acting then," I said, "or was up to a week ago. But this is most important, Tom. I've got to get hold of him. Any way of finding out his private address?"

I heard him mumbling to himself while he thought.

"Don't know," he said. "I can try. I can get hold of Croydon. Someone in the company ought to know something."

He brushed off the thanks. Tom has an idea that he owes me an enormous deal and I'll never convince him to the contrary. But I was feeling pretty pleased and even perhaps a trifle smug. And relieved. I couldn't bear to think of the fool I'd have looked if I'd gone back to Mainford and had had to tell Jewle I'd talked out of my turn.

It was just after eleven o'clock when Tom rang again. He had the address—7 Bolton Avenue, Westbury.

I rang Norris in the morning and he paid us a visit, though he wouldn't stay to lunch. I was optimistic. I told him I'd probably be back in harness before the week was over and that the job might be more profitable than we'd thought, especially if Weddall's estate took care of our charges.

That evening I'd hoped to take the seven o'clock from Euston but I didn't mention any definite train to Bernice. She only knew I was going fairly early, but what I had in mind was to go to Westbury and from there to my train. Westbury, as I call it, is a north-western suburb and handy for town by the Tube. I took a train from Leicester Square and it took me direct to where I wanted to go. I had to make a few enquiries before I found Bolton Avenue, a fairly modern street of semi-detached houses with trees planted in the verges to justify its name. I knocked at the door of number 7. I found a bell and pushed it. I went round to the back but the windows were dark. I knocked on the back door but only as a matter of form. It was clear that Delver was out.

Lights were on at the front of Number 9 and I could hear a wireless set going full blast. I knocked at the door. The sound of the wireless was suddenly less clear and in a minute a man came to the door—a middle-aged man in his shirt-sleeves and wearing slippers. I told him I was wanting to see his neighbour but no one seemed to be home.

"He lives by himself," he said, "and we don't see a lot of him. Tell you where you might find him."

He came out to the step and pointed to the left.

"Go along there for about a hundred yards and take the first on the left and you'll see the traffic lights, and just before you get there you'll see the King William. He might be there."

I found the King William, just down that side street short of the main shopping centre. It was a Sunday night and not many people were about, but the pub was well enough lighted. The main bar had quite a lot of patrons but none of them seemed to have the look of an actor. I went back and through the door to the saloon bar. That was even more full, and it suddenly struck me that I'd been in far too great a hurry. The best thing to do was to go back to Bolton Avenue and get a description of Delver and I was just about to turn when I caught sight of a man. He was at a table with three other men, and I had a good view of his profile. I doubt if I'd ever been more surprised in my life.

I moved across to the bar so that Delver had his back to me and while I drank the double scotch and splash I watched Delver and his three pals. They were having quite a good time. There was a lot of laughing and in the middle of it a short, fat man, who looked like a bookmaker, was snapping his fingers to the waiter. Another round of drinks was being ordered. The waiter came back to the bar and I finished my drink and went over to the table. Delver looked up and saw me. It didn't take him long to recognise me. That's the worst of me. Once seen, I'm never forgotten.

"You're Mr. Delver," I said.

"That's me," he said, eyes still on me.

"May I have a private word with you? It's very important."

"Don't know," he said, and gave the others a look. "What's it all about?"

I told him just as much as I thought he ought to know. The mention of Mainford seemed no surprise to him.

"Haven't seen her for years," he said, and shook his head with a kind of regret. Then he was giving me a quick look. "Where do you come in?"

I said I was a friend of his late uncle and had been at Hinchbrook on business connected with the estate. The police had been making enquiries, too, and I'd had to work with them. Then I had to come to town just after the murder had been discovered and I'd said I might find the dead woman's husband and I'd run him to earth through a friend, a theatrical agent.

"You'll be expected at Mainford in the morning," I told him. "You're her husband and the police'll certainly want to ask some questions."

"But why? What have I got to do with it? I didn't even know she was dead."

He took some convincing and then he said he'd go.

"Much better than their having to fetch you," I said. "As a matter of fact I'm going back there now. I can rely on you?"

"I'll be there," he said. "And damned glad to get it over."

He told me where I might find a taxi. I had to wait for one to come in. The driver stared when I said I wanted the police station.

"You can walk there, guv'nor, in a couple o' minutes."

"You take me," I said. "You can wait while I'm inside and then take me to Euston."

He took me to the police station and it was hardly worth while changing gears. The duty man said he doubted if he could get hold of his inspector at short notice. Then he had a look at my credentials and agreed to get Mainford for me. It took a good ten minutes before he handed me the receiver. I asked for Jewle. He was somewhere about and would I hold the line. It took another five minutes before Jewle was there.

"Travers here," I said. "I'm just on my way to Euston. I found your man, by the way. He's promised faithfully to be along in the morning. . . . Yes, at Mainford. If he isn't he can always be picked up. I have his address. You'd better take it down."

He said he'd be seeing me and then I got in a final word.

"You're due for a bit of a shock," I told him.

"How do you mean?"

"What I say. Jeffrey Delver's the running man."

12. THE RUNNING MAN

I WONDERED why Jewle had wanted to know more about my finding Delver since he'd only to wait till I got back to Hinchbrook to hear everything in detail, but maybe he didn't quite credit my belief that Delver himself had every intention of taking a morning train to Mainford. At any rate, when I got to the pub that night only Matthews was there. Jewle, he said, hadn't waited for a train. Within ten minutes of getting my news he'd been on his way to London in a Mainford police car, and he was going straight to Westbury.

"There wasn't even time to ring the Yard," Matthews told me, "but he left me to handle it. Someone'll be at the King William when he gets there or else at Delver's house. Depends where Delver is."

There was nothing else worth telling me, and as it was pretty late we both turned in. In the morning we breakfasted early and we didn't need to stir from the room to be reminded of what the day would mean. Both our newspapers had headlines and photographs. The popular London one had only the official account: it was the *Mainford Gazette* on which the police were pinning hopes. It had, for instance, a photograph and full description of the station-waggon. It had a full description of the murdered woman and the clothes she'd been wearing, and a drawing and description of the missing gloves. And there was the usual appeal. Anyone who had seen either the car or the murdered woman or could throw any light whatever on the crime was asked to come forward.

Matthews, optimistic as ever, thought that before the day was out we ought to have at least someone who'd seen something. I wasn't so sure. Grace Amble herself had planned too carefully. She hadn't wanted to be seen. And the crime, too, struck me as just as well planned. Grace had been clever but she'd been lured into a trap by someone far cleverer than herself. As for identifying a station-waggon at night, that couldn't have been done unless the car had been stationary. People in Mainford would be far too occupied with driving in traffic to take note of other cars. And that station-waggon had been of quite a popular type.

At Mainford police station that morning there was nothing to do but hope that someone would come in with information, and to wait for news from Jewle. I hadn't exactly thrown a damper on the Delver side of things but I had offered odds of five-to-one that Delver had an alibi for the murder of his wife. His manner, I said, had been too assured. Any uneasiness had been because of something else.

"We know that," Matthews said. "I don't mean about the alibi but what he's sweating about is Weddall."

"You think so? I'll lay the same odds he's dead sure no one has the faintest idea he was at Hinchbrook Hall that evening."

"Then what's he worrying about? You said he was uneasy about something."

"About the whole business that led up to a couple of murders," I said. "And my having seen him with Joe Borne. And I'll also bet that within five minutes of my seeing him last night, he was on the phone to Borne. Borne may even be giving him his alibi."

Matthews grinned.

"Bit of a ruddy optimist this morning, aren't you? You think he can outsmart Jewle?"

I didn't have to answer that one. Jewle was on the phone. Matthews grabbed paper and pencil and took instructions down. It took him best part of five minutes, and as soon as the call was over he got to his feet.

"A good job I didn't take your bet," he said. "Delver's got an alibi. He was with two of those pals of his you saw him with and Jewle says it's okay."

He ran another eye over the notes he'd taken.

"They'll be here on the eleven-twenty. I've got to fix a private identity parade with Mrs. Gribling and that bus conductor. It won't take long. We know where they are. You stay here and I'll send you in some coffee."

Ansen's room had been given us: a quite large room at the head of the main stairs. From the window I saw Matthews move out from the garage in his car and a police car followed him. The wall clock said a quarter to eleven. I moved the chair at Ansen's desk round towards the electric fire. It was another bitter morning outside but snug in there, and I lighted my pipe and stretched out my long legs to the warmth. I began wondering what technique Jewle would employ with Delver, and I thought I could see the pattern. As it happened I wasn't to be too far out.

Coffee came in and time was passing. At every sound of a car below the window I looked out. At a quarter-past eleven Matthews came back, but it was Jewle I was looking for. Then Ansen came in and began rearranging the room. He told me Jewle had just arrived. Delver was with him downstairs. Joe Borne had also come with him but he wasn't due for an interview till we'd finished with Delver. A stenographer came in and took his seat at the small desk in the corner by the window. Then at last Jewle came in, alone. He gave me a cheerful nod.

"Matthews put you wise?"

"Yes," I said. "A pity about that alibi."

"Don't worry," he said. "There'll still be some fireworks." He settled himself at the big desk. "Right-ho, Ansen. Bring him in."

Delver came in. Ansen closed the door and stood there with his back towards it. Delver gave me a nod. He seemed to be wearing the same clothes as on that evening of Weddall's death but his tie was black. I wouldn't have called his a dissipated face: it was pale, almost yellowish: the face of a man who keeps late hours and short days. His speaking voice was far from unpleasant and with just a trace of a London accent.

"Sit down, Mr. Delver," Jewle said quietly. "I expect the sight of your wife has been a bit of a shock to you."

"Yes," Delver said, and even more quietly. "It wasn't exactly the way I ever expected to see her again."

"It wouldn't be," Jewle told him. "But we want you to help us. Just a few questions we think might throw a little light on this dreadful business. For instance, when did you last see your wife?"

Delver frowned. He looked up at the ceiling.

"It'd be just before she came to Hinchbrook. I told her if she went there, that was the end of it. But she went and that was that."

"And you haven't clapped eyes on her since?"

"No. That was the last time."

"Hinchbrook Hall," Jewle said meditatively. "You ever there yourself?"

"Yes." His lip curled. "I went there with my mother and I'd be about twelve. She went to see my grandfather to ask him for help and he turned her down."

"And you've never been back there since?"

"Never. I hated the whole damn lot of them. I expect you've heard all about that."

"We've had their account but not yours. Still, you can't deny that you're not going to come too badly out of things now your wife's dead. What about the legacy?"

"Oh, that." He stopped, and I could guess he was wishing he'd bitten his tongue out. Then he pulled himself together. He leaned forward. "Sorry, I didn't quite catch that. Did you say a legacy?"

Jewle told him about it. Five thousand pounds and there was no trace of his wife's will.

"First I knew of it. I don't say I'll take it, though."

"I would, and like a shot," Jewle told him. "But let's talk about something personal. Just why did you give up your job?"

"I told you before. I was ill. A dose of 'flu." His eyes narrowed. "But what's the point? Surely that's my business? And I resent it."

"Now, now, now," Jewle said placatingly. "I'm only a subordinate. I have to make a report to my superiors and, believe me, Mr. Delver, they're highly suspicious men. Someone might even say that you knew about that legacy soon after the will was read and you decided you needn't work any more." He held up a quick hand. "Wait a minute. Let me finish. They may even ask me if the illness was faked and did you have a doctor. *Did* you have a doctor, Mr. Delver?"

"I didn't." He glared. "I didn't need one. Two or three days quiet and some stuff I got from the chemist and I was practically all right again."

"But you didn't feel like getting another engagement."

"Why should I? I didn't like the one I had. And I'm not all that hard-up."

"Well, there we are," Jewle said resignedly. "But just one last thing. Mr. Travers here reported something you might throw some light on. He saw you one day last week in the shop of your uncle, Mr. Borne, and he had the idea that Mr. Borne didn't want him to speak to you. And after what Mr. Borne whispered to you, you didn't want to speak to Mr. Travers either. Can you explain that?"

"Nothing to explain," he said. "My uncle's been a good friend to me. He's the only one who has, and that's why I often drop in on him. I did that morning and he told me he was busy with a possible customer and I could come back later. That's all there was to it."

"I see." He leaned forward. "But the curious thing is that when Mr. Travers asked your uncle who you were, he said you were a bit of a crank whose name was Brown. Can you explain that?"

"Easy," he said and the lip curled again. "Why should my uncle tell everybody his business?"

"What business?"

"Well, that I was his nephew and did odd jobs for him at various times." He smiled. "Besides, my uncle is a bit of a joker. He was just having a bit of a joke at Mr. . . . I didn't catch your name?"

"Travers," I said. "And you heard it often enough last night."

"Just forgot," he said. "But that's how it was. Just a humorous way of brushing Mr. Travers off."

Jewle leaned back again.

"Well, that seems to be all. I expect you'd like to have it read back, just in case there's anything you'd like to change or modify."

The statement was read back.

"Everything okay?"

"Yes. Everything's okay."

"Nothing whatever you'd like to alter and nothing you want to add?"

"Don't think so."

"That's all right, then. Just read those last few words over, stenographer, so that it's complete."

They were read.

"You're prepared to sign the full statement?"

"Why not? It's all true."

Jewle waved to the stenographer. Ansen opened the door and closed it after him. Jewle looked at Delver, eyes narrowing.

"I'm afraid we'll have to hold you, Delver."

"Hold me?" He stared. "What for?"

"Well," Jewle told him urbanely. "You probably know the old army phrase, *dumb insolence*. There's also the expression *mute of malice*. Another one is *conspiring to defeat the ends of justice*. I can think of quite a lot of reasons for holding you."

Delver looked at him. He looked at me.

"But this is ridiculous! Every question you asked me, I answered."

"I know," Jewle said, and leaned right forward again. "And there wasn't a single answer that was not a deliberate lie."

Delver moistened his lips. His fingers were fidgetting nervously. Then he decided to be bellicose.

"I resent that. I don't allow anyone to call me a liar."

"You're probably the biggest liar who ever opened his mouth in this room," Jewle told him evenly.

"Prove it."

"We're going to. That man and woman you were with in the waiting-room downstairs, for instance. One will swear that you were seen running away from Hinchbrook Hall on the evening and at the time Mr. William Weddall fell from a window, accidentally or otherwise. The other will swear you were on the half-past five bus from Hinchbrook that took you to Mainford railway station. I have another witness who'll swear that your wife had for months been seeing you at Bolton Avenue on the Tuesdays when she came to town. And that's only a start."

He leaned back. Delver was staring at him, lips clamped tight.

"Well?" Jewle said. "Like to start off again and make a wholly new statement?"

Delver said nothing. He didn't even shake his head.

"For the last time, Delver. Do you or do you not wish to make a fresh statement?"

He waited a moment.

"Right, Inspector. Take him away."

Ansen had almost to lift Delver from the chair. The door closed on them. Jewle let out a deep breath.

It had been a masterly performance and I told him so, but he didn't want my praise.

"Merely getting ready for a squeeze," he said. "Playing off him and Borne against each other. When Ansen comes back he'll be bringing Borne in."

This time there was no stenographer. Joe Borne came in looking only the least bit apprehensive, and maybe because he'd expected to see Delver.

"Ah, Mr. Borne," Jewle said almost jovially. "We meet again. Take a seat for a minute, will you? Only just a question or two. We think you may be able to help us."

Borne got his bulk settled in the chair.

"I don't know what use I can be to you. Inspector. I'd thought we'd talked over pretty near everything in the train."

"Well, loosen your coat and make yourself comfortable," Jewle said. "You've met Mr. Travers, I think?"

Borne had already given me a quick, suspicious look.

"Oh, yes. He's the gentleman who came into my place one day last week."

"Yes," Jewle said. "So he told me. But tell us something, Mr. Borne. Why *did* you tell him that extraordinary tale about your nephew?"

It was funny. It reminded me of old army days and the collusive stories of, say, a couple of delinquents in the orderly room, up for overstaying leave. Borne and Delver had certainly put their heads closely together. The two accounts varied in scarcely a word.

"Never could resist a joke," Borne said. "Not that it ever did me any harm in business."

"We all like a joke," Jewle told him amiably. "Let me tell you one. A sort of fairy-tale. It may tickle you and it may not. That's the way jokes are."

He was smiling as he leaned comfortably back in his chair.

"This is my little fairy-tale, Mr. Borne. It might even be serious. It might even have a whole lot to do with Grace Amble's death, and with your brother-in-law's. You see, Mr. Borne, people *will* think they're the only ones who can make up fairy-tales. But take this one: there was a picture dealer who had a niece and nephew by marriage, and a brother-in-law who suddenly thought he'd like to collect pictures. But it so happened that the brother-in-law's eyes began to go bad—"

"Now, sir, now! Let's stop this fairy-tale business and say what's on our minds. You suggested recently that I'd taken advantage of William Weddall's eyesight to try to sell him some fakes. I denied that. I still deny it. Whoever planted anything on him"—he looked round at poor, innocent me—"I wasn't the one. So what's all this about?"

"And you hadn't any hand in planting Grace Amble as a kind of spy in Hinchbrook Hall?"

"Preposterous! Utterly preposterous!"

"And you didn't know that Delver had always kept in touch with his wife?"

"Look," he said. "I don't know a thing. I mind my own business and Delver minds his. We're talking at cross-purposes, so if you haven't anything more sensible to ask me, I suggest you let me do any business I have to do and then go back to town."

"No," Jewle said tersely. "You're not going back to town; not till we tell you so. What we've heard from Delver doesn't even begin to tally with what you've said here. When you're in a more communicative frame of mind, then we'll see. Meanwhile, you can go to your son's place or anywhere else in town. Try to leave and I'll have you back here quicker than you can wink." He got to his feet and he leaned across the desk till his face wasn't a foot from Borne's. "Murder, Mr. Borne. Murder. Keep saying it over to yourself and see if it doesn't make you change your mind." He waved a hand. "And now get out!"

Borne, furious but deflated, went out with Ansen.

"A slimy crook if ever there was one," Jewle said.

"He's worried. And he'll be wondering where Delver is."

"And Delver where Borne is. I think Delver's going to crack first. I'll have him in later and hint that Borne is getting ready to throw him over."

He glanced up at the clock.

"Don't know about you but I'm ready for some lunch. Might as well have something up here."

He had a look at Ansen's buzzer and pressed a key. It worked.

"Who's next for questioning?"

"Humphrey," he said. "I can't keep *him* incommunicado, though. I'll have to think out some sort of new approach."

"But won't Borne be getting into touch with him? I wouldn't mind betting he's telephoning to him just now."

"Why not?" Jewle said. "He'll want to know his legal rights. I'll be surprised if Humphrey doesn't ring me."

Humphrey did ring, plumb in the middle of our meal. Jewle gave me a wink as soon as he heard the voice, but what Humphrey was saying reached me in reverberations that boomed about the room. Still, I could gather quite a lot from what Jewle was telling him.

"Sorry, but I want him here . . . Certainly he can go back to town, but I might have decided meanwhile that I want him again and someone would be there to bring him straight back. . . . The funny thing is I *do* think he's a liar. In fact I know he is. . . . His story doesn't agree with Delver's, for one thing. And Delver's ready to tell us a whole lot more . . . Oh, no. The only thing for Borne to do is come absolutely clean, or he's in for big trouble . . . Oh, yes I know what I'm saying. I'm giving him good advice . . . No, I'm sorry, Delver isn't available at the minute . . . Murder, Mr. Weddall. Two murders . . . Sorry, but I can't tell you that either . . . You'll be here for a little while? . . . Well, I might be able to see you. You're at your office? Right, I'll give you a ring."

He grimaced as he replaced the receiver.

"You got that? Borne was almost certainly with him."

He made a fresh start on his meal. I left him to eat for a minute or two.

"Humphrey was questioning your authority?"

"In a roundabout way, yes. But Borne's helpless and he knows it."

He pushed the plate aside. What was left didn't look too appetising.

"They were both anxious about Delver?"

"You bet they were!" He smiled. "And Delver's getting just as anxious about Borne. But Borne won't talk."

He saw my look of surprise.

"Borne's not directly implicated in murder except that the murders followed as a consequence of something he had a hand in starting. And he knows we'll have a hard job in pinning those faked pictures on him, now they've been got rid of. Delver's a different proposition. He's directly implicated in Weddall's murder and he knows we know it. If he doesn't tell the truth to us, he'll have to do so in court. And we can produce that statement he made."

Matthews, not Ansen, came in with some coffee. He asked when we were having Delver in again. Some chance word had brought something back to my mind.

"Wasn't it Delver who rang me up that night and lured me away to Liverpool?"

"Yes," Jewle said. "I've been thinking about that. He was here with his wife and she knew Humphrey was due in the study for the signing of the will. My guess is she did some listening, even peeping, and heard Weddall tell Sam about the special letter. It wouldn't have taken her a minute to slip back and tell Delver."

"Just my own idea," I said. "That letter sounded as if it might be dynamite and Delver knew it. He nipped down and knocked Sam out, and when the two read the letter they knew something had to be done about me. Grace knew something about me and what she didn't know might have been even more scaring. Also she must have looked me up in *Who's Who*, and almost certainly seen that card of mine with the Agency number. And Delver's an actor. He could put in a northern accent. For all we know he may have played a northern part or two."

"Yes," Jewle said, and frowned. "If only we knew what was in that damn letter!"

"What about timing?" Matthews put in. "How long would all that take?"

I said I knew the times. I thought if we checked them we'd find a perfect fit. And a perfect fit it was.

4.40. Sam took the letter.

4.45. Sam knocked out. Ten minutes for a consultation between Delver and Grace. Allow five minutes to get my number.

5.00. Delver rang me as Hugh Browning. Grace waited till I'd taken the bait and then did some more listening at the study door.

5.20. approx. Weddall killed.

5.25. Delver seen running to catch the bus.

"Pretty damning for Delver," Jewle said. "No wonder he's keeping his mouth shut."

"Why not give him some more to think about?" I said. "Let him be told that when he's seen again he'll be asked about a Hugh Browning."

"Yes," Jewle said. "Not a bad idea. Ansen had better do it. Then we'll let Delver chew it over for an hour or so."

Matthews went out with the coffee cups. Jewle took out his pipe and I passed him my pouch.

"Just a minute," he said. "I've remembered something. I ought to ring Humphrey's wife. She'd be a likely one to find out from attendants and so on whether anyone actually saw Grace Amble at the show that night. She might just have looked in to throw everyone off the scent. She might have wanted to be able to prove later that she'd really seen the opening of the show.

"Look," he said. "You do it. I ought to see Ansen before he speaks to Delver. We don't want Mrs. H. herself to do it. Just get her to tell us someone who'd be likely to know. She'll be flattered."

In a couple of minutes I could hear the bell ringing at Humphrey's house. It must have been almost a minute more before there was an answering voice. Not Rachel Weddall's voice.

"May I speak to Mrs. Weddall?"

"Sorry, sir, but she isn't here."

"When will she be back?"

"I don't know, sir. It mightn't be for a week or two. She didn't say."

"She's gone away?"

"That's right, sir. Heard from her sister at Stratford this morning, who isn't very well. She hasn't been gone much more than an hour."

I didn't see the need to tell her who I was, so before she could ask me, I thanked her and rang off. Not that the absence of Rachel Weddall was any great loss. In fact, I thought it more of an asset.

And Jewle should think so, too. Give the lady an inch and she'd take a yard, and we'd have her round our necks from then on.

13. NOTHING BUT THE TRUTH

I WAS right. Jewle didn't shed any tears over the departure of Rachel Weddall. He'd meant it, he said, as a kind of ingratiation. If we were well in with the lady, she might let something slip about Borne and her husband.

"Just what is going on between those two?" I said.

He shrugged his shoulders.

"Don't know. But Humphrey'd be the natural one for Borne to go to about any trouble in this part of the world. Remember what happened after you saw Delver in Borne's shop? And after Humphrey had rung Borne about those fakes? Humphrey as good as told him to get down here and he'd see him personally. And he did see him—at young Borne's shop."

"There's something wrong," I said. "The right place for the Bornes to go to was Humphrey's office. And why did Humphrey sneak in by Oliver's back door?"

"Don't know," he said. "I can't possibly see how either of the Bornes can have any hold over Humphrey. Humphrey's a pompous bore but he's a reputable citizen. He and his wife rank among the Big Bugs here. She certainly does."

"What about that other matter: fear of scandal."

"That's it," he said. "That's what's behind it. You bet your life Humphrey has to tell his wife everything. She's the one who's been pulling the strings. For her Weddall and Grace Amble were relations by marriage only, but that didn't make much difference. So were the Bornes. Scandal about any one of them wouldn't do her own name any good, and women like her usually tread on plenty of toes. Must be quite a lot of people who wouldn't mind Mrs. Humphrey getting a bit smeared."

"Any possibility of this visit to a sick sister being a fake?"

He laughed.

"Hadn't thought of it but I wouldn't bet against it. She may have gone off to lie doggo till she sees how things pan out. Which means that Humphrey knows a damn sight more than we've given him credit for."

Ansen came in, all smiles and affability.

"He thinks he'd like to talk."

"Fine," Jewle said. "And we're just the ones to listen. Get him up here, Ansen."

The room was back to what it had been before: stenographer by the window, Ansen by the door. Delver looked no different to me.

"Glad you've decided to come clean," Jewle told him. "You did yourself an awful lot of harm by that first statement but we're prepared to forget it."

"What am I being charged with?"

"Nothing," Jewle said. "I think you can help us in that matter of the death of William Weddall and I'm asking you if you'd like to tell us anything that might throw light on it."

"And if I don't?"

"Frankly, I don't know. A charge may be made. But you'll certainly be remanded, and maybe in custody."

Delver thought it over.

"All right, then. I'll tell you the whole truth."

"Fine. Like to smoke?"

He waved back Jewle's case and lighted a cigarette of his own. He blew the smoke out in one deep draw.

"Where d'you want me to begin?"

"It's up to you. A purely voluntary statement and you're the one who's making it."

It was a good performance: an actor's performance. Every word and gesture so harmonised that the whole thing rang true. Grace had decided, he said, that she'd been more in love with him than she'd thought and she'd written to him about a year after she'd gone to Hinchbrook and suggested a meeting, and after it they'd decided to come together again. But she didn't want to give up the job at the Hall. The money was good and he himself wasn't making all that much, so all they did was see each other on Tuesdays when it was possible. Once or twice he'd risked a visit to the Hall: just out of curiosity and for a change.

On the Monday before Weddall's death he got a letter from her asking him to come to the Hall the following afternoon. She didn't say why, only that it was urgent. She'd arranged for the coast to be clear and he went in by the back and she took him as usual up to her room. It was then about half-past two. She told him that Weddall was signing a new will that afternoon and she might possibly be able to find out if he'd left anything to her.

What happened between then and four-thirty was no one's business, but at four-thirty she went down to the kitchen and brought up tea, ostensibly her own. She then went off again and he locked the door after her. She didn't get back till quite ten minutes later and then she was all agitated. She showed him a letter.

Jewle interrupted for the first time.

"Did she say how and where she got it?"

She'd said nothing except tell him to read the letter and before he could do it, she changed her mind. She said the one whom the letter was addressed to had to be stopped from coming next day to the Hall. Anything to make time till she could think things over. He asked what things, and she said she'd tell him later, but something had to be done at once. She knew all about the addressee and she showed him the study copy of *Who's Who* and she also had the Agency telephone number, and that was when he thought of the scheme. As soon as he'd rung me, she went out again, saying she'd be back in a minute. She didn't get back till about twenty past five and she said Humphrey Weddall had gone to see the children and she'd had to make herself agreeable and see him off. And that didn't leave him any time to catch his bus, after, that is, he'd wanted her to tell him what it was all about. She said she'd write the next day and then she made sure the coast was clear and let him out at the back again.

The next morning he'd dropped in, as he often did, on Joe Borne and it was then he learned that Weddall was dead. If he remembered rightly, it was Humphrey Weddall who'd rung Joe up. Later Delver rang his wife from a call-box and she confirmed the news and said she didn't want to talk about anything over the telephone. He did hear, however, that the funeral was on the Saturday and he arranged for her to ring him up at the King William at seven o'clock on the Saturday night in case Weddall had left her anything. He'd been staggered to hear she'd been left five thousand pounds and he owned up that it was because of it that he'd left the company.

On the Monday he'd had a brief note from her saying she couldn't make town the next day and it might be risky for him to come to Hinchbrook. She'd let him know when she could get to town again but unless he heard anything to the contrary, it'd be the following Tuesday.

"And that's the last I heard," he said. "The next thing was Sunday night when this gentleman here saw me in the King William and told me she was dead."

"A very clear statement," Jewle told him. "But about any relationship between you and your uncle, Mr. Borne. Nothing you'd like to alter?"

"No," he said. "That's all true. It's just as I told you."

The statement was read. Delver said it was okay.

"As soon as it's typed you can sign it," Jewle told him. "Read it through carefully before you do." He turned to the stenographer. "Put that last bit down."

The stenographer went out.

"What about me now?" Delver wanted to know.

Jewle looked up at the clock.

"When you've signed the statement, you can go. You'll be able to catch the four-twenty. A car'll take you to the station and all your expenses'll be paid. Inspector Ansen will see to all that. And when you're back in town, don't talk. And be on hand if we should want you again."

Delver looked as much puzzled as relieved. He'd been in deep water and he could hardly believe he'd got himself out. A hand moved as if he wanted to offer it to Jewle, but Jewle wasn't seeing it. Delver drew himself up and Ansen stepped back to let him out.

Jewle gave me one of his quizzical looks.

"Well?"

"Still wondering," I said. "It dovetails in remarkably well. One or two lies but the bulk of it fits. I'm honestly beginning to wonder if he did kill Weddall."

"What were the lies?"

"I think, for one thing, he did read the letter. She couldn't have gone on keeping him on the end of a string. She had to tell him far more than he's said."

"Don't know," he said. "She was a very clever woman. Anything else?"

"Only that it was he who coshed Sam."

He shook a dubious head.

"I'm not so sure. A woman could have knocked Sam out. The mark on his skull was consonant with something like a spanner and there's a big box of tools just inside the garage— or was. She'd only to be there before him and pick one up. Besides, if anything had gone wrong, she was the one who'd have had a perfectly good excuse for being in the garage. Delver wouldn't."

"And Borne. Delver's still covering up?"

"Not a doubt of it. And that reminds me. Might as well ring Humphrey and tell him I'm free." His hand went to the buzzer and then back. "Wait a minute, though. What about a change of scene? Why shouldn't we see him there?"

I thought it an excellent idea. There was a lot of curiosity in it, of course: the wish to see Humphrey in his own *milieu* and the *milieu* itself. And we both agreed that under his own vine and fig-tree, so to speak, Humphrey might talk far more freely, even if he didn't let his hair quite down. So we walked the shortish distance to Church Row.

If ever an establishment had an air of stability and class it was that of Weddall, Weddall and Spurn. All that Row consists of Queen Anne and Early Georgian survivals, some still private dwellings and the rest offices. But not drab-looking properties or even gaudy ones: just places where everything was decorously conducted and voices were never raised. Humphrey's was a Georgian house of two storeys, with a beautiful door and an exquisite fanlight. The plate was polished and the two steps were perfectly clean.

Humphrey admitted us. It was a Monday afternoon and, but for his making it a special occasion, the offices would have been open. Or maybe they always closed at four. At any rate, everything sounded hollow and empty as we went up the wide stairs to Humphrey's own room: a handsome, lofty room that overlooked the Row. The chairs were comfortable and a fire was burning in the Georgian basket set back beneath a marble mantelpiece.

"A nice place you have here," Jewle said, and took a cigarette from the box that Humphrey offered us. "Those are family portraits?"

Humphrey said they were. They were interesting, especially the one of Old Gus. Humphrey's father and mother seemed to me to be ironically placed, as if regarding Gus with a certain disapproval.

"Your grandfather seems to have been quite a character," Jewle said, and Humphrey actually smiled.

"Yes," he said. "A very shrewd man. And headstrong. When I was a boy I was really frightened of him. You never knew what mood he was going to be in."

He looked at us as if to let us know that we hadn't come there to hear ancestral voices. Jewle took him up.

"Well," he said, "you can tell Mr. Borne that he can go back to town. We've had a full statement now from Delver and if we should happen to want Mr. Borne again, then we'll see him in town."

Humphrey looked relieved.

"That's capital." He gave us a nod or two. "I had the idea that Delver might be trying to incriminate Borne in something quite fictitious but just to save his own skin. A bad character, I fear. And Borne's been quite good to him from time to time."

The tips of his fingers went together.

"You—er—think he's deeply implicated in this dreadful business of his wife?" He gave a quick, deprecatory smile. "That's purely in confidence, of course."

"Implicated, yes. How deeply we don't know. But we hope to know. We've let him go back to town. We can always pick him up if we want him."

"Of course."

He seemed to be hunting for words. Jewle helped him out.

"Still speaking in confidence, he didn't implicate Mr. Borne. But, before I forget it, I wonder if you could tell us something. We have an idea that Grace Amble might have looked in at the town hall when the show started—just to prove she'd been there, so to speak—and then went away again to wherever she was murdered. You didn't happen to see her?"

"No," he said. "I was at the front, of course. I doubt if I'd have seen anything even if I'd turned my head. It's a very big hall, you know."

"Well, I just wondered," Jewle said. "We rang your wife to ask the same thing but were told she was away."

Humphrey frowned.

"Yes. I came away pretty earlier: matter of fact, I had to let myself in, so I only just saw her, then she rang me later to say she'd had a call from her sister. Still, you probably know that. I didn't think she should go. The grandchildren, you know. In view of this tragedy, some new arrangement ought to be made, and she stands out as the right person to make it. I told her so." He waved a hand. "Still, there we are. She didn't seem to think it as important as I do."

"But the women there," I said. "Can't they look after the children? They struck me as very nice people."

"Well, yes. But the Queen's English, my dear fellow. What about that?"

"Frankly, I don't think it matters all that much," I said bluntly. "It's their school contacts that would largely form their speech. Still, that's your concern. I'm speaking out of turn."

He smiled and waved a genial hand.

"Not at all, my dear fellow: not at all. Still, I shall get into touch with the trustees of their father's estate. It's their primary concern."

He'd risen tentatively from his chair. We took the hint and rose, too. Jewle said we could find our way downstairs but he insisted on accompanying us. He shook hands with us at the door, thanked us and hoped we'd keep him informed. He didn't say about what.

"Luckily we didn't have anything else to talk about," Jewle said, as we walked back, "but he certainly wasn't prolonging the interview. Expect he was anxious to tell Joe the good tidings."

We talked about the Humphrey Weddalls till we were nearly back at police headquarters, then I asked what the programme was from then on. I'd thought, by the way, that Humphrey had been looking a bit pale and tired, but I didn't say so to Jewle. And he had eyes of his own.

"I just don't know," he said. "Wait, perhaps, for someone to come forward with information. Chew things over and hope for daylight. I just can't say."

"You won't want me," I said, "and there's something I'd like to do. Something that anticipates that report from Colgate. Remember those pictures in the dining-room that Old Gus was supposed to have wheedled out of the old lady for next to nothing? The ones Colgate's busy on? Why shouldn't Mrs. Larkwell be able to tell us when the switchover was made from originals to fakes? She's a kind of oldest inhabitant?"

"Why not?" he said. "You never know what's going to be important. We haven't got to clutching at straws yet but I wouldn't be surprised if we soon shall be."

I didn't see why I shouldn't accept his offer of a police car. It dropped me at the Hall and I went along to the far door. Mrs.

Larkwell let me in. She seemed quite glad to see me. Her motherly face was all smiles.

"Have you any news yet, sir? And have you had your tea? Just given the children theirs and going to have my own. Daisy has slipped home for a minute or two. She lives in the village, you know, right the far end."

I said I'd share her tea in the kitchen. It was beautifully warm in there and everything, from floor to copperware, seemed to shine beneath the electric light. It was a good tea that we had and all the time we were talking sixteen to the dozen. It was the easiest thing in the world to bring in the matter of those pictures.

"You'd be the one to write a history of the Hall," I told her. "I bet you remember practically everything that's happened here all the time you've been here."

"Well, I do remember a lot," she told me, with a modesty that was patently false. Then she broke off, with an, "Excuse me, sir."

I'd heard nothing but she had. She went to the foot of the stairs and called something up. She was smiling when she came back.

"Always up to mischief, those two. Still, I suppose gentry's children aren't no different from no one else's."

"Something I thought of while you were out," I said. "I have an idea that some of those pictures in the dining-room were reframed some years ago. Do you remember anything about it."

"I remember that," she said. "But not reframed." She paused for a minute, nodded to herself once or twice and then it came back to her.

"No, sir, not reframed, as you call it. They was sent away to be cleaned. Mr. Joe see to it. It was when they come back they had new frames. The old ones was worm-eaten. Well, something was wrong with 'em and they had to be changed."

"The old master had it done?"

"Yes, sir, not long before he died. He had that stroke and I reckon he knew he hadn't long to go. He got over it but he had another and that carried him off. Reckon he wanted to have everything proper before he died and that's why he had them pictures seen to."

"What'd Miss Evelyn think about it?"

She laughed.

"She didn't have much truck with downstairs. The drawing-room and upstairs was what she took an interest in. Mr. Paul —that's the Major as he was. He was a Colonel when he was killed—he reckoned that dining-room ought to've been turned into a billiard-room, and if he'd have lived I wouldn't have been surprised if that was what'd have happened."

I didn't stay much longer. I wanted to drop in on Sam for a minute, but when I was outside I stopped for a moment or two in the lee of the house corner and thought over what I'd learned. Joe Borne hadn't worked that change-over of the dining-room pictures: what he'd done had been at Gus Weddall's orders. But Gus had left a comparatively small sum, and it was as I remembered that, that I remembered something else: something that had happened to me when I was a young collector and my father was still alive.

It arose out of a visit to a certain antique shop and my father had been with me: in Ipswich, once a hive of fakes and reproducers. My father had enquired about something which the dealer didn't have but which he thought his father, then a very old man, might have, so he rang his father up and we went round to the private address.

The old man had been an auctioneer and his house was full of good things. He hadn't what my father wanted but we did have some fascinating talk, chiefly about swindles, and the old man must have taken to my father, for he suddenly said he had something upstairs he might like to see. So we went upstairs to the old man's bedroom. He pulled a box out from under the bed, found a key and unlocked it.

"This is just between you and me, sir," he said.

"Quite so," my father said, and I think I nodded.

The lid of the box was lifted and our eyes popped out of our heads. It was full of rat-tailed silver!

"Good God!" my father said. "You've got a young fortune there. Why don't you sell it?"

The old man—he was an amusing old scoundrel—merely winked. The box was relocked and put back and we went downstairs again. When we left the house I asked my father what it all meant, guileless as I was.

"The moment he dies, his son'll collect that box," I was told. "He'll take it into his shop and later on the contents will be sold. That will pay all his death duties."

An ingenious scheme and the mere memory of it made me smile. And I thought that the very same thing had been done in the matter of those dining-room pictures. Copies had been made and the originals would be sold, on Gus's death, to pay death duties.

But that wasn't right! He'd left very little, though if the house and contents were included, it might have come to as much as twenty-thousand pounds. Maybe as much as thirty or forty, depending on the rise in value of some of those Edwardian pictures. In any case the proceeds of the sold pictures would have covered death duties with a great deal to spare. And so what?

I thought things out a bit more and then I went on to the garage and knocked at Sam's door.

"Not coming in, Sam, but could you run me into Mainford and back. I shan't be there more than five minutes."

He slipped on his chauffeur's coat and cap for warmth and we were off almost at once. I told him to park in the police garage and I wouldn't keep him long.

Jewle and Matthews were in Ansen's room. They looked surprised to see me. What I had to tell them took quite a deal of careful explaining.

"Let's anticipate Colgate's report and say those pictures were sold in New York," Jewle said. "What might they have fetched?"

"Honestly, I don't know," I said. "Give me a minute or two and I'll try to get some idea."

I had the list in my notebook and began totting prices up.

"It's very, very approximate," I said. "I might be as much as five thousand out. Sales depend on so many things. But let's take a conservative figure. Say twenty thousand pounds. May be much less, may be even more."

"That's a lot of money," Jewle said. "And it definitely didn't appear in the estate. So who had it?"

"I thought you'd like to find out. The obvious answer is Joe Borne. In any case it's something you can get your teeth into."

"Yes," he said. "And thanks for finding it. Looks as if it might be a case for the Commissioners of Inland Revenue."

I thought the same. They'd work underground and no one would know a thing till they had a case. Far better than poking our noses where they might be seen.

That was how we left it. Jewle said he and Matthews mightn't be at the pub till very late and I'd have to feed alone. Matthews told me to keep off the beer, and I said I'd leave some at least for him, and with that supposed-to-be-merry quip I went out.

We drove slowly back, and because I was telling Sam what it was safe to tell him about Grace Amble. I warned him that he still wasn't to tell Jewle about her snooping, since I hadn't been able to tell him myself. When we got to the Hall Sam ran the car straight into the garage.

"Don't know about you, sir, but I ain't none too hot. What about a cup o'coffee?"

"Sam, that's about the best thing you've said tonight," I told him, and followed him up the stairs.

I've often wondered since what might have happened if he hadn't offered me that coffee.

14. SECRET MISSION

SAM certainly made a good cup of coffee. I'd told him so before and I said so again. There was plenty in the percolator and we each had a second cup.

"What's going to happen to you, Sam?" I asked him. "Made your mind up yet?"

"Jest don't know, sir. Jest don't know. I like most everybody here but I jest don't know."

As we agreed, there was plenty of time in which to make up his mind, and meanwhile his wages would be paid by the estate. When we'd finished the coffee and he'd taken the cups back, we talked about the job for which he was paying me, though he'd have been the last person to put it like that. I told him that things were working up to a head and he must trust me till the time for the show-down came. When I glanced at my watch I was amazed to see how late it was.

"Still re-reading the same book, I see."

It was opened and lay on top of the same bookcase.

"Yes, sir. I'm what they call a slow reader," he told me. "But that's a mighty interestin' book. Jest comin' to that place again where the old man what they suppose is dead comes up alive." He chuckled. "Man! I can't get to that bit too fast. No-sir."

That's what I began thinking about as I walked back to the pub. Weddall had wanted Sam to read that book. There'd been a certain emphasis. Sam had been given it specially by Weddall and had been told that he—Weddall—would like to hear later what Sam's opinion of it was. And something was telling me that Sam had been given that book for a special reason. In the book, as Sam had just told me, a dead man turned up alive, but that had no bearing on Weddall himself who was even deader than most. What then was there so special about that book?

For there *was* something special. I was sure of that. Sam was Weddall's confidant and Weddall had been telling Sam something obscurely: something he either expected him to find out from a reading of that book or from the circumstance in which he had been given it, and almost certainly the former. The book itself had been a mystery: strange happenings that ended in a stranger climax—that the old man, supposed to be dead, was not only alive but had been the *deus ex machina* of those happenings. So what had Weddall been trying, through that book, to convey to Sam?

I was actually at the pub door when the answer came to me. It was fantastic but that made it only the more likely. And the more I thought about that hunch, the more I knew I was right. I *had* to be right. There was nothing else—no other flux —that bound the whole thing together. As to what I ought to do, that had to be done pretty fast.

Jewle must have rung, for my cold supper was laid out and while I was eating I looked at the time-table. There was plenty of time to catch the nine o'clock, and there was a convenient bus. I rang Bernice and left a note for Jewle where he couldn't miss it, on his bedroom mantelpiece.

Gone to test an idea which might help.
Back tomorrow—with luck. L.T.

All I thought I had to do then was to put a few necessaries in my bag and see the landlady, but it was fortunate that I still had ten minutes to spare, for there was something else which I'd suddenly thought of. I rang Mrs. Larkwell. Had she by any chance a photograph of the late master? She hadn't, but she knew there was one in the nursery. I asked if I could borrow it for just a day and would she let Daisy bring it to the end of the drive.

I still had time to catch my bus at the stop by the rectory gate. I had a look at the photograph as soon as we were on the move. It was probably about three years old but still a speaking likeness of the man I'd met—and months ago it now seemed—in St. James's Square on the way to Christie's.

There was no need to get up any earlier in the morning. The train that Weddall had taken at Charing Cross on that 30th of December was still running and I was proposing to take it, too.

I knew, of course, that the whole thing was a gamble. Everything depended on Weddall's real destination. That train stopped at both Waterloo and London Bridge, both big termini, before its further non-stop journey to Tonbridge, and Weddall might have got off at either, but it was a gamble that had to be taken. What I was proposing to do was to get off at Tonbridge and try to have a word with every driver of a taxi. Something in my favour was that it was a cold, dry day: had it been raining I should have been far less optimistic and eager.

I was to be lucky in about twenty different ways, but that's how things go. I've taken part in my time in a hunt that went on for weeks and for someone who all the time had been almost under our noses. And a lot of it was due to a sudden switch in plans: the man I took for a foreman porter. I asked him if he were and he said he was.

"You've a chance to earn some money," I told him and took a pound note from my wallet. "Anywhere we can have a quick talk?"

We went into the almost deserted restaurant. I asked if he'd like some coffee, and I took a couple of cups of that nondescript British Railways beverage to a table. I showed him Weddall's photograph and added a few extras by way of description.

"Did he have any luggage?" he wanted to know.

"Two fairly large bags. I believe they were in the compartment with him. Almost certainly a first-class."

"Well, I didn't see him myself," he said. "Someone must have taken his luggage up, though. The 30th December, you say."

The coffee was too hot for me but he emptied his cup as if it were lukewarm.

"You stop here, sir, and I'll have a look at my book and make a few enquiries. You'd better let me have that photograph."

For about a quarter of an hour I sat on in that none-too-cheerful room with its faint smell of soot and steam, but when he came back he had a man with him: a short, sturdy-looking porter.

"Here you are, sir. This is Bill White, the one who carried his bags up."

I handed over the tip and went out with Bill.

"You remember him, Bill?"

"Remember him well, sir. Something wrong with his eyes, he told me. Walked sort of stiff and took his time." He smiled.

"Tipped me half-a-quid, too. 'Tain't often you get gents who tip you like that."

We went up the steps to the street. I'd been asking if he knew what taxi Weddall had taken, and he said it wasn't a taxi at all but a private car. A real smart car, he said: an almost new Daimler. A lady had been driving it. In a minute or two we'd arrived at the fact that she'd been about forty or just over, tall for a woman and wearing a light-brown fur coat.

"We're up a gum-tree, Bill," I said. "How're we going to find her?"

Just across the street there was a filling station, a biggish one. Bill said the car had driven off west along the Tunbridge Wells road. There was just the chance that she'd had the car filled or the oil topped, so we went across. And we struck lucky at once. The proprietor knew the car and the owner, and because Mrs. Chantry drove her husband to the station five mornings a week and collected him again in the evenings. Their house was called The Croft, about a mile down the road. I asked if he ran a taxi service.

"That'd be robbing you," he said. "There're buses every few minutes. You can't miss the house. Less than a mile down, on your left. You'll see the big white gates just before you come to it."

I tipped Bill, waited for a bus and caught one inside five minutes, and in less than no time I was getting off near those white gates. I went through them and along a short, gravelled drive to a big Edwardian house set in quite spacious grounds. I rang the bell. A tall, good-looking woman of about forty-two opened the door. Her look was enquiring but pleasant.

"Mrs. Chantry?" I said.

"Yes. I'm Mrs. Chantry."

"Then may I come in for a moment?" I gave my best smile. "I'm not selling anything. I'd just like a word with you on a perfectly private matter."

She hesitated for only a moment.

"Will you come in? Perhaps we'd better go in here."

We went through a door just to the right of the entrance hall and into a dining-room. There was no fire but it was quite warm.

"Won't you sit down?"

"Thank you," I said. "And may I ask a rather rude question? Are you by any chance American?"

She smiled.

"I am," she said. "But I've been in England now for—ah, twenty-three years. My husband is English."

"And you like it here?"

"But of course! Why do you ask?"

"Yes," I said. "Why *did* I ask. But let me tell you why I'm here. It's on purely private business connected with Mr. William Weddall. You know him?"

I needn't have asked. The mere mention of Weddall's name had been almost a shock.

"Yes," she said. "I knew him in New York, long before I was married. But would you mind waiting here a moment? I'd like to speak to my father."

She was back in less than a couple of minutes.

"My father would like to see you," she told me. "Will you come this way."

I followed her across the hall to a door on the far left. She halted, hand on the knob.

"I forgot to ask you your name."

"Travers."

She opened the door for me.

"Mr. Travers, Daddy."

It was a smallish, real man's room, with wide windows that gave a good view of the gardens. The man who'd been reading *The Times* before the old-fashioned open fire got to his feet. He was tall and erect. His still ample hair was white and his neat moustache white. He had little colour in his face and his eyes were blue. There was about him an air of authority and distinction. He gave me a searching look before holding out his hand: a warm, dry hand.

"Sit down, Mr. Travers. Take your coat off first. Just put it anywhere."

I took the chair that faced his own across the fire.

"May I ask *your* name, sir?"

"Latwin," he said. "Mervin Latwin."

I smiled.

"Either you write a bad hand, Mr. Latwin, or I'm bad at deciphering. I refer to your signature on a cheque that reached me. I imagine Mr. Weddall gave you fifty pounds and you wrote one of your own cheques. But I'd better show you my credentials."

He had a good look at them and most of the time was a stall while he thought things out.

"You're a private detective, Mr. Travers."

"Yes," I said. "I own a detective agency. I met Mr. Weddall late last year and, if I may put it that way, I think we had confidence in each other."

"I see. And before I ask you what this special business of yours is, how is he?"

"You haven't heard from him?"

"No," he said. "I expect there'll be a letter in New York when I get back. I'm leaving at the end of the week. Just spending a short vacation with my daughter. I should have left a fortnight ago but my grandson—he's doing his military service in Germany—had an unexpected leave, and I decided to stay on."

There was a moment's silence. I made up my mind to come straight to the point.

"Mr. . . . . Sorry, I've forgotten your name again."

"Latwin."

"Thank you. I've some bad news for you, Mr. Latwin, or maybe it isn't news. Mr. Weddall's dead."

There wasn't a doubt about it being news.

"Dead? Bill Weddall dead!"

"Yes," I said. "It's a long story, Mr. Latwin, and I have an idea you'll want to hear it. You're a man of honour and there's no need to remind you that it's implicitly secret."

I began at the very beginning and I left nothing out except the Bornes, Delver and the death of Grace Amble. That last I might tell him if it were necessary. When I'd finished I invited him to ring Jewle for a check on my credentials.

"No need for that, Mr. Travers," he said. "I'm just as much a judge of men as you are. But what you've told me is absolutely incredible. Something's very badly wrong."

"With that queer business of throwing everyone off the scent and coming here instead of going to Italy?"

"Not that," he said. "That was all arranged. He was always a joker. And shrewd as they come."

"I'm trespassing on your time," I told him, "but would you care to give me your side of things? Strictly in confidence, if you so prefer it."

"I don't think it need be that, at least between me and your police. You'd like me to begin at the beginning?"

"If you don't mind, sir. When you first knew him, for instance, and how."

This is the story, edited from a conversation that lasted well over half an hour. Weddall's wife was Latwin's first cousin and the two men became close friends. Latwin was an eye specialist and, I gathered, a man of international reputation. His offices were within a stone's-throw of Weddall's though he commuted from Arlington, New Jersey. The two men shared a cabin in the Catskills when Weddall could get away from work. Evelyn Weddall and his own daughter Ruth had gone to the same school and the two families were very close. When Weddall ultimately retired, the two men corresponded at fairly frequent intervals.

And so to that fall when Weddall damaged the retinas of both eyes: the damage, perhaps, more an annoyance than serious. Such damage was unpredictable, Latwin said. People might have serious falls and suffer no damage whatever, and then someone else might have the slightest of falls that might bring the condition on. Weddall wrote and reported the matter to Latwin and he advised a consultation with Sir Hugo Bronsen. Sir Hugo advised local treatment—eye-drops or something of that sort, I imagined—and was against an operation. If the sight should deteriorate, however, there should be another consultation. And that was apparently why Weddall always walked so carefully and erectly. What he didn't want was another fall.

I'm putting all this in layman's language. To tell the truth I didn't follow all the technicalities myself and I didn't want to interrupt the flow of talk. But the next thing that happened was a slight deterioration in Weddall's sight, and you will note that it was Latwin who used that word *slight*. Weddall wrote to Latwin about it and that was just before Latwin was coming to England. That was how Weddall's visit to Tonbridge came to be arranged. Sir Hugo was there and the two specialists made a thorough examination. An operation was decided on: not too serious a one, so Latwin stressed. It was performed by Sir Hugo himself at a private nursing home, and after it Weddall had to be motionless and in the dark for about a month. When the bandages were removed, Weddall's sight was almost as good as ever, and, but for something unforeseen, would stay so till the rest of his days.

When Latwin had finished he glanced at the clock.

"You'll stay to lunch?" he asked me. "No inconvenience whatever and we'd like to have you. I'll just have a word with my daughter."

I had plenty of questions for him when he came back.

"Tell me if I'm right, sir, and in view of what I've told you and you've told me. Weddall suspected certain people were taking advantage of his slow deterioration of eyesight and he took advantage of it himself to pretend his eyes were far worse than they really were."

"An inescapable conclusion."

"And when he got back after his operation he carried the deception still further."

"Yes," he said. "That's an undoubted fact."

"You find it in keeping with what you knew of him?"

"Oh, yes," he said. "He was an extraordinary character. One of the most likeable and generous of men, but always the boy at heart. There was nothing he liked better than engineering some sort of practical joke." He smiled. "I remember once he rang me and asked if I'd heard that cabin of ours had been burnt out. Said I'd better pack a bag and we'd get down there, and when we got there the cabin was just as it always was. Said he'd thought I was due for a small vacation."

"Well, we're getting things into alignment," I said. "You knew, by the way, that his seventieth birthday was due?"

"Oh, yes. I was intending to send him something when I got back home. Hadn't made up my mind what. Something that'd bring back the old days." He shook his head. "I shan't have to think about it now."

I left him to his thoughts for a minute before I put the last questions.

"What I told you about making a new will surprised you?"

"No," he said slowly. "When a man reaches seventy he ought to be sure his affairs are in order. As a matter of fact I made my final will at seventy. That was four years ago."

I told him I wouldn't have thought it.

"I suppose when he was here he didn't mention to you anything about donating an art gallery to Mainford?"

"Yes," he said, and slowly again. "I remember he did. And I think that's all. We certainly didn't discuss it at any length. He must have been quite a wealthy man and it ought to have been well within his means. Something unpretentious, of course."

Ruth Chantry looked in and told us lunch was on the table. It was a modest but excellent meal and we chatted all the time. She told me that while Evelyn was alive, they had met occasionally in town. Evelyn was much younger, of course, and the two hadn't been contemporaries at school, but they'd known each other for much of their younger lives. After Evelyn's tragic death she had lost touch, though she and Weddall had always exchanged cards at Christmas. Once she had asked him down but he hadn't been able to come.

I asked her if she remembered Sam Martin, and she certainly did. Her father laughed. Weddall and Sam, he said, had been sort of complementary. Both characters in their way. He told us a funny story about Sam's getting lost up in the Catskills: something that Weddall had engineered. When he came to the part about Sam going round in circles and hollering for help, it was as if Sam were in the room.

Latwin and I had coffee in that small lounge and we talked some more about Bill Weddall. We manoeuvred each other into talking about ourselves and I could have sat there for the rest of the afternoon. What a fine character Latwin was, and when I rose at last to go he gave me his home address and made me promise that when I was next in the States I'd let him know.

Ruth Chantry insisted on driving me to the station to catch the train we'd looked up. She, too, was a charming person. Her husband was a stockbroker and she had a daughter at Oxford as well as the son in Germany. When I thanked her she said she was only sorry that I hadn't come with better news but I must be sure to come again when her father was over. She hoped he'd be retiring in a year or two.

I had plenty to think about in the train, even if everything was dominated by the close memory of two delightful people. Latwin, by the way, had promised to write to me at Mainford if he should remember anything else that might be in any way important: not that I thought he could tell us anything comparable with that day's revelations. Rarely in my life had there been so lucky a day. Or so pleasant a one, and it was mainly that that kept me from too serious thought. Later, on the way back to Mainford, the whole perspective would have changed and that would be the time to start fitting things in.

I rang Jewle from the flat while Bernice was making tea.

"Hallo," he said. "What bug bit you?"

I said I'd tell him the whole story when I saw him. I'd be taking the train that got me to Mainford at half-past seven.

"Then come to the pub," he said. "Things have been pretty quiet here."

"No news at all?"

"Nothing much. Colgate's report came by the afternoon post. I'm keeping it for you. You know more about it than I."

"Anything specially interesting in it?"

"Fairly big money involved. Still, you'll see it when you get here. Oh, and one other thing. Old Pepson wants to see us some time tomorrow. He said he'd ring again in the morning. That bee's still in his bonnet, or so we think. You know, that new art gallery business."

"It mayn't be a bee," I told him. "If it is it may be one in *our* bonnets. I'll tell you the whole story later but I've partly corroborated certain things today. Pepson's entitled to his grievance."

"Interesting. Like to give me a bit more?"

Bernice was making signs that my tea was getting cold and I told him he'd have to wait.

15. REVELATIONS

JEWLE wasn't so surprised as I'd thought he'd be. He said it was easy to be wise after the event, but he'd put in a lot of thought about those eyes of Weddall's. Not, of course, that he'd arrived at the point of even so much as suspecting what we'd now discovered.

That was what had bothered me, too, all along. There'd never been a uniformity about those eyes, and I'd known that from things that Sam had told me as well as from what I'd seen for myself. It had taken sharp eyes, for instance, to spot an experienced operative like Mander. The same eyes had seen the merest slit of a door when Grace Amble had been snooping. Those eyes had needed glasses at one moment and none at the next. Then there was that letter which had been given to Sam and for which he'd been coshed. Who had written it? Not Mrs. Gray. And a man with eyes as bad as Weddall's had been could hardly have written it either. According to Sam, the writing on the envelope had been normal, whereas it ought to have been something of a scrawl.

"What beats me is how you discovered about the operation," Jewle said. "And what made you guess he hadn't been in Italy?"

I had the answer ready.

"The second arose out of the first. But let me put it to you. Weddall was a wealthy man and if his eyes were troubling him who would he go to? The very best. Very well then. Find out, say, the three or four biggest authorities and make a few enquiries, using, of course, any influence you happen to have. You have some luck. The name of Sir Hugo Bronsen pops up and you go on from there."

"Yes," Jewle said. "Sounds easy when you've thought of it. And have the right connections. But it's the last clincher in Weddall's death. A man with eyes as good as yours"—he smiled—"well, as good as mine, wouldn't have fallen out of that window. And that brings us right back to Delver again."

I said I'd been thinking a lot about Delver on my journey down and I was far from sure that he'd been telling the truth about a reconciliation with his wife. What I'd come back to was that it'd been a put-up affair from the beginning, and the fact that in his final statement he'd shielded Joe Borne seemed to prove it. It was Borne who'd been the prime mover in planting Grace Amble at the Hall, and with, of course, Delver's connivance.

We'd been talking during our meal and now Jewle was taking out his pipe. Matthews was putting the debris on the side-table.

"I think we can fit that in with Colgate's report. What I read into it is that Borne must have had plenty to worry about. You have a look at it and see what you think."

We pushed back the table and drew our chairs towards the fire. Colgate's report was quite short. I thought at first glance that the bill he enclosed was a bit steep, but that was before I read the explanations.

Dear Inspector,

I hope I haven't kept you waiting about this report but it turned out to be a tougher job and took more time—cables, two trans-Atlantic telephone calls, etc.—than I'd expected. Fortunately I have a nephew who's a responsible employee of the Parke-Bernet Galleries, and who also happened to have a personal pull in the affairs of Hentzel, Groome. All the same I'm afraid you can't use the information as coming from my nephew.

I don't want to tell you your business but I'm sure you can think of ways and means of getting the same information considering what this report tells you, through the New York police, I mean if you need it as evidence.

Briefly, and I admit it doesn't seem much for the thirty guineas I have to charge you, what happened is this. Hentzel, Groome of Madison Avenue acted as selling agents for Borne and Son. The pictures were received from England in October, 1953. The three English ones were sold by the Parke-Bernet Galleries and were described as the property of an English nobleman! That's a nice little touch of Joe Borne's, of course, but it didn't matter to anybody since the pictures were obviously genuine, catalogued or not. None were of the best quality: the Turner and the Gainsborough, for instance, were both early work, and they created no furore. The other pictures were sold privately by Hentzel, Groome, the Metropolitan taking the Matsu. Sale commission to the Galleries would be about 20 per cent and what commission Hentzel, Groome took would be a matter of arrangement between them and Borne.

The important point is this, that the total sums sent to Borne amounted at the then rate of exchange to slightly under twenty thousand pounds. May I repeat that this information is confidential. The Parke-Bernet cheque reached Borne shortly after the sale, and the rest as Hentzel, Groome made their own sales. The final cheque was sent in March, 1954.

I hope this information may be of use to you and I shall look forward to receiving your cheque in due course.

I took off my glasses, blinked a bit and hooked them on again.

"A lot of money, as you say. And it wasn't paid into the estate. Old Gus Weddall was hardly in his grave before those pictures were shipped to America and Borne pocketed a very nice cheque."

"And you bet your life he was always sweating about it," Matthews said. "You see how it all works in? William Weddall wasn't a danger till he began thinking about that new art gallery and taking an interest in pictures, and that's when Grace Amble was planted. I don't say she knew just what she was there for. Perhaps she had what they call a roving commission. You know: keeping her eyes and ears open generally."

I asked Jewle what he'd done about getting into touch with the Tax Commissioners and he said he'd changed his mind. He'd thought he'd wait till the report arrived. Even now he wasn't sure of his best course: to pass on information to the Commissioners or use the report to squeeze admissions from Joe Borne.

We hadn't got much further overnight and there didn't seem to be anything particular on the agenda next morning when we set off for Mainford, except, of course, a possible meeting with old Pepson. It was not long after we arrived when he rang Jewle about that. He said there was a little restaurant sort of place that did morning coffees, just as you came into Reddiford on the left-hand side, and he'd meet Jewle there at ten-thirty prompt.

"Reddiford's five miles away," Jewle told us. "And a mile off the Mainford-Peterborough Road. He's certainly taking precautions. Almost looks as if he's unearthed something."

He thought there was no reason why I shouldn't go with him. After all, if Pepson objected when he saw me, I could always go back to the car.

"Might be lucky for you," he said, "if he's going to get all het-up about that art gallery again."

"Remember what I told you last night?" I said. "Pepson's a right to be annoyed—and puzzled. As I said, I don't know when Weddall mentioned that art gallery to Latwin but even if it was just before the operation, that wasn't all that time before his death."

"If necessary we can check with Dr. Latwin later," he said. "But I can't see how it *can* be necessary. And Weddall's far more likely to have mentioned it when he first wrote him about his eyes. All that working on those plans might have helped to aggravate the eye condition."

I didn't think that was too logical, but I didn't argue. We set off for Reddiford. The weather had changed. It was almost muggy and very overcast and the forecast had promised rain. But it was easy to read the board set in the near-side hedge as we approached the village:

THE OLD BARN

300 yards

TEAS. LUNCHES. MORNING COFFEE.

There was a big, unmetalled car park. The restaurant itself was an old, converted barn with living quarters above. We waited a minute or two till we saw Pepson's car turning into the drive and then we went on ahead and through a door to a warm, pleasantly furnished room with its tables not too closely spaced. By the time Jewle had ordered coffee for three with cakes, Pepson was with us. There was the faintest of smiles on his gaunt, lined face as he held out a bony hand.

We had the place to ourselves and chose a table well away from the fire. As soon as Pepson had sipped the scalding coffee he began to talk, and he kept his voice low, as far, at least, as that voice of his could be muffled at all.

"This is highly confidential," he began. "No doubt you guessed that from my choosing this place to talk in, but I'm a public figure and I daren't risk being seen in the company of you two gentlemen." The gaunt smile flickered again. "No offence, of course. You know what I mean."

There was no doubt that Pepson had a keen and glacial sort of brain. If he hadn't, he wouldn't have held down that job of his for so many years. And he'd obviously thought over what he was going to tell us. Everything was logical and ordered.

He began by stressing the need for absolute secrecy. He was proposing, he said, to tell us certain facts: things he'd be prepared, if necessary, to help in substantiating. It was up to Jewle to attach his own importance to them and to act as he then thought fit. Pepson thought it would be better that way, and for himself, after that morning, temporarily to retire, as it were, behind the scenes.

He moved on to his own position and status in Mainford. He had innumerable friends. He had access to information denied to others. He was often asked privately for advice and he was the custodian of a good many secrets. Were he ever to write an auto-biography, Mainford and district could be set by the ears. And so to what he had to tell us.

It had gone badly against the grain, he said, when Humphrey Weddall had virtually made a fool of him that night at Hinch-brook Hall.

"I knew I was right, gentlemen. I even knew more than I told, and when I began thinking things over that night I was positive that something remarkably tricky had taken place. What Humphrey must have done was to tell his uncle nothing short of a pack of monstrous and vicious lies to induce him to change his mind about that art gallery.

"Hallo," I thought. "Here we go again."

I was wrong. If that were the case, Pepson was going on, then he had his own very good reasons. And a couple of days later Pepson began to see daylight. It arose out of a talk with a certain elderly lady who was a friend of his. Humphrey, he reminded us, like all solicitors, advised clients on investments and executed the necessary deeds to put certain investments into effect. This particular old lady had advanced just over five thousand pounds to be invested in a mortgage.

"You see?" Pepson said with a definite triumph. "The one thing where the law as it stands affords a loophole. The Law of Property Act of 1945 says that a mortgagee making a loan is not entitled to inspect the lessor's title. And that's what Humphrey Weddall took advantage of to carry out his transactions."

"Legal terms are beyond me," Jewle said, "but let me put it like this. Humphrey used that five thousand pounds for his own private purposes."

"Yes, that's what it amounts to," Pepson said. "And another curious thing is that within a few days of the terms of his uncle's will being known publicly, he advised my friend to change her investment. He had the new investment so much in mind that it was carried through almost at once. I may tell you that this time it's a genuine one."

"You think there were other and similar cases?" I asked him.

"Yes," he said. "I'm making a very cautious investigation into one now. An institution which had advanced him money: this time a much bigger sum. In this case a change of investment was advised and completed a week or two before Weddall's death."

"Yes," Jewle said. "He drew the will and he knew what was in it. Unless something went badly wrong he could straighten out the irregularity by borrowing—"

"And probably from Joe Borne," I said.

"Maybe," he said. "But these legal technicalities are a bit beyond me, not that we haven't people at the Yard who're more than competent to handle them. But let me ask you a plain question, Mr. Pepson. Why should Humphrey be pressed for money?"

The grunt was almost a snort.

"Plenty of reasons. The people who were his father's clients haven't any money nowadays. Old Spurn is just a figurehead and those two have been running what business there is, plus two or three girls in the office. Then, fairly late in life, he married a woman much younger than himself. A marriage of convenience if ever there was one. He was supposed to have the money and she and her sister were poor as church mice even if they were county. Their father, if you don't know it, was old General Sir John Stearne and he only left the house and about ten thousand."

"And Mrs. H. is a spender?"

He snorted again.

"A spender! Lady High-Muckamuck. Has her nose in everything. And he's besotted. Makes an absolute fool of himself over the woman."

He got to his feet and brought some loose change from his pocket. Jewle said he'd pay, but Pepson insisted. And he didn't say anything else till we were outside.

"As I told you, here's where I retire. I think I've given you enough to prove I was right about that art gallery."

We let him get a mile or two along the road before we moved off.

"Talk about throwing a spanner into the works!" Jewle said. "When you come to think it out, this is the very devil."

"You mean because Humphrey couldn't have killed his uncle?"

"What else?" he said. "That's the one thing that's dead certain about this whole business. And he couldn't have killed Grace Amble. He has an alibi and he hasn't a motive. Whoever planted her at the Hall has far more motive and he hadn't a hand in that."

"It always gets back to Joe Borne," I told him consolingly. "And we know now the hold Joe had over Humphrey: if Humphrey borrowed that money from him, that is."

He had the road to watch and he obviously wanted to think, so I didn't say any more till we got to the town. He turned left and down a short-cut that was taking us away from the police station. We drew up before the main Mainford branch of William Weddall's bank.

"Shan't be a minute," he told me. "Just something I want to see."

His minute turned out to be a quarter of an hour. But he looked quite pleased.

"A stroke of luck," he told me. "The tax people are here assessing the amount of liability in conjunction with the executors, so the will was in the bank safe. I wanted to be sure that everything was right and proper."

"Could it be anything else?"

"Everything looked perfect to me," he said, and moved the car on. "And it's satisfied those concerned. One more little thing to do and I'll be still more satisfied."

I didn't know what that thing was till we got back to Ansen's room and he began giving Matthews instructions.

"Want you to slip along at once to the Hall and see the under-gardener and housemaid who witnessed Weddall's will. Warn them I want them here just short of two o'clock and you'll be fetching them."

At just after two o'clock we were in the manager's room at that bank. The safe was unlocked and the will laid out on the table, face downwards so that little more than the signatures was showing.

Horless was a young fellow of about twenty-five, and he was looking none too much at ease in his best clothes. Daisy might have been a rabbit in front of us three stoats. It took quite a lot of talk from Jewle to get them to loosen up. If he hadn't asked Horless to give his version first I don't think Daisy would have helped us at all. Or maybe I was wrong. There was one place where she actually tittered.

What Jewel wanted was everything that happened from the moment the two stepped into the study that night, and when the slow mental regurgitations had at last been produced, the picture we had was this. Weddall, wearing his dark glasses, had been seated at the small table. Humphrey Weddall had let the two of them in and accompanied them to the far side of the table. He seemed to have been rather jocular. Had they ever witnessed any signature before? And, nothing to get alarmed about. Just watch while the master wrote his name and then write their own names at the place which he'd show them.

During those soothing explanations Humphrey had brought the will, a sort of book bound with ribbon, from his attaché case and had been running an eye over it. He placed it on the table before his uncle. He put a finger on the spot to indicate where the signature had to be written. And when we got as far as that, Daisy gave a little titter.

"Something funny happened?" Jewle said.

Horless, by now far more at ease, explained. The master had bent down till his nose almost touched the paper. It was just as if he was trying to smell it!

"Don't forget his eyes were very bad," Jewel told them. "He had to have his eyes very close to anything in order to be able to read it. And what happened then?"

Weddall kept a finger of his left hand on the place, took the pen Humphrey gave him, and wrote his name. Humphrey blotted the ink, then turned the document round and showed Horless where to sign his name. Underneath, he explained, was written his address and occupation. Horless signed his name in full and Daisy signed hers.

"Well, that's all," Humphrey had said, and then Weddall spoke.

"How're you keeping, Horless? Haven't seen you for some time."

"Keeping very well, sir, thank you."

"That's fine. Thank you for coming up. And you, too, Daisy."

And that really was all, and one could imagine them, still a bit awestruck, filing quietly out.

"That's just how I imagined it," Jewle told them. "Now look here, Mr. Horless. That your signature?"

Horless had a good look and said it was. Then Daisy verified hers.

"That's all right, then," Jewle told them and gave them a cheerful smile. "Nothing very terrifying. Just the usual way these things have to be done. So if neither of you wants to go anywhere in the town, the sergeant will take you home. Thank you both very much indeed."

The manager saw them out.

"Well, everything was done perfectly regularly," Jewle was to tell him as he held out his hand. "Thank you for being so co-operative. And don't forget. No one—no one at all—is to know what's just transpired here. I'm sure we can rely on you for that."

It was not till we were walking back to the police-station that Jewle made any comment.

"No jiggery-pokery of any sort. That was obviously the authentic will." He grunted. "Wonder what it was that Humphrey told Weddall that made him change his mind over that art gallery business?"

I said I'd been wondering that, too.

"A dead end," Jewle said. "We might guess a dozen things and never have a bit of proof. What was said was just between the two of them. That's plain as the nose on your face."

I decided to let something out. There wasn't much risk. He knew that I'd seen Sam quite recently.

"Did Sam ever tell you about Grace Amble listening at the study door and his reporting it to Weddall and Weddall saying he knew all about it?"

"Can't say he did. Or maybe he did say something. I don't remember, but we guessed it in any case."

"Then doesn't a question arise?" I said. "If Weddall knew she was spying on him, why did he leave her quite a handsome legacy?"

"I've thought about that, too," he said. "Even if he did know she was up to some game or other he could still have been grateful to her for looking after the house and the grandchildren. And don't forget everything wasn't over. He wasn't expecting to die. That particular will might have been only a stop-gap till he'd reconsidered a whole lot of things. That art gallery, for instance."

I wasn't so sure. I was going to ask him about that seventieth birthday business and the showdown we'd thought he'd planned for the family, but I thought better of it.

"What about the Bornes?"

"Just a token legacy," he said. "And I still think that will was a stopgap."

We went up to Ansen's room, hung up our hats and coats and looked about us as if the place was suddenly strange. For my part I felt adrift in some curiously unknown space: thought and thoughts and nothing substantial to clutch. Too much and too little.

"Think I'll get away for an hour or two," Jewle suddenly said. "We've heard some queer things today and I'd like to let them settle for a bit."

He began filling his pipe and then he stopped and his head went sideways as if he was listening. What he heard was a new idea.

"The sooner we stop dithering and dallying, the better," he told me. "I'm going to try to blow this thing sky-high. I'll get along to the Yard and put everything on the table."

"Everything?"

"The whole caboodle. If things are seen my way, and I think they will be, old Borne can be brought in for questioning. And we'll get someone down here to do a bit of ferreting. Pepson ought to be a help. He hates Humphrey like sin."

I said I'd push off. A little loneliness might help me, too. He was already so busy with his plans that I don't think he even heard me go.

It was to be thirty hours later when I saw him again. I strolled about in the town, had a look in the windows of young Borne's shop, wondered if I should go in and buy, perhaps some small present for Bernice, and then changed my mind: not from any special frugality but because I didn't want particularly to add Borne to the rest of my thoughts. I went to the Homeways and had tea. Someone who'd been at the table I took had left behind him that day's issue of the *Mainford Gazette*. I had a quick look at it while my tea was coming, but it wasn't then that I got a certain idea. All I got was something that was to merge with other ideas. For the moment it was only a raindrop on a window: not noticeable till it slowly moved and joined another drop and then another till the whole weight of it sent it slithering down the pane.

It was just after six o'clock and the pub was open when I got back to Hinchbrook. Just before seven Matthews came in. Jewle had gone, he told me. The two had come back to the pub for Jewle's bag and Matthews had driven him to the train.

16. DAY IN THE COUNTRY

I HAD a good night. I didn't even know that while I was sleeping a drop of water had moved down from the top of a pane, had gathered others in its accelerating course and finally slithered like a miniature rivulet down to the glazing-bar. What I did know when I woke was that there was something that I ought to try out. It was a long shot. It was even fantastic, and yet I knew it was something that had to be done.

Matthews opened the way at breakfast.

"Well, sir, what's the menu for today?"

"Don't know," I said. "What about the mice doing a bit of playing now the cat's away?"

"Never a hope," he said. "I've got to be near the telephone. Can't take a chance."

I let it lie for a bit, then I asked almost casually if he'd be using the car. If he weren't, then I'd like to have a little run round. He said I'd chosen a hell of a month for sightseeing.

"No fool like an old fool," I told him. "But I *would* like just to look round a bit while I'm here."

No reason at all why I shouldn't have the car, he said. Plenty of police cars if he wanted one, and he probably wouldn't. So when we got to Mainford the car was mine. And I kept the illusion up by refusing to have the tank filled at the public's expense.

I didn't drive far. At the post office I bought some threepenny stamps and then used a call-box to ring Pepson. He'd only just arrived at his office.

"Travers here," I said, voice kept low. "You remember me from yesterday?"

He caught the subtle allusion.

"In connection with that," I went on, "I'd be grateful if you could give me the address of a certain general's daughter. I think it's at Stratford."

I had to wait a couple of minutes.

"The Little Manor, Yelden. That's about two miles this side of Stratford-on-Avon."

"She's married?"

"A spinster. They sold the family house when her sister married, and she bought the one at Yelden."

I thanked him and said he'd probably be hearing from us later.

I nosed the car into the traffic. In the first suburban shopping area I caught sight of the stationer's shop I was on the look out for and there I bought some sheets of very cheap writing paper and a few envelopes that didn't match. And I kept my gloves on.

Those preliminaries might be sheer waste. Much more depended on what I learned at Castledene. Almost at the far end of the village, just beyond the filling-station, was another stationer's shop. I drew up the car and through the glazed upper half of the door I could see that the shop was empty. Two or three newspaper placards stood on boards outside.

An old-fashioned bell tinkled as I went in and in a few seconds a dumpy, elderly woman came in from the back. "Good morning," I said pleasantly.

"Good morning, sir. Not a very nice morning."

We had a few more words about the weather and then I flashed my agency card.

"I'm here on rather private business. I'm one of the detective force enquiring into the murder."

She'd looked a bit wary; now she was almost agog.

"You may not see the importance of what I'm going to ask you, but it's this. We want to know all the people in Castledene who regularly took the *Mainford Gazette*."

"Oh dear," she said, and sighed. "Quite a lot to do."

"Let me help you. Let's begin at the first house when you're coming in from Mainford and work our way up to here."

"Yes," she said. "Now let me see. I ought to know. Mr. Radford, he do, and Mr. Weddall. . . ."

I let her go right through her list. When she'd finished I shook a doleful head.

"Nobody of the name of Fisher?"

"No," she said, surprised. "There ain't no one of that name in the village."

A little more general talk and I thanked her and went out.

I drove straight on, intending to stop when I saw someone who could tell me of a short cut round to the Stratford Road. I saw no one but in about half a mile I came to a road that went to the left and the direction post said it was the way to Buttington and Stratford.

On a straight stretch just short of Buttington I pulled up on the verge and wrote a letter with gloved hands. Only a few words, but they had to be carefully shaped and to be a nice blend of literacy and low cunning. I addressed the envelope in the same careful hand, stamped it and moved the car on.

I still had thirty miles to go, and I took them fairly quickly. Yelden was a mile off even that secondary road and it was about half-past ten when I reached it.

It was a much bigger place than I'd thought. Probably eight or nine hundred people. Quite a thriving little place. The notice outside the post office-store said there were three outward mails a day—at nine, twelve and six. There were two deliveries, the second at three. I dropped my letter in the box, moved the car on and came to a right turn that would take me to Stratford.

Stratford is a tree-less depressing sort of place except in the old town by the church and the Memorial Theatre, and on that dull day, with its threat of drizzle, even the river with its spidery skeletons of trees and the flat green beyond had a queer sort of suburban-like melancholy. In the town itself I wondered, as I'd done before, what writhing and twistings the Bard was making in his grave when on his midnight prowls he remembered what the town had been before big business had even begun to discern its possibilities. At any rate, I killed a lot of time and then had lunch, and it was about a quarter to three when I got back to Yelden.

I learned where the Old Manor was and began reconnoitring. It was just past the church, down a side lane: an old, half-timbered house that I wouldn't have minded living in myself, and the sudden remembering that Shakespeare himself might have seen it added quite a lot to its charm. It was fronted by a low, mellowed wall above which was about a foot of evergreen hedge. From a corner of the churchyard I had an even better look at it. It was bigger than I'd thought from the road and in the summer its front garden would be quite a dream.

I moved the car and settled down to what might be a considerable wait. It was not till quite half an hour later that I caught sight of the postman making his way towards the church. I watched him make a few deliveries and only at last, when he'd turned into the lane, did I follow him. I overtook him and was at the front door first. He put a couple of letters through the slot of the door and we passed the time of day before he turned back to his rounds. If I hadn't seen my letter in his hand I should have made some excuse and gone away.

An elderly, sprightly woman opened the door: a family retainer by the look of the black dress and little white cap.

"Mrs. Weddall," I said. "Is she in?"

"Who is it, please?"

"Travers. Will you tell her I'd like to see her on some rather important business. I'm from Mainford. I'm sure she remembers me."

The entrance hall was so small that a swung cat could have lost its brains. She asked me to come in and, I don't know why, laid the two letters on a brass tray on a little side table just inside the door.

"Just wait a minute, sir, and I'll see."

The only thing to look at was a rather nice convex mirror that hung above the table. There was a faint scent of lavender. Beyond the door through which she had gone was an even fainter sound of voices. It was a couple of minutes before she came back.

"Will you come this way, sir?"

I was ushered into what was the main living-room and the smell of lavender was at once more strong. The room had a low, timbered ceiling and its long windows were latticed. It was all chintz, cushions, knick-knacks and pictures: that was the quick impression I had as I went in and Rachel Weddall rose from an easy chair. I gave her my most reassuring smile. "How nice to see you again, Mrs. Weddall."

"How d'you do," she said, and gave me a little inclination of the head. She was looking watchful, I thought, but had herself well in hand. "Won't you sit down?"

I launched out into quite a lot more reassuring words. I'd thought I'd like to look at Stratford-on-Avon before I finally went back to town and I'd remembered her maid had said something about her being at Yelden when we'd telephoned. That's when she interrupted me.

"Telephoned? To me?"

I explained. Someone had apparently had the idea that she might have caught sight of Grace Amble near the town hall before the show began.

"I'm sure I told them quite to the contrary," she said severely. "I had to be there very early to receive people. I was far too busy to notice anything else."

"Of course. They should have realised that." I made a very half-hearted attempt to rise. "Still, it has given me the pleasure of seeing you again before I return to town."

"You're going to Mainford first?"

"Just to collect my belongings. Then on to London. My uncle, Sir Charles Trevor, wants me to go down to his place in Hampshire."

I suppose that was outrageous. Still, the only way to be on equal terms with snobbery is to out-snob the snobs. And I had to stay in that room till the afternoon mail was brought in.

"Trevor," she said. "Was he in the Army? I remember my father talking about a Colonel Trevor, an old friend of his. I *think* he was in the Hampshires."

"That wouldn't be my uncle." I had to do some quick thinking. "He was at the Foreign Office."

"How interesting."

"Yes," I said. "He's a very charming man."

I hesitated a moment, then said I'd better be on my way. "But you must stay to tea."

I said the usual things: couldn't give her all that trouble and I really ought to be getting along, and then let myself be over-ruled. She went out through the far door. I sat on, and I was hunting for more details in the life of that fictitious uncle. Then almost at once the door opened again and another woman was coming in.

"How do you do? I'm Margaret Stearne."

She looked about forty, and surprisingly pleasant: the outdoor type—cropped hair, tanned face and a certain masculinity. I doubted if she'd had an illness since her measles days.

I introduced myself and just as we were seating ourselves Rachel came back.

"You've been staying in Mainford?" Margaret asked me.

"Heaven forbid," I said, and she laughed. "I've really been at Hinchbrook Hall. I'm an art expert, you know. They called me in for a preliminary valuation."

Harriet came in with a tea trolley. I fetched the low table and placed it as directed but I noticed there were no letters. Margaret presided: she was quite a hearty eater. I didn't do too badly myself. Rachel scarcely ate a thing, yet it was she who, strangely enough, picked up a thread of thought that seemed so harshly out of place in that atmosphere of Davenport china and chintz and cushions, and all the fluffy, lavender-scented proprieties of that room.

"Poor Mr. Weddall. Such a charming man. Very sad about his death, don't you think? And the way he died."

"I'd never met him except about twice," I said. "But I certainly agree with you. By the way, this is confidential, but the police are now convinced his death was an accident."

"Stupid of them to have thought otherwise." That was a flash of the old Rachel who hadn't been too visible. "And that other dreadful affair. Have the police discovered anything yet?"

"They don't take me into their confidence," I said, "but it certainly was a shocking business."

"Poor soul," Margaret said. "One hardly likes to say it, but she wasn't a very nice person."

Rachel sniffed.

"A hard, common woman. The worst person in the world for those children. No wonder they're so boisterous. Thank goodness Paul's going to a prep. school next term."

Margaret peered across the table.

"More tea, Mr. Travers?"

"Thank you, no. It's been a delightful meal."

"Then I might as well ring for Harriet."

She tinkled the little bell that had come with the trolley. Harriet came in carrying that brass tray. On it were the two letters.

"Ah, letters!" Margaret said. "Wonder if there's one from Henry." She gave a little squeal of delight. "There is! Our only nephew," she explained. "His father, Colonel Stearne, was killed at Anzio. And here's a letter for you, dear."

Rachel looked at the letter. She frowned. Harriet went out with the trolley and I went forward and opened the door for her.

"Do read your letters," I said, and tried to make it archly. "Someone might have won something from Premium Bonds."

"No such good fortune," Margaret said smilingly. "At least, I haven't any. Who's your letter from, Rachel?"

It happened quickly. Rachel must have opened her letter during that badinage and there hadn't been much to read. The whiteness of her face made me gasp, and then suddenly she went sideways, hands groping blindly. There was a crash of china as she slithered across the side of the table to the floor.

Margaret gave a gasping, "Oh!" I pushed the table aside and we collided as we bent down.

"A faint," I said, and felt for the pulse. "I'll try to put her on the chesterfield. Perhaps there's something you can get."

She scurried out and I heard her calling to Harriet. Letter and envelope were on the floor. I pocketed the one and left the other. Then I got my arms under the heavy body and managed somehow to stagger with it to the chesterfield. Harriet came in.

"Just a faint," I said. "I'm pretty sure it's nothing worse."

"Miss Margaret's calling the doctor," she said. "He lives quite close." She had a look at the unconscious woman and gave a sad shake of the head. "She hasn't really been well ever since she came. She wouldn't admit it, but I knew."

Margaret came back.

"The doctor's coming," she told us. "Said we were to leave her as she is. How is she, Mr. Travers?"

"No difference," I said. "But it'll take a few minutes for her to come round. Anything else I can do? If not I think I should be going."

"You've been splendid," she said, "and I'm very grateful."

I picked up my coat and hat from the chair on which I'd laid them, said again how sorry I was, and then Harriet went with me to the door. The doctor's car passed me as I went down the short lane.

Back in my own car I took that letter from my pocket. It was wet with split milk and a corner was jagged where a broken cup had pressed on it, and I left it on the seat where the heater might dry it. It was twenty-to-five by the dashboard clock and I had a long way to go and still another job to do, and once I was clear of the village I travelled fast. And this time I knew something about the road. All the same, dusk was in the sky when I came to Castledene. Lights were on in the repair-shop behind the garage. The letter was dry enough to smooth out and I put it in my pocket-book.

A lorry was jacked up in the repair-shop and the owner of the garage and a young mechanic were working on it. I asked for a private word and the owner took me into his cubby-hole of an office. I let him just see the Agency card. I told him I was working with the police on the Amble murder and that, if he wished, he could ring Mainford and verify it.

"No need to do that, sir. But just what is it you want?"

"Secrecy, for one thing, and possibly some information. Keep this strictly under your hat, but we're looking for a man who might have had an accident in the village that Friday night round about half-past seven or eight. It might have been just a minor accident. Or only a puncture. So will you look at your books?"

"No need to do that, sir. Nothing came in here. I ought to know. I was working in here till late."

"And early the next morning?"

"Nothing," he said, and then remembered something. I held my breath.

"Only thing that did happen was when Mr. Weddall give me a call. You know him?"

"Weddall? . . . Weddall?"

"A lawyer. He lives here but has his office in Mainford."

"Of course. Mr. Humphrey Weddall."

"That's him, sir, and, as I was saying, he rang me about half-past seven. Said he was going out and found his car had a flat and would we see to it first thing in the morning. Which we did."

I shook a dismal head.

"Well, I'm afraid that's nothing like what we're looking for. The man we want is a stranger. Much obliged to you all the same."

It was almost dark as I drove on towards Mainford and I was asking myself a lot of questions. Had Rachel recovered from that fainting fit? Would she be almost certain that it was I who'd taken that letter? And that the whole business of that afternoon had been planned? And had she already rung her husband? If so, Humphrey Weddall would by now be a remarkably thoughtful man. I hadn't said so to Jewle, but the last time we'd seen him I'd thought he was a man with a lot of worries on his mind, but that would be nothing to what he was thinking now.

I ought to have been feeling pleased with myself, but I wasn't. What had been surmise was now almost fact, and yet I felt somehow that we were still very far from the heart of the case. If Humphrey were not implicated, then the events of the afternoon couldn't have happened. And he *couldn't* be involved, which meant again that surmise was still surmise, in spite of what had happened.

And that reminds me that I didn't tell you the contents of that letter. It had no address and no date—just these few words:

What did you do with those gloves? And hadn't you ought to tell the police?

Matthews was having a peaceful time: feet up on a chair, fire full on, and reading that night's *Evening Gazette*. He looked round quite casually at the sound of the door, then beamed as he got to his feet.

"Hallo, sir. Thought you'd got lost. Just thought of having the local ponds dragged."

"Don't make me cry," I said, and hung up my coat. "Matter of fact, I thought I'd have a look at Stratford-on-Avon."

"Wish I'd known," he said. "I could've asked him if he was Bacon."

"Good lord!" I said. "Every day you reveal some new and startling side of yourself. Who'd have guessed you even knew Shakespeare?"

"Me?" He looked indignant. "Had to learn chunks of him at school. Like to hear some?"

"God forbid," I said. "You tell me the news instead."

He said there wasn't any, except that Jewle was due back early next morning.

"Things are moving," he said. "Everything's fixed for a quiet look at Humphrey's affairs. And they had old Borne in. Still at it when he rang."

"Humphrey," I said, and let it rest for a moment or two. Then I looked at him.

"Wonder if you'd do something. And straight away. Find out where Humphrey is and put a man on his tail."

"Wait a minute," he said. "What's been happening? What've you found out?"

"That's just quibbling," I told him. "How could I have found out anything that you don't know already? And isn't that enough? A man with a guilty conscience like his must know that Pepson's after his blood."

"You really mean it?"

"I do. And to this extent. If anything slips up, then you're responsible. I hate to say it, but I'll have no scruples about putting everything on you."

"Oh," he said, and thought for a moment. "Well, it can't do any harm. I'd better see Ansen and get it fixed."

He was back in a quarter of an hour and he said it was all fixed. An accusing look accompanied the information but I didn't rise to it.

"And what now?" I said.

"Might as well have a quiet night at the pub. Anything that comes along can be put through."

When we were clear of the town I couldn't help noticing that he was driving uncommonly slowly. I guessed he was wanting to talk and, sure enough, a question came.

"Look, sir, just between you and me, what new dope have you got on Humphrey?"

"What a fellow you are!" I said. "If he really thinks we're on to those frauds of his, wouldn't he be likely to bolt?"

"I can't see how he could be." His tone changed and I could hear the ersatz smile in his voice. "Now if he was mixed up in a couple of murders, that'd be different."

"True enough. And why shouldn't he be?"

"You serious?"

"Well . . . yes. But do something for me. I never quite got all the details of that alibi of his for the Weddall murder."

"Unbreakable," he said. "Admitted Grace Amble's dead and can't help but it's this. She joined him in the nursery with the children at ten-past five or before and she was with him from then on till he drove off in his car. And he didn't come back and we can prove that by then he was at his office."

"Yes," I said. "Unbreakable, as you say. And Weddall was alive and ringing Sam at about twenty-past. I suppose it *was* Weddall who rang?"

Matthews snorted.

"Or else the one who did him in was a ruddy impressionist. And wouldn't Sam know? Besides, what about what we got from Mrs. Gribling? Weddall wasn't killed till at least five-twenty."

"You're right," I said. "Let's leave it. And push this damn car on or else we'll be arrested for loitering."

17. Ex Ore Infantium

A QUIET evening. A drink, supper, darts, maybe more beer than was strictly necessary and so to bed, and, for my part, to a good night. There was no need to worry about Matthews. I woke twice and each time I could hear his snores in the next room.

Morning brought no brainwaves but something was somewhere at the back of my mind. It wasn't till after I'd shaved and dressed that I knew what it was—the feeling that if anything was ever to be discovered it was at the Hall. What and how had apparently nothing to do with it. It was just a feeling: a sort of hunch. I think that if I'd had anything else definite to do I'd have chased it from my mind.

As it was I told Matthews that I had one or two things to do and I'd come along to Mainford later. When he looked suspicious I mentioned private letters and ringing the Agency. At any rate he went off alone and at about half-past nine I began walking towards the Hall. Just as I was passing the rectory drive I saw Brenda coming my way and I waited for her.

"Hallo, Brenda! What's happened? No school today?"

"It's half-term," she told me primly. "We always have half-term."

"Fine," I said. "No half-terms in my young days. When do you go back?"

"Tuesday morning."

"And where're you going now?" I smiled. "If I'm not asking too many questions."

"Just to the Hall," she said. "We may help Gribling in the greenhouse. He's taking cuttings."

I couldn't help smiling. She smiled, too, as we walked along.

"Gribling's pretty strict?"

"Well, not too strict. But he doesn't allow any nonsense."

I thought of something and it made me stop in my tracks. "Tell me something, Brenda. You were there when Mrs. Amble told Jean I was a policeman—"

"Oh, but I've told them you aren't really a policeman."

"That's very kind of you," I said, "and I appreciate it. But why was Jean so scared?"

The old superior smile was back.

"Oh, just because she was scared. She and Paul are always doing silly things."

"Such as what?"

"Well, once they hid Sam's cap."

"That wasn't very bad," I said. "Was Sam annoyed?"

"He just *told* them," she said with very definite satisfaction. "And another time when he caught them making faces at people through the window. And that shows how stupid they are. They didn't think about how he could see them in the mirror."

"That certainly was stupid," I said. "Anything else did they do?"

"Yes," she said. "The most stupidest of all. . . ."

It was quite five minutes after she left me before I went to the side door. Elizabeth Larkwell opened it.

"Morning, Mrs. Larkwell. Anyone here besides yourselves?"

"No one, sir. There was all yesterday and the day before, but they've gone now. I'll make you a cup of tea."

"Only just had breakfast," I said. "The children aren't at school, so Brenda just told me."

I heard about half-term and Gribling and the greenhouse. Gribling, she said, was very good with children.

"Something I'd like to do," I said. "May I have a look at the nursery? And we can replace the photograph you so kindly let me have."

We went up the stairs. Daisy looked out of a door, then shot back again.

The nursery was like a hundred others. It wasn't vastly different from the one in which my sister and I had spent so many years: the same smells, toys and books everywhere, and even a bed in the far corner. Mrs. Larkwell began replacing the photograph in its frame.

"Where's that door lead to?"

"To Master Paul's bedroom, sir. Miss Jean sleep in that bed there." She smiled. "Many a time, though, she's been catched in his bed. And him in hers, too. A couple of regular young imps, they are."

I said it was a fine, airy room and we went back downstairs. I stopped in the lobby. I could hear someone in the kitchen.

"In the dining-room," I said quietly. "I'd like to have a word with you. Just ourselves."

She was looking a bit apprehensive till I told her what it was I wanted and how important it might be.

"What time do the children have their lunch?"

"Half-past twelve, sir."

"And after it?"

"Well, a fine day like this they'll go out and play. I don't hold with them staying indoors."

"Right," I said. "This is highly confidential but unless you hear from me to the contrary Inspector Jewle and I will be here at half-past one. The main door and we'll go to the nursery. When I give you the signal you'll call the children in. Say there's someone to see them in the nursery. You've got that?" She repeated it pat.

"Now something else. Any particular toy or anything the children would like?"

"Well, Master Paul keeps on to me about one o' them space suits what you read about now. And Miss Jean? . . . Well, I reckon she'd like one, too. What one have, the other always have to have or else there's squabbling."

I told her that it must all sound very mysterious but we had good reasons. I even went further and told her that if what we were going to do turned out successful, we'd know a lot more about two deaths. She listened intently, eyes never leaving my face. We went over everything yet again and it was she who suggested a modification. The staff lunch could be early and the children's correspondingly late, and then she could let them stay in the kitchen till we were ready. And that was how we left it.

I went out by the front door and round to the greenhouses and I was glad there was no sign of Sam. The smaller of the two was the scene of the morning's activities and I waited for a moment or two, wondering how to make my visit seem natural.

It was warm in there with the heating on. Gribling was preparing chrysanthemum cuttings from a bed of stools. Paul, with a large beach spade, was turning over the potting mixture: Brenda was filling the boxes and Jean was squatting by her, watching.

"Morning, Mr. Gribling. You're busy here."

He laughed.

"Yes, sir: only some's more busy than others. Still, they're not bad workers, though."

"I'm sure they aren't."

Paul had stopped work and he gave me a smile. Brenda looked up too. Jean's look was shy but she was no longer afraid.

"By the way, when's pay-day?"

"Well, I haven't worked it out yet, sir. Might be when Easter Monday fall on a Tuesday."

Brenda gave a little titter. She understood.

"Oh, no," I said. "No pay, no work. What about sixpence an hour?"

"You'll ruin us, sir!"

"Sixpence an hour," Paul said. He said it again. It became a chant and Jean took it up. Brenda told them to be quiet. She gave me a private look which said I could see for myself how babyish they could be.

"I might do something about it myself," I said.

"You're going to pay us sixpence an hour?" Paul asked.

"You'll get no sixpence nor nothing else if you don't get on turning that heap," Gribling told him. Paul gave me a confidential sort of look before resuming.

"I'll do something," I announced. "Have you read *Alice in Wonderland*, Brenda?"

"Some of it," she said, "but I haven't got it."

"Well, I don't think it's in there, but I think people who have birthdays, like me, should give other people presents and not have presents themselves."

Brenda smiled.

"Coo!" said Paul. "I wouldn't like to do that. It'd take all my money." Then it dawned on him. "Are you going to give *us* presents? You must be rich."

"That'll do, Master Paul," Gribling told him sharply. "You just mind your manners."

Paul looked a bit abashed. I said he hadn't meant to be rude. And maybe I would do something about presents. Then I looked at my watch and said I'd have to be going. I said goodbye to the children and hinted that I might see them later. Gribling went with me to the door.

"Was there anything you wished to see me about, sir?"

"Just looked in to see the children," I said.

"They're company," he said, "and it keep them out o' mischief. Come again, sir, and cheer us all up."

I didn't tell him so but it was myself who'd been cheered up. I went across by the cottage and waited for a bus. In Mainford

I went to the big toy shop in Market Street. They had plenty of space suits in different sizes and at different prices. I bought two and had them separately wrapped. Then I went to the book shop and bought *Alice in Wonderland* and *Little Women* for Brenda. I was pretty well loaded with parcels when I went on to the police station. I asked if Jewle had returned. He had.

Just short of half-past one Elizabeth Larkwell let Jewle and myself in at the front door. She told me the children were still in the kitchen. Only the two, of course. Brenda had gone home to lunch.

Jewle and I went up the stairs, along the short corridor and into the nursery. The round kitchen clock above the mantelpiece said exactly half-past one. Jewle set the tape-recorder down. He said he didn't think we ought to risk opening the door to Paul's bedroom. Then he moved a table to the far corner, put the tape-recorder under it and masked it with some books. I set two chairs by another table just inside the door and put two parcels on it.

"All set?"

"All set."

I went to the head of the stairs and called down. In a minute there was a scampering across the lobby and up the stairs. Paul came in first and stopped dead at the sight of me. Jean came in, her chubby face red as a tomato.

"You've really brought some presents?" Paul said.

"Yes," I said. "But only for good children." I smiled. "Both of you sit down there and I'm going to find out who's good and who's bad."

It was a fine game. Paul didn't wait to be questioned. "We're both good."

"Oh?" I said, and made a face to show I wasn't too serious. "I'm not so sure about that. A little bird was telling me about some children who hid Sam's cap."

He moistened his lip. Then he smiled.

"Oh, that! Well, that wasn't being bad."

"Well, perhaps it wasn't," I told him after a little consideration. "But what about the clock?"

His face went a bit red.

"Well, that wasn't bad either. It was just so we shouldn't have to go to bed so soon."

"I didn't touch the clock," Jean said.

"She's too small," Paul told me. "I had to get on the chair to do it. But it wasn't bad, really it wasn't."

Both were looking at those two parcels.

"And why wasn't it bad?" I went over to the parcels myself as if preparing to hand them over.

"Because Aunt Grace always found out. And the last time she said if we ever told anyone about it she'd have to tell the police."

"Oh, she did, did she? And that was the night when your Uncle Humphrey came to see you?"

"Yes," he said.

"You'd already altered the clock that night?"

"Yes, I had. But not very much. Only about ten minutes."

"He crackled!"

I smiled. What Jean meant I hadn't even an idea.

"Crackled? Who crackled?"

Paul explained.

"She said Uncle Humphrey crackled when he kissed her."

"You mean a sort of crackling noise?"

"It was all inside him," Jean said and began to giggle.

"Ah, well," I said, "I think on the whole you're both very good children, so here's your presents."

"May we open them?"

I cut the string with my pen-knife. In a moment there was a little pandemonium. I had almost to shout to get silence.

"You'd better take them down to the kitchen and show them to everyone. And wait a moment. Here's a present for Brenda. You can take it to the rectory for her later on."

"Cool—and thanks!" Paul said, and when he was already through the door. There was the rush of feet across the lobby and the children's excited voices. Jewle stepped out of the bedroom. He took out the tape recorder, switched it off and we quietly made our way back to the front door.

At six o'clock that night there were five of us in Ansen's room: Ansen himself, Chief-Constable Meers, Jewle, Matthews and, as they used to say, your humble. Jewle looked round at us and picked up his notes.

"This is how things stand, gentlemen, and I began at the beginning. Everything originated with two men who were in need of money, or thought they were. Borne might have been: Humphrey Weddall certainly was. If we start at the time when William Weddall's eyesight really began to be affected, the position was this. Old Gus Weddall had a scheme for evading death duties and had instructed his son-in-law to have copies made of eight of his best pictures. On his death the originals were to be sold and the proceeds would pay those duties. Borne knew that only Humphrey and himself were aware of that swindle—after Gus died, that is—and he practically admitted when we had him at the Yard yesterday that he and Humphrey shared the proceeds. That was, of course, before William Weddall had settled in at the Hall and suddenly begun to take an interest in pictures himself.

"That was what made Borne alarmed and when a lucky chance presented itself—the death of Evelyn Weddall—he and his son, and possibly Humphrey, managed to get Grace Amble at the hall to keep her eyes and ears open, especially about anything to do with pictures, and to report. There also had to be the connivance of Delver.

"But let's leave Borne out for the moment. His case, a comparatively minor one, won't come up for quite a time, so we'll concentrate on the murders. And here I've got to anticipate a little, for unless Humphrey breaks down, then there'll have to be a lot of spade work before we know just how deeply he was involved in swindles of his own, but what we know from the little we already have is that Humphrey was in pretty desperate need of money, and when his uncle began talking about a new will, and the main estate going to an art gallery, then he had to do something.

"What he did was prepare two wills: one strictly according to instructions and the other the one the executors now have. You'll remember that his uncle stressed secrecy, and that Humphrey himself, and no one else, had to draw up that will. And that brings us to the night of the first murder.

"William Weddall was an architect, gentlemen," Jewle smiled dryly as he said that. "He was also the architect of his own death. By that elaborate pretence of having virtually lost his sight—I admit it all arose out of certain suspicions he'd begun to have— he definitely killed himself. Humphrey turned up that morning and read the will to him, and everything was ready for the afternoon. Weddall's prints are on each page, so the will might have been left for him to look through as far as his eyesight permitted. Humphrey arrived that late afternoon at just before five o'clock and he contrived at once to substitute the other will. It was signed and the witnesses went out.

"And now we have to imagine things. We see it like this. Weddall was now going to play with Humphrey as a cat plays with a mouse. Humphrey would naturally reach for the will to put it in his case, but Weddall kept his hands on it. He knew there'd been something curious happening even if he hadn't seen the actual substitution. So he kept Humphrey talking and listening and then, when he'd had enough, he took off his glasses and picked up the will. He began to read, and to read like a normal person. He riffled the pages, and then he gave Humphrey an ironic look. He reached round for the telephone and spoke to Sam. Said he wanted him up there at once. And that's when Humphrey hit him on the head with the paper-weight and faked the accident. He put that will in his case and he had to get out of there before Sam came up. He couldn't go by the lift or main stairs as he couldn't tell which way Sam would come, so he went through the work-room and then remembered the art gallery plans. They were too big to put in his attaché case so he stuffed them under his coat and went on to the nursery, hoping to establish some kind of alibi. To his amazement he saw that the clock said only ten past five. He had a word with the children, then Grace Amble came in. She went downstairs with him and duly furnished his alibi. And now, Chief, and you, Ansen, we'd like you to hear a tape recording that was made this afternoon. I think it'll surprise you."

The recording was played. The room had a deadly silence when Jewle switched off.

"My God!" Meers said. "Who'd ever have believed it! Play it over again, Jewle. Play it over again."

"Better leave it till we let Humphrey Weddall listen to it," Jewle told him. "He's at home at the moment but we don't know how long he'll be there. But you see what must have happened? Grace Amble tried to blackmail him and he lured her out to his house and strangled her. It was a handy night for them both. Mrs. Weddall went early to that show and he was going later. We can prove he didn't take his own car that night. He drove Grace in her own car to where it was found. He'll probably say that when he found his car was punctured he got a lift from a passing motorist and didn't take his name. As for what the little girl said about the crackling sound, you'll have guessed that that was the paper crackling: the art gallery plans he had inside his overcoat.

"But there's one other thing." There was the dry smile again. "Once more it arises from the unconventional methods of Mr. Travers. Let him tell you about it."

"It was just a fortunate guess," I said. "On the morning when news of the Amble murder was spread across the front of the *Mainford Gazette*, Mrs. Weddall, after her husband left for his office, rang him to say her sister was ill and she had to go to her. My idea was that she might have found those gloves, a drawing of which was in the paper, and knew whose they were. She'd have been faced, you see, with two equally bad alternatives: tell the police and so inherit fifty thousand pounds, plus all the scandal, or keep quiet, avoid all scandal, and subsequently hold what she knew over Humphrey's head and so put herself in absolute control. So

I took a chance by sending her an anonymous letter and being there by good luck when she read it. The effect was terrific. She fell in a dead faint and enquiries this afternoon reveal she's still badly shaken. I think you might see the actual letter."

They had a look at it. Meers was good enough to say it was most ingenious. Ansen said it was damning.

"Not altogether," I said. "She can't be made to give evidence against her husband. All that could be done is produce the letter and have the sister as evidence. Still, that's a long way ahead and it mayn't be wanted."

"That all?" Meers said.

Jewle said it was. Ansen wanted to ask a question. What about the substitute will?

"What arises from Humphrey's trial will settle that," Jewle told him. "But when Humphrey left tonight we spoke to Spurn confidentially and says he thinks the old will is in the Weddall boxes. If not he definitely has an abstract. I'm pretty sure the courts would uphold, if that's the term, that old will. The provisions for employees are virtually the same though Grace Amble got only one thousand instead of five."

"And that's really all?" Meers asked again. "If so, what are we waiting for? The quicker we bring Humphrey in, the better."

They went out, Jewle last with the tape recorder.

"You not coming?" he said to me.

"Don't think so," I said. "You can tell me all about it at the pub. And I've got one or two things to fix up."

That's the worst of me; never really cut out for a detective—not, at least, a hard-boiled one. The problem was solved and the chase over, and that was what really mattered; I hadn't the heart somehow, to gloat over a man, even one like Humphrey Weddall, at the moment when truth was brought shatteringly home. So I took a bus to Hinchbrook and made my way round to the garage. Sam was in and he beamed at the sight of me.

"Come on up, sir. Come and have some coffee."

I went up the stairs and in. The room was snug as ever.

"Give me your hat and coat, sir, and I'll hang 'em up."

"Thank you, Sam, but I'm not staying. Just dropped in to give you some news."

He didn't speak but the question was in his eyes.

"The job's over, Sam. And you were right. The boss didn't fall out of that window. He was killed."

The eyes were getting bigger and bigger.

"We know who did it: his nephew, Humphrey Weddall."

Sam's whole body stiffened. The fists were tightly clenched and the stare was so wild that I thought for a moment he was going to attack me.

"Bad men!" he said. "Bad men!"

That was all he could say: the words just wouldn't come. Then tears came instead and he was moving away, and wiping his eyes with his sleeve. In that queer moment of another man's grief I could almost have cried myself.

It took a minute or two before he could speak and then his voice was quiet.

"What for did he have to kill the boss?"

"Greed, Sam, greed. He wanted his money and he couldn't wait."

He sat down at the table and did some thinking.

"Reckon I shan't stay here now. Couldn't go on livin' here now. Reckon I'll go some place back home."

"Why not?" I said. "Perhaps later on you'll feel like coming back again."

Then he remembered something, that he owed me money.

"No you don't, Sam," I said. "What you paid me was enough. Anything else the estate will pay."

He still wanted to pay. He told me again that all his life he'd been the saving-est man, and he didn't need to do no more work: no-sir, not for the rest of his life. But I convinced him and at last I held out my hand.

"I mayn't be seeing you again, Sam, before you go, but promise me something."

"Anything, sir. Anything."

"Then promise me you'll write to me as soon as you get settled back home."

He smiled.

"I sure will, sir. I sure will."

He came down the stairs with me and again I held out my hand.

"Goodbye, Sam, and good luck to you. I shan't forget you, Sam. And I'll be looking forward to that letter."

He grasped my hand but he didn't speak. I think he was afraid to trust himself to say even a word.

Humphrey Weddall tried to commit suicide in Mainford jail and that did his case no good. At his trial he had a first-class counsel all of whose emphasis was on the fact that the prosecution's case rested wholly on unsubstantiated evidence that was in substance purely circumstantial. I was a bit nervous when the jury were out so long, but I needn't have been.

Borne's case had come up well before Humphrey was hanged, and he'd been given two years. He was actually brought from jail to be a prosecution witness, and his shiftiness carried even more weight with the jury than if he'd told all he knew.

Sam didn't write to me till the following July. I'd found out that he'd received his legacy and I'd begun to give him up when the letter came.

He wrote quite a good hand, did Sam, but I smiled to myself at the thought of him settling down to compose it, and when I shut my eyes I could see him as clearly as if he were in the room. He said he'd gone first to New York but hadn't liked it there. Probably too many memories, though he didn't exactly say so. But he'd moved on to Akron and was living with some of his mother's folks, but he didn't think he'd be there long either. He'd heard of a filling-station in Philadelphia that he might buy as it didn't do for a man to have nothing to occupy his mind. But as soon as he got really settled he'd send his address and when I was in the

States again I was to be sure to look him up. I told myself that I certainly would.

Long, long before that I'd had a couple of letters, and they arrived the day after I left Hinchbrook. I'd given Elizabeth Larkwell my private address and I could imagine her supervising the writing of one letter: the joint letter of thanks from Paul and Jean. Jean's part of it was in big print and I doubt if she even did it herself.

Brenda's letter was very nicely written. Even for someone so grown up.

THE END